C000092628

Death Pays a Visit

A Myrtle Clover Cozy Mystery, Volume 6

Elizabeth Spann Craig

Published by Elizabeth Spann Craig, 2014.

DEATH PAYS A VISIT

First edition. September 9, 2014.

Written by Elizabeth Spann Craig.

In fond memory of my grandmother, Mary Ligon Spann
(Amma)

Chapter One

"Hello, Myrtle," said Miles calmly opening his front door.

Miles wore his customary plaid pajamas, slippers, and navy-blue bathrobe. His silver hair was neatly combed. Myrtle patted her own poof of gray hair and found that it appeared to be standing on end like Einstein's. She impatiently smoothed it down.

"Hi, Miles," said Myrtle. It was three forty-five in the morning, but somehow Miles didn't seem at all surprised to see her there. But then, Miles frequently seemed to have a sixth sense when it came to Myrtle's nocturnal visits.

Myrtle, dressed in her oldest and warmest robe, socks, and slippers, and bearing a cane, walked into Miles's tidy kitchen. It was a bachelor's kitchen with sensible pull-down shades in the windows, a sturdy wooden table and chairs that seated four, and appliances meant to cut his cooking time considerably. He had set out a carafe of coffee, cream, sugar, and two coffee cups. There was also a small platter of what appeared to be homemade cookies on the table, alongside two plates. Myrtle looked suspiciously at the cookies, not wanting to believe them homemade since her own efforts at cookies had recently gone very poorly. But they appeared to be genuine.

"Sure of yourself, weren't you?" asked Myrtle. "Confident that I was visiting tonight?"

Miles shrugged. "I hoped you were coming to help me pass the time. I haven't slept much this week. I didn't get around to watching the last episode of *Tomorrow's Promise* and thought we could have a snack and watch it if you came over."

Myrtle squinted at the cookies again. "Not getting domesticated, are you?"

Miles considered this thoughtfully. "I'm baking. I believe I must be bored."

"I can't say I didn't warn you," said Myrtle rather smugly. "I've lived in Bradley, North Carolina, my entire life and it just doesn't get more exciting than the church bake sale or the craft fair in the fall. Have you joined all the Organizations for the Aged?" She poured herself a generous cup of coffee and stared into the mug. The coffee appeared very, very dark and she'd unfortunately not left much room for cream. She made up for the lack of cream by putting in several tablespoons of sugar and cautiously stirring the brew so that it wouldn't slosh.

Miles looked annoyed. "I'm not particularly aged, Myrtle. Sixty is the new...."

"Right, right. I've heard all that poppycock. Sixty is the new forty or something. Well, you're over sixty. And you sure don't feel forty, do you?" said Myrtle. She spilled some coffee onto her robe and stared down at the small puddle in irritation.

Miles pushed a pile of napkins in her direction with a sigh. "What Organizations for the Aged are you referring to? Maybe there's one that I've missed."

Myrtle held up her fingers, enumerating them. "The historical society. Friends of the Library. The Bradley Museum board. Garden club. Our book club."

"Done, done, done, done, done," said Miles morosely.

"Played bingo in the church rec hall? You can win stamps," said Myrtle succinctly.

"No thanks." Miles made a face. "I don't seem to be lucky at bingo. Or, when I think I've won, I'll find out they were playing a special variation where you only win if you get the outside corners or something. Sometimes I only end up with the free space marked out."

"So no bingo. Although you really should play. It's a silly game, but there are those prizes, you know. I haven't had to buy stamps for years. Let's see. Sometimes the community theater has good musicals," said Myrtle. "I think they're playing *Oklahoma* next. I'll go see it with you."

"But there are never any male actors at the community theater," said Miles. His voice was starting to get plaintive. "It's distracting to watch Tilly Cranston play the male leads."

"I think of it as Shakespearean theater in reverse," said Myrtle. "It helps."

Miles reached for a cookie, shaking his head. "Tilly Cranston as Curly in *Oklahoma*. It's just all wrong."

"You know what the problem is? You're retiring from a big city. You should never have moved from Atlanta to a tiny town like Bradley. You've done it all backwards," said Myrtle with sweeping movements meant to show the disastrous mess Miles was making of his life, sloshing more coffee on her bathrobe in the process. "In fact, you likely shouldn't have retired at all. You're in full possession of your faculties. You could still be selling insurance."

Miles gave her a baleful look. "I was an engineer, Myrtle, not an insurance salesman. For heaven's sake."

"Whatever. You retired early, you made the tremendous error of moving to a small town, and now you've done it all. Everything that Bradley has to offer. You'll be waving at cars from your front porch now, cheating at solitaire. You've already started baking cookies, Miles. It's a slippery slope." Myrtle gave him a knowing look over her coffee cup.

"Have you got any better suggestions?"

"Murder," said Myrtle simply.

Miles said, "I'm assuming you're meaning that we'll solve another murder together instead of taking the next natural step of committing it. I don't think I'm *that* bored yet. But as far as I'm aware, there hasn't been any murder recently. Unless you know something that I don't."

"Oh, give it time. This little town is rife with murder. Besides, when the cat's away, the mice will play. And the cat is on a walker," said Myrtle.

Myrtle's son, Red, was the police chief of the town of Bradley, North Carolina, population one thousand five hundred. He was usually on top of Myrtle, trying to keep her out of trouble. But now Myrtle was enjoying being unsupervised while Red was recovering from knee replacement surgery.

"How is Red doing?" asked Miles. "I made extra cookies so that I could take Red and Elaine some tomorrow." He glanced at the clock and corrected himself. "Today, I mean."

"He's doing fine from a *physical* standpoint. The surgeon said that the knee replacement went really well and that Red will eventually feel better than new. But Red hates not being able to take care of himself or drive or do his job. Elaine has had to rearrange furniture so that Red can get around on his walker. And remove the throw rugs so he won't trip. He's keeping his leg raised when he's seated and has ice on his knee a lot. Red is fairly incapacitated." Myrtle didn't sound remotely displeased at this.

"Remind me again who is policing the town when he's out?" asked Miles.

"The county sent a deputy to help him out since Bradley is between deputies right now. Someone named Darrell Smith," said Myrtle. She broke a cookie in half and cautiously tasted it. It was surprisingly very good.

"What's he like?" asked Miles.

Myrtle said, "He's not exactly mentally agile. But he's perfect for the kind of police issues facing the department right now...missing dogs, neighbor complaints, noise ordinance stuff. Red is taking a couple of weeks off, although it could turn into several weeks if he doesn't do his physical therapy exercises. He's out of my hair, at least. Bradley was getting *so* safe and quiet that he spent even more time than usual focusing on me. Thank heavens for that bum knee!"

Miles grinned and shook his head. "Motherly love."

"Motherly love is easier to scrounge up when there's a bit of distance between mother and child," said Myrtle with a shrug. Red lived directly across the street.

Miles bobbed his head in the direction of Myrtle's house. "I saw the gnomes were out. What infraction caused their eruption in your yard this time?"

Myrtle had extensive gnome collection. What had started out as a small, fanciful yard accent had blossomed into a tremendous army of gnomes when she'd made the pleasing discovery that the sight of the gnomes was very upsetting to her son. Whenever Red stepped out of line, Myrtle was there to lug out the ceramic men, all in a variety of precious poses, to fill her front yard.

"He suggested that he could take over 'worrying about my bills' for me. The nerve! He's just nosy, that's all. Curious over my expenses. I told him I had plenty of time to handle my financial affairs, but perhaps he'd like it if *I* gave *him* a hand. And then the gnomes made an appearance."

They thoughtfully considered this as they munched on their cookies.

"Want to watch the soap?" asked Myrtle.

"Have you already seen it?" asked Miles.

"I watched it yesterday afternoon. But there was a whole storyline where one character came back from the dead...you know how it is on *Tomorrow's Promise*. So they brought the character back, but he's a different actor than before—and younger. Most distracting. I think I need to watch the episode again just to absorb it," said Myrtle, feeling annoyed.

"Are you sure it's supposed to be the same character, or is it his twin? That soap is wild about twins...evil twins, good twins. Twins all over the place," said Miles.

"And weddings ... and twins at weddings ... twins interrupting weddings to kidnap brides or otherwise completely disrupt weddings. They must run out of ideas when they're coming up with the scripts." Myrtle walked into Miles's living room and plopped on his sofa in front of the TV.

"But we're still hooked," said Miles morosely.

"Like a fish gobbling up a worm," agreed Myrtle.

Miles picked up the remote and clicked on the TV, absently smoothing down his navy bathrobe. Myrtle felt a slight chill in the air and pulled down an afghan from the back of the sofa, snuggling into it as she curled up on the sofa.

And then there was an insistent knock at Miles's front door.

Myrtle and Miles stared at each other.

"Did anyone know you were here?" asked Miles, putting the remote down on a table and quickly standing up.

"No. I mean, sometimes Red spots me through a window, but he's incapacitated, as we were saying," said Myrtle, throwing off the afghan. "Go ahead and answer the door—I'll cover you." She grabbed her cane and brandished it in the air.

Miles rolled his eyes. "I'm sure that won't be necessary." He walked quickly to the door and peered out a side window. He turned around to Myrtle, eyebrows raised. "It's Wanda."

"Our favorite psychic? In the middle of the night? Well, let her in!"

Miles opened the door and ushered in Wanda. Wanda was skinny as a shadow, practically non-existent in her thinness. She had yellowed leathery skin and a raspy voice from years of smoking far too many cigarettes. Her smile revealed teeth that were hit or miss. Miles had learned to his horror that he and Wanda were cousins, and since then had felt some sort of responsibility toward her. Myrtle had developed a real fondness for the straggly woman, even though Wanda always seemed intent on offering her dire prophesies and warning her away from investigating mysteries.

Miles frowned, and then opened his door again to scan the street. "Where's your car?" he asked sharply.

Wanda shrugged an emaciated shoulder. "Up on cement blocks."

"You didn't walk here! It's freezing cold out there ... it's December, Wanda. Besides, it would have taken you all day."

Wanda lived with her brother, Crazy Dan, in a hubcap-covered shack on a gravel road off the rural route highway.

Wanda shrugged again. "Nothing else to do. And car was broke."

"You should have called me! I'd come pick you up, Wanda." Miles sounded anxious.

"Dan didn't pay the phone bill," explained Wanda succinctly.

Myrtle said, "What about email? You have a computer, I know. You said one time that your psychic services had a Facebook page."

"Computer is broke," said Wanda with a shrug. "And I ain't good at writin' emails, anyway."

Miles sighed. "Let me at least get you a glass of water."

Wanda gave Myrtle an apologetic grin, showing several missing teeth. "Sorry to mess up your TV time."

Myrtle wasn't surprised in the least that Wanda would know that was what they were about to do or even that they were convening in Miles's living room in the middle of the night. She knew that, unlikely as it may seem, Wanda had Powers. "It's taped," said Myrtle with a shrug. "Here, you've got to be exhausted from your walk. Have a seat." She patted the sofa next to her and Wanda perched on the edge of the sofa, seemingly unable to really relax.

Miles came back in the room with a pitcher of water, a tall glass full of ice, and the remainder of the cookies, which Myrtle assumed were for Wanda. Wanda eyed them hungrily.

"Please, eat them up," said Miles, putting the tray down on the coffee table in front of Wanda. "I'll make more later on." He sat down in the leather recliner next to them.

Myrtle and Miles watched in wonder as Wanda prepared to turn the cookies into a distant memory.

Miles cleared his throat. "I'm going to presume that you weren't walking for your general health. Was there something that I needed to do for you? Or something Myrtle can do?"

Wanda nodded and delicately covered her mouth with a nicotine stained hand as she finished chewing. She took a sip of ice water and said, "I need help."

Myrtle stared at her, a bit stunned. "*You* need help? You're usually the one who's doling it out."

Miles leaned forward in the recliner. "How can we help you, Wanda?"

Wanda sat up even straighter as she perched on the edge of the sofa. She intoned mysteriously, "There is great evil at Greener Pastures Retirement Home."

Myrtle slapped herself on the leg. "I *knew* it! Haven't I always said so, Miles?"

"To *ad nauseum*," agreed Miles dryly. "But I don't think Wanda is referring to the way that Red is trying to force you into residing there. What *do* you mean, Wanda?"

"I can guess," said Myrtle. "The management there is denying their poor inmates their basic human rights?"

"They're residents, Myrtle. Not inmates," said Miles.

"Says who?" Myrtle narrowed her eyes at him.

"Not the management," said Wanda in her gravelly voice.

"Is it the food?" asked Myrtle helpfully. "Because the food is really crummy there. Do they poison the food?"

"Not the food." Wanda gave Myrtle a grave look. "One of the old folks is a killer."

Chapter Two

Myrtle and Miles stared at her again.

"Repeat that again, please," said Miles slowly.

"Someone at the Home is a killer. But hasn't killed anyone. Yet." Wanda ate another cookie and watched their reactions.

Myrtle and Miles glanced at each other.

Myrtle said, "So Wanda, you know that there is someone at Greener Pastures who is planning to kill. So you're wanting us to investigate?"

Wanda nodded.

"You can see that someone is going to kill, but you can't see who the killer is? Because, obviously, knowing who it is would be very helpful." Myrtle tried to be patient. Wanda could be so cryptic. But she was somehow always right.

"It don't work that way," said Wanda morosely.

"Doesn't it?"

"No. It's like the hiccups. The Sight shows up and then it goes. I saw the plan. I saw the victim—the woman. I don't see the killer." Wanda looked sad now.

Myrtle felt more cheerful, though. "Oh! Okay, a victim. Now *that* we can work with. We could get to know her and try to prevent the crime from happening."

"What's her name?" asked Miles. He reached into the drawer of the end table next to his recliner and pulled out a small notepad and sharpened pencil.

"Don't know." Wanda studied her shoes, which were looking pretty beat up. The walk likely hadn't helped, either.

Myrtle rubbed her temples. Her head was starting to hurt. But it certainly wasn't going to help things to snap at poor Wanda.

She said slowly and carefully, choosing her words wisely, "I think I'm looking at this from the wrong angle. Wanda, why don't you tell us what you *do* know?"

Wanda nodded again and stared at the floor. She spoke without the hint of any inflection in her voice, "They haven't killed yet. But they will and will try to more than once. Justice must be meted out."

Now Myrtle and Miles gaped at her. Because *meted* wasn't a word they necessarily thought was in Wanda's vocabulary. Where did these visions come from?

"Victim is a hard woman. Sharp tongue. She ... writes." Wanda shrugged. "That's all I know about her."

"Writes ... books?" asked Miles.

"Writes letters? Poetry? Tweets on Twitter?" Myrtle felt her frustration rising.

Wanda shrugged again and ate another cookie.

"How do you know all this, Wanda?" asked Myrtle. "Did a vision just interrupt you at the breakfast table one day?"

Wanda gave her a reproachful look. "The Sight just shows up. I do have a cousin there at the home, though. Cleans there. Randy. He thinks something's up, too. He dropped by to visit me yesterday and said so."

Myrtle said, "Are you sure you need an *investigator*? It sounds as if a security guard who just stood around and looked ominous might be better."

"Or maybe a bodyguard for the future victim?" asked Miles.

Wanda leveled them a look. "Y'all know how crazy it'd sound if Randy told them a psychic saw a death there? Greener Pastures'd just laugh and laugh."

She did have a point.

Myrtle said thoughtfully, "Well, usually I investigate crimes that have already happened. That, you might say, is my forte. But under the circumstances, and considering who is doing the asking, I'll go over to Greener Pastures and start poking around."

She took Miles's notepad and pencil from him and thrust them at Wanda. "Here. Draw her. The future victim."

Wanda squinted at the pencil mistrustfully. "Not so good with them things."

"No writing necessary. Just a sketch," said Myrtle in a bolstering-up type of voice.

Sadly, however, Wanda didn't appear to be any better with drawing than she was with writing. The sketch that Myrtle received back from her could have represented anything from Marilyn Monroe to Santa Claus. She sighed.

Miles diplomatically decided that the verbal description would perhaps be best. He repeated, "So...a writer. A hard woman with a sharp tongue. Right?"

Wanda nodded. She drained the water, picked up and ate a cookie crumb that was miniscule and stood up. "Need to head back."

At these words, there was a peal of thunder that shook the house.

"Well, you're certainly not walking back in the freezing cold during a storm. I'll get my keys." Miles stood up.

"Wait just a minute and I'll put some snacks and things in a bag," said Myrtle briskly.

Of Miles's food, of course. But Miles didn't offer any objections.

She then threw a few apples, some flaky croissants, a few slices of glazed ham, and what appeared to be half a cheesecake into various plastic containers and into a grocery bag.

Wanda looked rather touched as she peered into the bag. "Thanks," she said gruffly.

Miles said wryly, "Myrtle is a softy at heart, even though she sometimes seems a bit intimidating."

"I'm really just a sweet, white-haired old lady," said Myrtle with a shrug.

"I wouldn't go that far," said Miles.

Myrtle snapped her fingers. "The phone line. Wanda, how much is the bill to put you current?"

Wanda grimaced and muttered, "Probably one hundred twenty-five. Or more."

Myrtle made a face and Miles put his hands up in the air in surrender. It was definitely more than either of them wanted to pay.

"How about stamps and envelopes?" asked Myrtle. "At least Wanda would be able to reach us the following day. Mail delivery is fairly reliable."

Wanda looked alarmed, an expression one didn't see often on her laconic face. "My writin's not so good," she muttered.

Myrtle waved her hand dismissively. "Doesn't matter! We'll figure it out. Or you can just write *visit me* and we'll know to run by. Okay?"

Wanda nodded, still looking anxious.

Miles walked over to his desk. He found some postcards and postcard stamps.

"Does anyone send postcards anymore?" asked Myrtle doubtfully. "Why wouldn't you just send an email? And how old are those stamps? Will they still be enough to *send* a postcard?"

"I only recently got these," said Miles stiffly. "They'll be fine. And I rather like sending postcards."

Myrtle rolled her eyes at Wanda. "He would."

Miles opened the front door a little to peek out and the wind slammed it all the way into the wall. Rain blew at their faces as Miles struggled to push the door shut.

"Well." Miles took a folded tissue out of his bathrobe pocket and dabbed at his wet face.

"Where did this storm come from?" grumbled Myrtle. "I don't remember this being forecast."

"We could check the weather on TV," said Miles. "Maybe it's about to move out of here."

Wanda had already sat back down on the sofa and was working through the grocery bag of food.

Miles fiddled with the remote until he got the Weather Channel up. "This is actually one of my favorite stations," he said. "I keep it on in the background during the day."

"Exciting stuff," said Myrtle dryly.

"It can be. There is absolutely frightening weather going on in this country at any given minute." He paused as he studied the weather map. "And right now, it looks as if the frightening weather is moving through here."

"Great." Myrtle morosely squinted at the map. "And it looks as if it's not going anywhere if that map is right. Wanda, can you foresee the weather for the next few hours?"

Wanda violently shook her head. "Weather is quirky."

"Well, judging from the map there's absolutely no way around it. No one needs to be driving in a raging storm. And I'm not making a run for it to get home. You're going to have to host a sleepover party, Miles." Myrtle tried unsuccessfully to keep a gleeful smile repressed.

Miles's long face grew longer, if that were possible. "But Dan will be worried about Wanda. And we can't even call him."

Wanda finished chewing the cheesecake and said, "Naw! Dan don't know where I am half the time, and don't care, neither. He's my brother, not my keeper."

Myrtle said, "For heaven's sake, Miles. It's already after three in the morning. You won't have company for very long. It's not like it's only eight p.m. and you're trying to decide if we're going to paint nails or play Truth or Dare."

Miles looked deeply unhappy. "All right. Well, there's the one guest bedroom with two twin beds. Or someone could take the sofa if they wanted."

Myrtle said, "I'm pretty sure there's a golden rule somewhere that octogenarians no longer have to consider sleeping on sofas. I'll take a twin bed." She looked over at Wanda. "I don't snore."

Wanda bit her lip and looked away. Myrtle sighed.

"I have ear plugs," said Miles. "For when the neighborhood dogs bark. I'll put them out here on the coffee table and make them available to anyone who needs them. We're only talking about a few hours, anyway, as Myrtle said."

"Do you need to dig out linens from the closet for us?" asked Myrtle.

"No, I keep the beds in there made up and ready to go in case I ever have company," said Miles. "But I'll pull out some towels and washcloths for you. Oh, and I have some individually-wrapped, brand-new toothbrushes and travel size toothpaste."

Miles scurried away. "He's so *fastidious*," said Myrtle to Wanda. Wanda wasn't really paying attention to Myrtle though and Myrtle noticed that Wanda was looking quite bemused at all the fussing over. But then, Wanda lived in a very dark, cluttered, hubcap-covered hut with her nutty brother off the rural highway. She might not have experienced this level of hospitality before. In fact, she may not have ever had the opportunity to even be an overnight guest somewhere before.

Miles quickly returned with a basket he'd apparently put together for his rare overnight guests. It included toothbrushes and travel-sized toothpaste, a shower cap, soap, and travel-sized bottles of shampoo, and mouthwash. He also carried two sets of fluffy towels. He flipped on the lights in the small bedroom, put his hands on his hips and looked around him with a critical eye. Finally he said, "I think it's all set up. The last time the cleaning lady was in here, she dusted and vacuumed so it looks fairly tidy."

"It's immaculate compared to my guest bedroom," drawled Myrtle. "I can't ever get Puddin to clean in there. Puddin says she's allergic to dust. Isn't that convenient? A housekeeper with a dust allergy. The foolishness I have to put up with!"

Miles gave her a sympathetic look, having seen Puddin in action. Or rather, in inaction.

"All right," he said. "Well, I guess we all should try to get a little sleep since it'll be dawn before we know it." There was another loud peal of thunder and Miles grimaced. "Or, perhaps there won't be any dawn at all with the cloud cover out there."

Miles retired to his bedroom, turning off lights in the living room as he went.

"All right, then! Bed for us." Myrtle turned down the bedspread and saw, unsurprisingly, hospital corners on sheets that were perfectly unwrinkled and folded precisely down at the top. "Wow. Did Miles use a ruler to make up this bed? Or should I be kidnapping his cleaning lady?"

Wanda gave a tremendous yawn, shoved the sheets aside and lay on the bed. Her dark eyes glanced around the room. "Too clean in here," she muttered. "Ain't natural. Might not sleep."

"Well, if we can't sleep, which is a frequent affliction of mine, then maybe we can at least read. Let's see what Miles has in the bedside table." Myrtle reached over to the wooden table, painted a bright white, and curiously pulled the drawer out. There was a slim volume inside. Myrtle peered at the cover. "*Essential Daily Devotions.*" She opened the book and started leafing through the pages. "With marginalia, no less. In Miles's own handwriting. Is Miles religious? I wouldn't have thought so."

Wanda didn't appear at all interested in Myrtle's fascinating discovery. "G-night," she mumbled, turning her bony back on Myrtle and seeming to instantly fall asleep.

Myrtle sighed. It was discouraging to see that other people were able to fall asleep so effortlessly. It made her wonder, as she had so often in the past, what it would actually be like to fall asleep at night and wake the next morning with absolutely no recollection of the previous eight hours.

She returned the book to its drawer, turned off the light, and lay down, prepared to do her usual sheep counting or ceiling staring. But, to her amazement, she felt a strong drowsiness sweep over her until she fell abruptly into a deep sleep.

Chapter Three

Myrtle woke later that morning to the smell of a Southern breakfast. She recognized bacon and sausage, garlic cheese grits, and waffles by their aroma. Myrtle glanced over to the other twin bed and didn't see Wanda there. Were Miles and Wanda already eating? Was she missing out? She quickly swung her legs out of the bed, pulled her robe on, and hurried to the kitchen.

There she stared in wonder at the sight of Wanda cooking her heart out at Miles's stove. She spotted fluffy-looking omelets in addition to the other breakfast foods she'd already been able to identify by smell. "Wanda! I didn't know you could cook."

Wanda, who'd been so deeply focused on the cooking, jumped before giving Myrtle a reproachful look. "Mama was a cook. She'd bring Dan and me leftovers. She showed me how."

Myrtle was also stunned to see Pasha, her feral cat, contentedly lying in a kitchen sunbeam next to Wanda's feet.

Wanda noticed the direction of her gaze and gave a smug smile. "Yer cat likes me."

"I'm surprised to see her here. Miles will have an absolute stroke. Who knows what kinds of fur she's leaving all over his house. I left a window cracked for her at home and figured she'd jump inside with the storm and all. Did you—well, I guess you let her in?" asked Myrtle, still feeling a little groggy from the unaccustomed sleep.

Wanda nodded, gently sliding hash browns onto a plate with a slotted spatula. "She was outside. In the storm. I opened the front door to let her in."

"So, did you *hear* her out there?" pressed Myrtle.

Wanda just shook her head, looking back at Myrtle. Myrtle gave up with the questioning. It was one of the unexplained things that simply happened around Wanda. "Okay, well, you're taking the rap when Miles starts fussing," she said.

"Starts fussing about what?" asked a suspicious voice behind them. They both turned to see Miles entering the kitchen. He'd apparently already showered and was dressed in khaki pants and a crisp blue button-down shirt. Then he caught sight of Pasha and took a step back.

"Now Miles! You know that you and Pasha have an understanding now," said Myrtle. "Remember? Pasha has become very fond of you. In her way."

Pasha gave Miles a disdainful look and curled closer to Wanda's foot.

"Was Pasha outside in that storm?" Now Miles looked a little horrified.

"Looked like a drowned rat when I pulled her in," grated Wanda.

"I guess she went searching for me when she found I wasn't at home. Loyal Pasha," said Myrtle.

Miles said, "And now onto surprise number two. Wanda, I had no idea that you were such a wonderful cook. This breakfast looks absolutely amazing." He walked closer to the stove and surveyed the food. "Garlic cheese grits? Hash browns? Omelets? Sausage and bacon? It's a feast. And I, for one, am hungry enough to gobble it all down."

The food was just as good as it looked and it was gone within no time. Then it was time for the cleaning up, which Myrtle and Miles insisted on doing as Wanda sat awkwardly by until Pasha leaped adoringly into her lap and Wanda's time was taken up with petting her.

"Okay," said Myrtle as she and Miles finished the last of the dishes. "The storm has cleared out. So the plan is to drive Wanda back home and then to head over to Greener Pastures. Right?

Because it does sound as if it is something of an emergency, if we're there to stop a murder."

"To *try* and stop a murder," said Wanda cautiously. "The Sight—it usually ain't wrong. But seems wrong to don't do nothing."

Myrtle was proud at herself for overlooking all of Wanda's double-negatives. Although the retired high school English teacher in her winced at every occurrence.

"Right," said Miles briskly. "And are you sure you don't want to come along, Wanda?"

"Nope. Won't help if I go. But tell my cousin Randy I said hi," said Wanda.

Myrtle looked down at her robe and slippers. "I should probably head home real quick and change."

"Might be a good idea," said Miles dryly. "Otherwise Greener Pastures might think that you're trying to apply for admittance to their memory care unit."

Myrtle made a face at him. "I'll be back in twenty minutes."

Miles stopped her. "Hey, what are your plans for Pasha? I don't think she needs to stay in here for the duration of our time away. There are no litter boxes here, for one thing." He gave Pasha an uncomfortable look. There was an uncertain peace still between them.

"Just open your back door and let her out that way. She spends her days hunting chipmunks and won't want to stay inside. Besides, I think Pasha was just checking on me." Myrtle opened the front door and walked out.

Unfortunately, at the same point that she was making her foray into Miles's front yard in her robe and slippers, Erma Sherman was outside getting the *Bradley Bugle*. Erma was Myrtle's nemesis and lived between Myrtle and Miles. Erma looked like a donkey, had atrocious breath, talked non-stop about her various disgusting medical issues, and was impossible to escape.

As Erma looked Myrtle up and down, she smiled an unpleasant smile. Which was when Myrtle also remembered something else about Erma—she was a horrible gossip. And Myrtle was now leaving Miles's house in the early morning hours in her nightgown and robe. Myrtle fumed.

At that very moment, however, Myrtle's reputation was saved by an unlikely source. Wanda quickly popped outside with her usual uncanny recognition of trouble and called out to Myrtle, "So—it's a plan, right? Thanks for setting that up with Miles and me."

Erma's face fell with disappointment. There was no fascinating bit of gossip at all—merely a boring meeting of some sort that Myrtle had dressed oddly for.

Myrtle called back, "That's right. Let me get changed real quick and we'll head out." She put her nose up in the air and sailed down the sidewalk, as much as someone with a cane can sail, past the dejected Erma and home again.

After they'd dropped Wanda back home, Myrtle and Miles headed off for Greener Pastures.

"Do you know what gets on my nerves about Greener Pastures?" asked Myrtle as they sped along at a fair clip.

"What's that?" asked Miles. "I thought everything about it got on your nerves. Its very existence."

"That too, yes. But what's really getting on my nerves lately is the way they're trying to rebrand the place as some sort of luxury resort. 'Greener Pastures Retirement *Village*' or some such nonsense. They're making it sound like we're heading to Little Switzerland or something."

Miles said mildly, "It's their right to try and sell openings. Naturally, they're going to want to want to make the place sound as appealing as possible."

"It's blatant false advertising!" snapped Myrtle. "They should be ashamed. They apparently have new management there, and they're intent on making the place seem chichi. Greener Pastures has an ad where everyone is in mid-laugh and clutching a wine glass. The ad copy reads, *enjoy an afternoon of relaxing classical music with a glass of wine.*" Myrtle snorted. "The residents probably *need* to drink to handle it there. And whoever does their print copy is really terrible at copywriting. Have you seen their ads in the *Bradley Bugle?*"

"Must have somehow missed it," said Miles with a sigh.

Myrtle said, "The ads read: *Greener Pastures: Don't follow the herd.*"

"Oh, okay. So pastures and herds. Clever."

Myrtle said, "Not clever. And this one is even worse: *Greener Pastures is your pastoral home—bet the farm on it.* They keep mentioning the new 'Villas' they're opening. It's all just a bunch of hooey. And Red keeps trying to sell me on it! Ridiculous. He waxes poetic about the place when it's actually a complete dump. I told him that if he liked it so much, *he* should move in."

Miles coughed. "Red is only in his late forties and in perfect health and mobility—ordinarily. I don't think he's their ideal applicant."

Myrtle was about to argue the point when Miles quickly continued, "So, tell me what our plan is for today. Whom are we allegedly visiting? I'm assuming we'll be saying we're at Greener Pastures to visit a resident. That sounds a lot better than saying we're there looking for a future murder victim that our psychic friend told us about."

Myrtle said, "I've been thinking on it. I know a few people over there, but we need to be careful whom we pick as our target. We need to be visiting someone who won't find our interest suspicious. Someone who is, perhaps, slightly dotty already and will just be glad to see us and not think twice. I think Ruby Sims will fit the bill nicely."

"Is she a little dotty?"

"She'll do. I was over at Greener Pastures in the last couple of weeks to eat Sunday dinner with a friend of mine. Ruby kept calling me by different names during the entire meal. She doesn't have any local family to act as gatekeepers, so that's good. She has gobs of children, but they don't live around here. We'll say we're visiting Ruby. Then I guess we'll look around for people who resemble the woman on Wanda's drawing. Ask a few questions ... you know ... our usual thing. And then maybe have a word with Wanda's cousin Randy," said Myrtle.

They drove on for a few minutes. Miles said thoughtfully, "Family is a funny thing, isn't it? I was surprised that Wanda had a cousin at Greener Pastures, but then I was surprised that she and I were cousins, too."

Surprised hadn't been the word that Myrtle would have used for *that* discovery.

Miles looked curiously at Myrtle. "And you've really got a very young family, haven't you? Younger than mine and I'm younger than you."

"How gallant of you to say so, Miles," growled Myrtle, staring stoically out the window.

"A son in his forties. A toddler grandson," continued Miles thoughtfully.

"What of it?" asked Myrtle, affecting a disinterested tone.

"Well, nothing, really. I mean, that's all fine. Nothing wrong with that. I was only wondering since most women from your generation ... uh, *our* generation ... married and had children fairly young. It just seems like an anomaly and anomalies are...interesting," said Miles. It appeared that his forehead was starting to dot with perspiration.

"You should know by now that I'm not *most people*, Miles. I didn't marry until quite late, as a matter of fact," said Myrtle stiffly. "I was forty when I married. So I was an older mother, that's all. A mature mother, I think they call it these days."

Miles said, "Forty when you married? I always just assumed you married young and then just...put having children off or something."

"Why on earth would I do that? It wasn't as if I couldn't teach and have a child at the same time." said Myrtle in a cross voice. "No, I simply put off being married. I was picky, okay?"

"Well, that I can certainly imagine," said Miles. He laughed, "You're even picky about peanut butter. I've never seen such loyalty to a particular peanut butter brand."

"Peanut butters vary widely," said Myrtle. "As do people." She was more than ready to move onto another topic, and fortunately, they were just approaching Greener Pastures. She raised her eyebrows. "This certainly looks different. And I was *just* here."

Where Greener Pastures had previously had a sad little sign out front that made it all too easy to drive past the retirement home, it now had a massive and grandiose sign consisting of two brick pillars with ironwork connecting them. *Greener Pastures Retirement Village* was written in script on the iron.

Miles said, "It certainly doesn't look like a dump, Myrtle."

"Appearances can be deceiving," she answered with a sniff.

They drove past carefully manicured beds with a variety of blooms. On their left was a newly constructed series of brick buildings with black shutters with *Greener Pastures Villas* on another iron sign in the front.

"Villas?" asked Miles.

Myrtle heaved a sigh. "I suppose they mean condos. Now they're trying to evoke Italy. Pathetic."

Miles pulled into a parking lot and parked the Volvo. They walked toward the front door. "Automatic doors," said Myrtle. "Hmm. Last time I was here I was battling a wooden door while holding onto my cane at the same time."

There was a chalkboard sign outside the automatic doors with *Today's Events* listed in excruciatingly neat handwriting. Miles studied the sign as Myrtle continued walking toward the doors, her cane thumping on the sidewalk as she went.

"Scrabble, checkers, chess, and a comedic play," said Miles in a musing voice.

"Come *on*, Miles!" said Myrtle testily. "Someone might be about to kick the bucket as we dawdle!"

An old woman walked out of the door right at that moment and gave Myrtle a thunderous glare.

Myrtle hissed to Miles, "You know what I mean. We've got to figure out who this victim is and stop the crime before it happens."

"Do we need to sign in?" asked Miles. He gave the front desk an apprehensive look. "I'd hate for us to have to state what our business here is."

"Nope. The front desk isn't the type where you sign in—it's the type where you ask directions. But I think we'll wander around a little first before we ask for Ruby's room number. Ruby might be in the dining hall—it's lunchtime, after all," said Myrtle.

Myrtle glanced around curiously as they walked down a wide hall with handrails lining either side. "I'd noticed last time that they'd given the place an overhaul. New carpeting. New paint." She stopped short and put her hands on her hips. "Wonder what they're up to," she said suspiciously.

"Improving the place, clearly," said Miles. "It seems very bright and cheerful to me."

"Hmm." Myrtle wasn't so sure. She frowned. "What's this mob up ahead?" she asked, gesturing to a group of people in wheelchairs and pushing walkers.

"Looks like a traffic jam," said Miles. "Is that the entrance to the dining room?"

"Unfortunately." They approached the group and stood in line behind them. "They need a fast lane here. These folks are poky."

Miles raised his eyebrows. "Just because you're so mobile doesn't mean you should be smug, Myrtle. And people can hear you," he said in a low voice as some residents turned to give Myrtle reproving looks.

"It's not *their* fault they're poky. But it's the management's fault for allowing these traffic jams. The same thing happens outside the health room and the chapel—they block up the halls with their walkers and wheelchairs and other contraptions. They're all lining up to go through the dining hall door like jockeys in the starting gate," said Myrtle.

An old woman with Coke-bottle glasses turned and gave Myrtle a baleful look, which Myrtle carefully ignored.

Miles scrutinized the dining hall as they finally entered. Then he smiled. "Reminds me of my old college dining hall," he said, a gleam in his eye. "Look—there are even little bouquets of fresh flowers on every table."

Myrtle snorted. "The food will remind you of your old college dining hall, too. The meatloaf is particularly treacherous. It should be avoided at all costs."

"What are the rules here?" asked Miles, still surveying the room. "Are we allowed to sit wherever we want?"

"Of course we are! I even saw it in their manual one time," scoffed Myrtle.

"Manual?" Miles looked bemused.

"Manual, welcome guide...whatever the thing is called. Point being, there are *no* reserved seats at Greener Pastures. It's supposed to be a bastion of friendly camaraderie. Let's just put my pocketbook down on one of the tables to hold our spot since I don't see Ruby in here right now. It can get very busy very quickly."

They approached one of the round tables covered with jaunty yellow tablecloths.

A thin woman with high cheekbones glared at Myrtle as they approached. "No room!" she said sternly.

"Why, there's plenty of room!" said Myrtle hotly, feeling suddenly a lot like Alice at the Mad Hatter's tea party.

"No room for you," said the thin woman rudely. She must have realized how she sounded because she tried again, still sounding ungracious, "I mean—these seats are taken."

"No worries. I wouldn't have wanted to sit at this table anyway," said Myrtle, eyes narrowed. She flounced away, glancing around to see if there were another free couple of spots somewhere.

"The nerve," muttered Myrtle, her feelings a bit stung.

"What about the Greener Pastures owner's manual forbidding reserved seats?" murmured Miles.

"I've half a mind to report her to the retirement home authorities," said Myrtle. "Here we are, hapless visitors, and we're rejected and dejected."

"You can sit here if you like," a reedy voice piped up behind them. "Or not, if you'd rather not. Either way is fine. No one cares at this table. At least, *we* don't care."

Myrtle turned to see a woman at a large round table. She had perfect posture and was gazing steadily at them. She sat with two other friendly looking ladies wearing brightly colored tops.

"The gallant ladies of the round table, saving me from embarrassment," said Myrtle with a smile.

Miles gave a small cough behind her.

"Miles is with me," said Myrtle. "It'll ruin the hen party—is that okay?"

Apparently, it was more than okay. The ladies all beamed at Miles and quickly moved their chairs to make room. Myrtle sighed. It was obvious why they'd gotten the table. Well, she didn't mind capitalizing on Miles's supposed sex appeal, either. Not if it meant they had a place to eat lunch.

They stood in line, sliding their trays along the metal shelf and pointing out what food they chose to the staff. There were chicken fillets filled with sage and onion, roast pork with applesauce, leek and cheese bake, and a quiche Lorraine. Myrtle remained stoic through the line. She'd made the mistake of having high expectations of the Greener Pastures food before, only to be disappointed.

This time, though, she was pleasantly surprised, although she wasn't about to let on that she was.

Miles took a cautious bite of his chicken. His eyebrows shot up. "Myrtle, this food isn't half bad." He took a second, more enthusiastic bite. "Actually, it's good. Much better, in fact, than what I made for myself for lunch yesterday."

"Don't be hasty. It's not really fair to judge a hot lunch against a pitiful cheese sandwich or whatever you made for yourself yesterday."

"It was a salad with vegetables from my own garden," said Miles rather indignantly.

A lady next to Miles beamed at him, giving a flutter of her eyelashes. "Do you really grow your own vegetables? I really do admire a man for living off the land."

Myrtle snorted. "Miles lives off the Piggly Wiggly grocery store. And then accents that food with tomatoes grown in his small garden." This lunch was getting to be irritating, although Miles seemed pleased.

"Have we seen you here before?" asked the lady next to Miles, completely ignoring Myrtle's presence.

Miles opened his mouth to answer but Myrtle quickly said, "Actually, we're here to visit a friend of ours who hasn't apparently made it to the dining room yet. Ruby Sims. I might be on a reconnaissance mission, myself—checking the place out to see if it might make a suitable future home."

She was surprised at how glibly the words came out, especially since they were complete lies. Miles gave her an admiring look at the smoothness in which she delivered the falsehoods.

The woman sitting next to Myrtle hadn't yet uttered a word, instead, continued eating her roast pork and studying her intently. She had sharp features that were carefully outlined in various earth-colored makeup. She wasn't unattractive, just hard looking. She wore clanking jewelry and a turquoise top with well-ironed white linen pants.

"Is something wrong?" asked Myrtle with some irritation. It was no fun to be so blatantly stared at.

Chapter Four

"Did you teach me?" asked the old woman, narrowing her eyes. "English? In high school?"

"Surely not," snapped Myrtle, feeling a rising horror that she might have taught someone who appeared nearly as old as she was.

Miles started choking on his chicken and Myrtle pounded on his back. He hastily sipped his iced tea until the coughing spell subsided. The entire time, the old woman continued staring at her.

"I was Inez Bridgebane," she said. "Now I'm Inez Wilson. And I'm positive you taught me. Miss Towers, wasn't it? I never forget a face. Never."

Myrtle sighed. "Yes, that was my maiden name. I suppose I did teach you. But it must have been early in my career—I'm not *that* old. I did start out as a substitute for a pregnant teacher and finished the year out for her. That probably was when you had me. I was barely older than my students that year."

Inez just gave her a smirking smile and didn't answer.

The woman sitting next to Miles tried to enter the conversation again. "So y'all are here visiting! How nice. Are you...siblings?" she asked hopefully.

Miles said, "No. We're not related ... we're friends."

The women at the table looked back and forth between Miles and Myrtle as if trying to figure out what *friends* might entail. Apparently, the woman next to Miles decided to accept it at face value. She said, "How nice!" and beamed at Miles in an encouraging manner.

"So, you're visiting Ruby?" asked Inez.

"That's right," said Myrtle. She tried a bit of her broccoli casserole. Not bad. She scooped up a larger portion.

"Funny Ruby didn't mention that," said Inez.

Myrtle got the impression that Inez was the kind of person who enjoyed a lot of drama. And, lacking drama, might be the type to generate some herself.

"You're friends with Ruby?" asked Miles quickly. He appeared to be both attempting to deflect attention from Inez's question and attention away from himself.

Inez's face muscles tightened up. It was clear that Miles hadn't won Inez over. Although the other women at the table were hanging on every word that was coming out of Miles's mouth.

"I live on her hall and spend maybe more time with her than I'd care to. Which makes it very odd that I know nothing about your visit," redirected Inez. She pursed her thin lips.

Myrtle made a breezy wave of her hand. "It's a surprise visit, that's all. A special treat for Ruby."

Miles grinned at her. Myrtle was concerned for a moment that he might burst into applause. She gave him an almost-imperceptible bow.

"Amazing. I haven't heard Ruby mention your name, Miss Towers," drawled Inez.

"It's *Clover*." Myrtle cut into her meat aggressively. "Has been for over forty years, for heaven's sake."

"Haven't heard her mention a Clover, either."

The woman was like a pit bull. She simply refused to let go. "Well, you know Ruby. She was probably being considerate and trying not to bore everyone with stories of our adventures together."

"I very much doubt that's the case, since Ruby is dull as dishwater and doesn't care a whit about boring all of us to tears." Inez scrutinized Myrtle again. "Although somehow I think *you're* probably not dull. Not one bit." Her gaze rested on Miles for a second before bouncing off again. She'd apparently passed judgment on him.

Miles gave Inez an indignant look. Then he returned to his evident fascination with his chicken.

"Besides, Ruby's mental acuity has plummeted recently. Absolutely plummeted. She might have been somewhat absentminded before. Maybe a little foggy. But now she's memory *impaired*," said Inez with great emphasis. "I'm sure the staff here is keeping an eye on her."

A jovial man with a neatly trimmed beard and a straw hat sat down at their table. Although there wasn't an empty seat, he pulled one over to make room. "Myrtle Towers!" he proclaimed in a booming voice, kissing Myrtle solidly on the cheek.

Myrtle recoiled, dabbing her cheek with her napkin. "What is this, an episode of *This is Your Life*?" she asked crabbily. It was annoying that she didn't recognize this old man when he so clearly recognized her. If he said that she'd taught him, she'd head back home and call it a day, Wanda or no Wanda.

"You don't remember me?" The man seemed crestfallen.

"I clearly taught for way too many years," said Myrtle with a sigh.

The old man's face was startled before he threw his head back and laughed. "I'd forgotten your delightfully dry sense of humor, Myrtle. You're teasing, aren't you? You remember that we were sweethearts years ago."

Miles, eyes watering, started choking on his chicken again and the old lady next to him timidly tapped him on his back in a way that wouldn't dislodge a crumb.

"Certainly not!" Myrtle gave the old man a horrified look.

Inez was enjoying the scene playing out in front of her. "Winston, she clearly has no idea who you are."

"Winston?" Myrtle frowned. "Surely you're not...."

"Winston Rouse, at your service," said the old man, taking off his straw hat and giving a deep bow.

Miles was downing iced tea quickly, trying to suppress his coughing so he could listen in.

Myrtle gave him a critical look before returning to her broccoli casserole. "I suppose age has done us both a disservice. Plus the fact, of course, that I haven't laid eyes on you for at least forty years."

"Well, it's a real pleasure to see you again, my dear. A real pleasure." He reached out and gave her a hug. It was an odd sort of hug since Myrtle was pulling back as Winston was leaning in.

Winston seemed either oblivious to the awkward moment or determined to ignore it. "So ... are you still a single pringle?"

"No. No, I married. I'm Myrtle Clover now, Winston."

Winston snapped his fingers and his expression was crestfallen. "Rats. Who's the lucky man? Don't tell me—it's this young fella here," he said, gesturing to Miles. "Aren't you the cougar, Myrtle?"

Before Miles could start another choking session, Myrtle hastily corrected him. "No, not Miles. He's a friend of mine. No, I married over forty years ago. And was widowed not long afterward."

Winston's heavy eyebrows drew together. "Sorry to hear that."

"It was a long time ago," said Myrtle with a dismissive wave of her hand.

Winston's eyes were hopeful. "So are you looking to move here, then? To Greener Pastures?"

Myrtle managed not to make a face. "Well ... I'm really here to visit a friend. But I'm taking notes of course, because I may be interested in living at Greener Pastures. I might be visiting quite a bit in the upcoming days."

Miles gave her an admiring look. It *was* amazing she carried off that particular statement.

"You should come, Myrtle," said Winston in a bit of a wheedling voice. "There's a lot going on at Greener Pastures."

Inez rolled her eyes. "Perhaps if you like bingo and Scrabble."

"I don't just mean the games, Inez," said Winston. "I'm talking about all the scandalous gossip. Inez knows more about them than she's letting on. She runs a newspaper here."

"What kinds of scandalous things?" asked Myrtle.

"Oh, it's just like high school again with the dating and the break-ups and all. Plus there are secrets from the past. Fascinating stuff," said Winston with a wink.

Miles said, "Do you like it here? At Greener Pastures?"

Winston looked at Miles with surprise. "Most *definitely*," he said with vigor. "What's not to like? I've got housekeeping to make up my bed and clean up after me. I've got my meals cooked for me and the dishes washed after I'm done. No yard to fertilize or aerate or seed or mow, no pesky flowers to plant. No home repairs to make. People to play games with or sing old songs with in the commons room. And women outnumber men by ten to one. It's paradise, man. It's like being on a cruise ship every single day of my life."

Myrtle grimaced. "I don't have the right kind of clothes for a cruise. It sounds as if I'd have to update my wardrobe to live in a place like this." She turned to Inez. "Tell me more about your newsletter."

Inez drawled, "It's a news*paper*. You know—the kind that you read in the mornings."

"Yes, thanks—I *know* that. I work for a newspaper, myself. For a *town*," said Myrtle a bit testily.

Inez looked at Myrtle through narrowed eyes. Myrtle realized that now she seemed like competition to Inez. A real newspaper reporter who might be moving to Greener Pastures? Before Inez could shut up like a clam, Myrtle hastily amended, "It's really just a column that I do for the paper. Helpful hints, that kind of thing. Nothing, really."

Inez said slowly, "The paper here is called *Home Life*. We print all the news everyone here is dying to read. They all say they look forward to seeing their names in print along with my descriptions of what they're wearing and their activities."

Winston winked at Myrtle again. "And all the gossip that's fit to print!"

Inez scowled. But Myrtle also saw a fleeting glimpse of wistfulness there. Was she an admirer of Winston's?

Myrtle said, "How about crime stories? Is there a problem with crime at all here? I'm just curious as a potential resident, you know."

"Oh sure, there's crime," said Inez.

One of the other ladies at the table looked at Inez reproachfully. "Not big crime, Inez. I won't hear you say things like that about Greener Pastures. I feel very safe here. Maybe there's a smattering of theft, but that's all I've ever heard about. You're making it sound as if people are getting murdered as they sleep."

"Are they?" asked Myrtle quickly.

"No!" said the old lady.

Myrtle tried not to show her disappointment. However *was* she going to gather clues and figure out who this victim was supposed to be if Greener Pastures was some sort of bastion of safety?

Inez said, "So...your relationship with Ruby Sims."

"It's close," snapped Myrtle.

"Naturally," said Inez smoothly. "It's just so odd that you didn't recognize her when she sat down just a few feet away."

Myrtle blinked as Inez pointed out a woman with fluffy, snow-white hair that framed her face like a halo. She somehow had a china doll-like face despite being somewhat plump.

"My vision isn't all that it used to be," said Myrtle weakly. As a matter of fact, she wouldn't have described Ruby Sims with any of the adjectives that leapt to mind upon seeing her.

Inez, seeming to enjoy stirring up trouble, called sharply to Ruby. "Ruby! Look who's here!" This didn't help matters as Ruby sloshed her glass of pink lemonade all over herself.

Ruby glanced nervously around her, eyes skipping right over Myrtle in the process. Inez smirked.

Miles gave Myrtle a rueful wince.

"No, Ruby, right here!" said Inez, pointing to Myrtle. "It's Myrtle Towers!"

"Clover!" said Myrtle with great irritation.

A confused look passed over Ruby's face and she squinted at Myrtle. Then she quickly recovered and said, "Hi, sweetie. You came here to visit me? How nice."

Inez said, "Would you like Myrtle and Miles to sit with you, now that you're in the dining room?"

Ruby bobbed her head and said, "Of course, sweetie."

It was quickly apparent that Ruby called *everyone* sweetie. It was also apparent that Ruby's fogginess had gotten worse and calling people sweetie was a great way to cover up the fact that you didn't remember anyone's name.

Myrtle leaned over to get her pocketbook and found that Winston's face was very close to hers. She jerked back with irritation, holding her purse in front of her protectively. "Leaving so soon, my fair lady?" he asked sadly.

Miles seemed to be choking again, although he wasn't even eating anything. His eyes were full of merriment.

"I'm paying a visit to my friend," said Myrtle.

"Her gain is my loss," said Winston gallantly, clutching his chest as if feeling pangs.

Myrtle carefully picked up her tray, hanging her cane and her pocketbook on one arm as Miles somehow handled both their drinks and his own tray. Winston stood respectfully until Myrtle had left the table.

"Thank goodness," muttered Myrtle to Miles. "I feel as if we had a lucky escape. That whole table was a nightmare."

"Will you still feel that way after spending an afternoon with Ruby Sims?" asked Miles under his breath.

Ruby was looking more confused as Miles and Myrtle pulled their chairs up around her table. "You and I are good friends, sweetie?" she asked in her broad Southern accent. Her bright blue eyes were a bit baffled.

Myrtle decided honesty was the best policy here. The sooner Ruby stopped asking questions and took their presence for granted, the better. "I wouldn't say we were *good* friends," said Myrtle in a quiet voice. "But I wanted to take a closer look at Greener Pastures and remembered that you were living here. I thought I'd pop by for a visit—to see you and to see the retirement home. And Miles decided to come along, too. Because Miles...." She paused. What *was* Miles's excuse for being here?

Miles smoothly filled in. "Because I'm interested in becoming a resident, too."

Myrtle stared at him. That statement sounded entirely too genuine.

Miles asked kindly, "Ruby, do you like it here at Greener Pastures?"

Ruby nodded happily, her white, fluffy curls bouncing. "I do. I really do. I've made so many good friends here and have done so many different activities. There's yoga and needlework groups. And we go to the mall or to the movies on the bus—that's always fun. I've made some very good friends. Like Mickey."

Myrtle nodded. This was more of the same: nice people, fun activities. No mention of potential murder from anyone, and it was all very frustrating.

"Would you like to meet her?" asked Ruby eagerly.

"Who?"

"Mickey! Let's go meet her," said Ruby.

Chapter Five

Myrtle gave Miles a startled look. "Ruby, you haven't even eaten your lunch yet." And Myrtle still had a bit of her rice pilaf left. She'd found it surprisingly palatable.

"It's okay—I'm not really that hungry, anyway." She abruptly stood and started walking toward the door.

Myrtle and Miles stared at her for a moment before quickly following her. "I think your choice of person to visit has real issues," he muttered.

"Don't be bitter just because you couldn't finish your lunch," said Myrtle.

"That corn pudding was pretty tasty," said Miles, sounding sad. "And what's the point of our following Ruby? Do you really think she's going to be able to help us find our victim? Or our future killer? I'm wondering if she even has the capacity to remember names minutes after hearing them."

"Well, she certainly remembers Mickey's name. Since Mickey seems to be such an important figure here, maybe *Mickey* can help us." Myrtle sighed. "What's Ruby prattling on about?"

Ruby was, in fact, prattling on about the wonderful food, the games and activities the staff planned, and the little pocket gardens that were in courtyards around the grounds.

"Completely brainwashed," muttered Myrtle.

But Miles seemed somehow interested in Ruby's ramblings.

Myrtle decided to redirect. It was good to meet as many people as she could at the home, surely. "So you and Mickey are friends, right? Who else do you hang out with?"

Ruby's eyes clouded with confusion again. "Hang out with?"

"You know. With whom do you eat? Or, go to activities with, do your yoga with, go to chapel with? That sort of thing," said Myrtle.

Ruby hesitated again and Myrtle realized that the names had probably escaped her. "Maybe some of the people Miles and I were eating lunch with?" asked Myrtle. "Inez? And ... uh, Winston?"

"Yes!" said Ruby, excited. "Inez lives in the room right next door to Mickey. And I live across the hall from both of them."

They entered an elevator from which an old man was exiting. He had a large collection of wrinkles that all settled into a frown. He was mainly bald except for a white fringe of hair around his head. He had brown eyes and a stony expression and walked past them without a greeting on his way to the dining room.

Ruby said in a small voice, "And he lives near us, too. In the room on the other side of Mickey." She added in an even smaller voice, "And he's mean."

"Mean to Mickey?" asked Myrtle as they descended to the bottom floor.

"Mean to everybody," said Ruby in a fervent drawl. "But especially to Mickey. Lots of people are mean to Mickey." She looked sad. But then she sprang out of whatever sadness she was feeling. "Just wait until you see our door decorations! They're the best."

Ruby chatted on about the benefits of using fake flowers on their floor. Myrtle nodded. They would definitely have to be fake since there appeared to be no natural light in the hallway. "Have they stuck you in the basement?" Myrtle asked in disbelief.

"It's the bottom floor," said Ruby in a cheery voice.

"The basement. Aren't the rooms gloomy? I should hope you'd get a discount for having a room in this location," said Myrtle.

"Oh, *no* ... no, we like it down here. It's ever so quiet. And there's plenty of light in the rooms ... you'll see. There are windows near the top of the walls that shine light down like a skylight," said Ruby.

"It's quiet, all right," said Myrtle. Eerily silent, as a matter of fact. And if the individual resident rooms had natural light, the hallway certainly didn't. "Like a dungeon."

Miles gave her a reproving look. Changing the subject, he politely asked Ruby, "Do you have any children?"

"Yes! I have six sons." Ruby gave them a proud look.

"Wow," said Myrtle. "Six sons. That's a lot of kids." She'd remembered Ruby having a lot of children, but not that large of a brood.

"And nary a one in jail," drawled Ruby with an emphatic nod of her head.

"Quite an accomplishment," said Myrtle dryly.

The residents of the dungeon-like floor had attempted to make their areas a bit more cheerful by putting out various welcome mats, flowerpots, (with silk flowers since there was no sun in the hall), door decorations, and entrance tables with baskets of candy on them.

"This is my room," said Ruby, beaming at her door. She'd put a poinsettia wreath on her door and had a small table with a cat on it. The cat was real enough to make Myrtle peer more closely at it, finally convincing herself that it was indeed stuffed.

"Do you own a cat?" asked Ruby wistfully.

Did anyone *own* a cat? Cats were sort of like independent contractors. At least Pasha was. But Myrtle knew what Ruby was getting at. "Yes. I have a black cat named Pasha."

Ruby stopped walking with a gasp. She fixed Myrtle with an intense stare. "Can you bring Pasha for a visit? To see me?"

Miles coughed. "She's not the kind of cat that goes on visits, really. She's a little...unpredictable."

Ruby's eyes filled up in response and Myrtle was suddenly very worried that Ruby was going to break into tears. She remembered a tactic that had worked well with Red when he was little and seemed to work well for Myrtle's grandson, Jack, too. "We'll see."

"Really?" Ruby's eyes lit up with hope.

"That's right—we'll see."

It seemed to satisfy Ruby. "Here's Mickey's room," said Ruby in a reverent tone. They knocked and a commanding voice barked at them to come in.

Myrtle couldn't comprehend why Mickey was spoken of as practically a deity by Ruby. She was a small woman dressed in workout clothes that had seen better days—and Mickey clearly wasn't doing any actual working out. She had high cheekbones and piercing eyes. She looked like the type of person who didn't suffer fools lightly—and yet she apparently spent time with Ruby, which was rather baffling. Mickey grunted a greeting to them and Ruby allowed Miles and Myrtle to handle their own introductions, having likely forgotten their names already.

"Good to meet you," said Mickey. "I'm technically Evelyn, but everyone has always called me Mickey. Last name Pelias." She shook their hands with a surprisingly firm grip.

A moment later, Myrtle was startled to realize that there was someone else in the room. The figure had been sitting so still in the corner that she could have been mistaken for a pile of laundry. But when Ruby said, "Hi sweetie" to the corner, Myrtle and Miles both turned to look more closely.

The quiet figure was middle-aged, had lackluster brown hair, bad skin, and a bit of a weight problem. Mickey arched her drawn-on eyebrows. "This is my daughter, Natalie," she said, waving her hand in the direction of the woman. It appeared as if she were making the introduction for Ruby's benefit as much as much for Myrtle and Miles.

Mickey fixed her piercing gaze on them. "Why are you here?" she asked.

"I have visitors," said Ruby breathlessly, giving Myrtle and Miles a look of wonderment.

"Here to visit Ruby?" Mickey studied them even more carefully.

"That's right—just visiting Ruby and getting acquainted with Greener Pastures," said Myrtle with a vague wave of her hand.

"Acquainted with Greener Pastures?" repeated Mickey. "As a prospective resident, you mean?" She snorted. "Why would you want to come here? It's dangerous."

Mickey's daughter, Natalie, rolled her eyes at this statement as if it were something she'd heard many times.

"That's right! I see your disbelieving eyes. My daughter won't believe the truth because she doesn't want the inconvenience of moving me." Mickey gave Natalie a resentful look. "This place is cutthroat. Dangerous."

Ruby bobbed her head in agreement, looking anxious.

Miles gave Myrtle a meaningful look. This certainly sounded promising—as long as Mickey wasn't simply demented.

Natalie interrupted in a nasal voice, "It's *perfectly* fine here. The staff is charming. There are wonderful activities and very nice people who live here."

"Bah!" Mickey glared at her daughter. "My life is constantly threatened. Constantly. I'm always watching my back. I sleep with one eye open."

"If you can manage that trick while snoring at the same time," said Natalie with a snort. "Seems you'd lock your door every now and then if you felt so endangered."

Mickey ignored Natalie's latest interjection. "The staff refuses to believe me."

"And *I* don't believe you, either. It's all pretty implausible, Mama. Why would someone possibly want to murder you?"

Mickey gave Natalie an inscrutable look.

Ruby said, eyes opened wide, "Oh! *I* believe you, Mickey. Every word."

"This is why you're my friend," said Mickey. "You're one of the very few people with any sense at this place."

Miles gave Myrtle a look that said that Greener Pastures was in a lot of trouble if Ruby Sims was the only one making sense.

Myrtle cleared her throat. "Why do you feel as if you're in danger? What's happened?"

"Crime," snapped Mickey. "Crime has happened. I've called the Bradley Chief of Police himself and can't seem to get any resolution to my complaints. He acts as if I'm making the entire thing up."

Myrtle nodded. "The Chief of Police is a most annoying man. Most annoying." She could easily picture Red unsuccessfully trying to smooth over Mickey's ruffled feathers. Naturally, he would think she was making it all up.

"For one thing," said Mickey, clearly warming up to a favorite topic, "And this is on the very smallest scale, but someone is stealing from me."

Mickey's daughter rolled her eyes. She picked up the celebrity magazine next to her and started reading with great determination.

Ruby said solemnly, "And people are stealing from me, too. I have a missing toothbrush and a missing deodorant. And a shoe from my favorite pair has been stolen, too."

Myrtle sighed. But Mickey nodded at Ruby, validating her delusion.

"Well, Ruby doesn't have a lot to steal, but I guess they steal what they can. Maybe it's the staff—they're a dangerous lot of people here. Maybe it's some of the sneaky, horrid inmates they have here. But I've had necklaces stolen, cash stolen, rings stolen." Mickey gave an exaggerated shrug.

Miles said carefully, "Not misplaced? Stolen?"

Mickey glared at him. "Stolen. I do know the difference. Do you really think I can misplace something in a room this size? Where on earth would it go?"

And, indeed, the room did appear very tidy and organized.

"As I was saying," she continued, giving Miles a repressive look, "that's just the tip of the iceberg. An annoyance. Something to report to the police to give them fodder later for not believing my most serious allegations. Now I know that my *life* is in danger."

"Why is that?" asked Myrtle. She was feeling a lot less skeptical than she might ordinarily have because of Wanda's prediction.

"Because I know too much," said Mickey simply. "I work on the Greener Pastures newspaper."

"News*letter*," corrected Natalie.

Mickey leveled a stern look at her daughter. She took a deep breath. "Natalie, I need you to go to the nurse's station and get me my afternoon medication. Now."

Natalie heaved a sigh, stood up, and slouched over to the door, letting it slam behind her on the way out.

"Now!" said Mickey. "Now maybe I can finally get a couple of words out. It's impossible to even think with Natalie hanging around like a vulture all the time."

Miles said stiffly, "Not a vulture, surely. It appears she's here to help you out."

"Don't let her fool you," snapped Mickey. "She's less dutiful than avaricious. She's worse than all the staff and all the nefarious residents put together. And she wields guilt trips like weapons. Now where was I? Oh yes—I know too much because I'm in charge of the Greener Pastures *newspaper. The Home Truth.*"

Miles knit his brows and glanced over at Myrtle in puzzlement.

"When we were in the dining room, a woman named Inez seemed to think that she was the editor of the paper," said Myrtle.

"*That* silly newsletter? Pah. Mine is hardcore, *real* news. I don't cover who is holding hands with whom at the Valentine's mixer. And mine doesn't function as a mouthpiece for the

Greener Pastures management. Mine has exposés. It has secrets. It has in-depth profiles on people who are influential or have been influential. Mine has the real truth. Like with the petty thievery—I know who's behind it all. The kind of stuff that people have covered up for years and now forget to cover up."

Myrtle blinked at her. This didn't somehow sound like something that Greener Pastures would be excited about endorsing. "And this publication is sanctioned by the home?"

"Of course not!" spat out Mickey. "It's not only discouraged, it's snatched up at every opportunity from every commons area and tossed away as if it were trash. That's because truth is dangerous and knowledge is power. Money is power too, and I have plenty of that." Mickey's eyes gleamed.

There was a loud knock on the door.

"Come in!" hollered Mickey. She snorted. "Am I having a party? Does this number of guests in one's room constitute a party?"

The door opened and a man of indeterminate age who bore a striking resemblance to Wanda except for a long ponytail stuck his head in. "Housekeeping, Miss Mickey," he drawled. He gave Myrtle a wink.

"Housekeeping? Now? For heaven's sake," said Mickey.

"Just taking your trash out," he answered mildly.

"Well, there's certainly plenty of that. All of Natalie's Ho-Ho and Twinkie wrappers. That girl's eating is deplorable."

The man nodded his head in an agreeable manner as he quickly and expertly cleared out the two trashcans in her room. "Also needed to let you know the bug man is coming through. Should be here in a minute."

"The bug man!" Now Mickey looked alarmed. "I don't like that guy. Talks my ears off when he's here and eats my peppermints. Why on earth is he here in the dead of winter anyway? Let's head out to the commons area."

Miles said, "What about Natalie?"

"She'll find us."

Each floor apparently had a small commons area with a table and chairs, a sofa, and some armchairs arranged around a large television. Although the furniture and carpeting looked nice and there were plenty of lamps, Myrtle still retained that rather claustrophobic feeling from the lack of windows and the sense of being underground.

Miles said under his breath, "At least this would be a great place to be if a tornado comes through."

"We *never* have tornadoes in Bradley," said Myrtle with a sniff. "Especially in December."

Miles said, "Are you thinking that Mickey is our possible victim?"

"Of course. But what other conclusion can I come to? After all, she's the only one talking about the dangerous environment here and her life being in danger. Everyone else is full of happy talk about sunbeams and kitties and good food."

They settled in two armchairs that were close to the sofa where Mickey and Ruby had plopped down. Mickey said in her fierce voice, "Now, what were we talking about? Before that blasted interruption?"

"I don't remember. But I know what I wanted to ask you about," said Myrtle.

"Then lay it on me," said Mickey, leaning back on the sofa and half-closing her eyes in either reflection or sleepiness.

"You sound like a truthful person," said Myrtle.

"You can bet your bippy I'm truthful."

"Then share your opinion of Greener Pastures with me. Really. You touched on some issues that were different from other people's views. I want to hear more about them."

Mickey gave her a hard look. "It's okay. It's had a face-lift recently, but don't let that fool you ... it's the same old place. They're trying to put some cosmetic upgrades on a home that needs a complete overhaul. Needs more nurses. And they need lots more security, since it's dangerous here. Now are you asking about the *people*? The poor inmates of this place? Because you really should be asking about them. And it's a mixed lot. Some of them are a little edgier than you'd think you'd find in an old folk's home. Lots of secrets here ... *lots* of secrets."

Myrtle asked, "And you like finding them out?"

Mickey was starting to look a little bored. "It's a hobby of mine."

Myrtle glanced over in Ruby's direction and noticed that Ruby had fallen asleep—her chin resting on her chest and her breath coming out in little regular puffs. Looking over at Miles, Myrtle saw that he was looking drowsy too and was blinking his eyes with great force to try to keep them from shutting permanently. The heavy Greener Pastures lunch must have gotten to him.

"I guess we'd better be going," said Myrtle with a small sigh. Mickey seemed to have spilled everything she was going to if the sudden expression of boredom had been any indication. And she needed Miles to drive her home before the sleepiness got too bad.

They stood up. Mickey just gave them a small smile, not bothering to stand. This choice might have been influenced by the fact that Ruby's head had now swung over to Mickey's shoulder. "Good to meet you," she said briskly.

As Myrtle and Miles walked back through the halls to the elevator, they saw the old man with the fringe of white hair again. "Uh oh," said Miles. "Ruby said that was the mean one."

And, indeed, the old man glared at them as they approached. "How are you?" murmured Myrtle.

"My business is my business!" grouched the man. His eyes were a fierce blue.

"Why wouldn't it be?" said Myrtle with a frown. "And what does that have to do with me?"

"I saw you hanging out with her. That motor-mouth Ruby. She tells Mickey everything. And it's not her business or anyone else's." The old man was nearly foaming at the mouth.

"We're not exactly part of their group or anything. We don't even live here. We were only visiting," said Miles in a soothing voice.

"Sure you are!" snarled the man. "But here comes Ruby running up behind you now. So apparently you're all closer than you say."

They turned around and sure enough, Ruby, looking amazingly fresh and not at all like someone who just woke up from a deep sleep, was rushing up as fast as possible. She skidded to a stop when she saw the old man however, giving him an apprehensive look.

"I'm sorry," she said to Myrtle and Miles. "I had visitors and didn't even say goodbye! I just got so sleepy." She edged away from the old man who was now looking even more agitated.

He said furiously to her, "You just stay away from me, Ruby. Don't want to see your face for a while. Telling tales! Thought you were a friend!"

"I *am* a friend," said Ruby, but her voice was uncertain.

The old man wasn't hearing of it, though, and quickly unlocked his door and disappeared into his room. Outside his door, ironically, was a miniature fishing pole with the name Fred on it, and a small table had a basket of fishing flies in it. Apparently, whatever peace or Zen that fishing gave him had worn off since his last trip.

Ruby gave a humorous large sigh of relief when he was gone. "Let me walk you back up to the front door," she said, beaming at them. "It's the least I can do. And it's like a maze in here sometimes."

As they continued toward the elevator, they ran into an exasperated Natalie holding a clear bathroom cup that held pills inside. "Have you seen Mother?" she asked.

"In the commons area," said Ruby stumbling over her words a little. "Escaping the bug man."

Natalie grunted a response when they told her goodbye and walked toward her mother like a martyr going off to the stake.

Ruby seemed very relieved to see that the halls were now free of people. She resumed her guileless chatter as they rode up in the elevator and walked through the halls upstairs. "Could I get your phone number, sweetie? In case I want to call you."

Myrtle opened her large pocketbook and pulled out a pad and pencil, handing her cane to Miles as she did. She wrote down her number in large print and, after a moment's hesitation, added her name to the paper since it was clear that Ruby had already forgotten her name.

Ruby carefully folded the piece of paper and put it in her blouse pocket. "There. I won't lose it now. Thank you."

She waved to Myrtle and Miles as they finally exited the building.

Myrtle and Miles discovered that the janitor with the ponytail was waiting for them outside the building. He was scrubbing diligently at a shiny-looking handrail as they approached and then stopped and smiled at them.

Myrtle said, "Randy, I presume?"

The janitor nodded, his wide grin showing a few gleaming gold teeth. "That's right. I'm Wanda's cousin. She told me y'all were coming out. Real glad you're here. Wanda said there was going to be some trouble."

"And you?" asked Myrtle. "Do *you* think there's going to be trouble?"

"I trust Wanda," answered Randy in his gritty voice. "Ain't got no reason not to trust her. Besides, I got eyes and ears, even if I don't have the Sight. And stuff ain't right here, Miss Myrtle. Not right at all. Wanda said you'd set things straight."

Myrtle frowned. "Am I on the right path, though? It's hard to know how to set things straight when I don't actually know what in direction I'm heading. Do you think that this trouble might involve Mickey Pelias? Wanda had spoken of a hard woman who writes. And she certainly fits that bill."

Randy absently scrubbed at the handrail as he considered the question. The sun shone down on his receding hairline and highlighted the blond strands in his ponytail. "It could. I think it does. People are right mad at Miss Mickey."

"Okay," said Myrtle briskly. "Well, unfortunately, it looked as if we were on the point of overstaying our welcome today, as far as Mickey was concerned. We'll try to make it back ... tomorrow?" Myrtle gave Miles a questioning look and he nodded. "We'll poke around some more, try to get more out of Mickey. And you—do you think you can talk to us tomorrow, too?"

Randy looked relieved. "Yes, I can. And thanks."

"Out of curiosity," said Miles, "why aren't you approaching the Greener Pastures management about this issue? Since it's an obvious safety concern."

Randy stared, openmouthed at Miles before starting to laugh—a guffawing laugh that quickly broke off into coughing. It appeared that Randy might share Wanda's smoking habit. Finally, he said, "Management just wants to keep the peace. They don't care nothin' about nobody."

Chapter Six

Myrtle put her seatbelt on as they climbed into Miles's car. "Well, what did you think? There was lots going on over there wasn't there? And I don't mean the Scrabble games we passed by."

"Well, she certainly seems like a rather difficult woman," muttered Miles as he put the key in the ignition and started the car.

"Natalie?" Myrtle snorted. "For sure!"

"No, I meant Mickey. I think she bosses Natalie around a lot."

Myrtle said, "But what is Natalie doing? Does she even have employment? Is that why Mickey referred to her as a vulture? Was she just hanging around Mickey for handouts?"

Miles gave her a startled look. "But Natalie has to take care of her mother. She's probably sacrificing a career to help out. All I'm saying is that if anyone's supposed to kill anyone, it would likely be Natalie doing her mother in."

"Natalie's mother is in a retirement home with a staff to take care of her. Whatever Natalie is doing, she's doing because she *wants* to for some reason. And apparently, Mickey thinks that Natalie's motives and other people's motives are monetarily-related," said Myrtle. "And you didn't think that insane old man acted as if he had a motive?"

"Which one? The one who was practically sitting on your lap in the dining room?" chortled Miles.

Myrtle gave Miles an icy glare. "I'm going to try to pretend that you didn't say that, Miles. Really!"

"Well, I have to admit that I'm curious. I haven't heard you ever mention the name 'Winston' before."

Myrtle said, "For good reason."

"And it was very intriguing to hear two people at lunch refer to you at Miss Towers."

"It simply goes to show that I've been in the area for a long, long time. And that I knew everyone, once upon a time, who lived here. I suppose that Inez must have moved away after graduation and just returned after retirement, or else surely she'd know that I married quite a while back," said Myrtle huffily.

"And why wouldn't Winston have kept up with your marital status—since he apparently was quite interested in it?" asked Miles, glancing sideways at her as they drove off the Greener Pastures property and onto the street.

"Why? Because he married someone else," snapped Myrtle. "And that's all I currently want to say about that since I'm trying to discuss potential murder suspects and a potential victim with you. Seriously, Miles!"

Miles had a rather abashed look on his face. "All right, sorry. I didn't realize it was a sensitive subject. I was waiting for you to eviscerate him completely at lunch, but you didn't do it. It made me curious."

"Let's just say that I was caught off-guard, that's all. Now, onto the ornery old man that Ruby says is mean. The one with "Fred" on his door. If we've determined that Mickey is a good pick for a potential victim—mainly on the fact that she practically stated that herself—then the old fellow could be a suspect since he obviously has some sort of grudge against her," said Myrtle. She pulled a peppermint out of her pocketbook and popped it into her mouth. She was putting her pocketbook back down on the floor of the car when she stopped and fished out a mint for Miles as an afterthought.

Miles smiled at her as he took it and somehow managed to unwrap it as he drove. "Right. So his business is his business and no one else's. Quite a character. So what I took from that, is that he had some kind of a secret. He wanted to get it off his chest so he spoke about it to Ruby who seems sweet and innocuous on the outside but is embedded with Scary Mickey who perhaps even published something about his secret in the underground newsletter that Mickey runs."

"Underground news*paper*, that is," corrected Myrtle, "lest we offend Mickey."

"And, yes, that would obviously give him a motive for potential violent action against Mickey. But he's not the only one. I really do think that Mickey's daughter, Natalie, has the stronger motive. And who can blame her?" said Miles.

"Well, we can't convict someone for a crime that hasn't happened, Miles. And we don't have enough information yet, either. So let's plan on heading back tomorrow. If you hurry back, we can watch *Tomorrow's Promise*. And I hope today's episode is really, really foolish today. I need to recharge after being in the soul-sucking Greener Pastures environment half the day," said Myrtle.

"I'm getting us home as fast as possible, Myrtle."

They were just pulling onto Magnolia Lane and heading in the direction of Myrtle's house when Myrtle started rifling through her large pocketbook. "Well, I'll be. Miles! Someone pickpocketed me."

"Are you sure?" asked Miles.

"Of course, I'm sure! I know when I have money and when I don't. And I don't have enough money not to keep track of it," said Myrtle. She dug all the way to the bottom of her purse, under the tissue container, under the mints, under the lipstick. Nothing.

"Now, you did pay for lunch, remember," said Miles.

"But I didn't pay *twenty dollars* for lunch. And that's what I had in there. I had a ten and two fives. All I have left is the change from the ten." Myrtle heaved a sigh. "How irritating."

"Maybe that's a clue," said Miles thoughtfully as he pulled up into Myrtle's driveway.

"A clue that I need to keep my pocketbook zipped up, maybe," grumbled Myrtle.

"And a clue that someone we associated closely with today isn't all that they seem," said Miles.

The next morning, Myrtle was giving Pasha a can of cat food when the sound of the phone ringing made her jump. She swung her head around to confirm that the clock actually did state that it was seven in the morning. Myrtle had been up for ages. But it wasn't ordinarily a time for her to be receiving phone calls.

She hurried to the wall phone under her rooster clock and picked up. "Hello? Hello?"

"Sweetie?" a sad voice whispered. The voice hesitated, and then said as if reading off a paper, "Myrtle?"

She *knew* she shouldn't have given Ruby her phone number. The poor thing was just too addled to handle the responsibility. "Ruby Sims? Is this you?"

Not bothering to answer the question, Ruby spoke in a tumbling rush. "Mickey was right! Her life *was* in danger. And now she's dead!"

"Dead?" Myrtle pulled a kitchen chair out and plopped down in it. "Dead, as in someone took her out before her time? Or dead as in—she lived a long life and it was a natural causes-type thing?"

Ruby said sadly, "Dead because somebody didn't like her, sweetie. I think—I think I must have heard something last night. I heard a lot of commotion next door. In the middle of the night, you know."

"A commotion?" asked Myrtle. "Thumping around, screaming, glass breaking?"

"Well—no. No," said Ruby sounding a little confused but earnest. "More like a door opening and closing. And maybe some footsteps. My hearing is pretty good and I don't sleep well at night. But I take lots of naps during the day, you know. And I thought—well, I'm trying to remember what I did last night. I want to say I looked out my door for just a second and saw a dark shape. That's what I think. But I thought it was Mickey. Now it looks like maybe it was a bad visitor."

The problem was that Ruby was not the best of witnesses. She was clearly unreliable at best. And she'd believed that every word out of Mickey's mouth was gospel. But it was at the very least, suspicious. "So what are they doing at Greener Pastures now? Has the staff called the police? The medical examiner? What's going on?"

Ruby said slowly, thoughtfully, "No. No, they called an ambulance. I asked what was going on and they said that Mickey had slipped away in her sleep. Except that the woman who didn't like Mickey was convinced Mickey hadn't died in her sleep. She was yelling at the staff about it. She had stopped by Mickey's room to see if she wanted to go to breakfast with her. And she...wasn't alive."

Myrtle mulled this over. Didn't like Mickey. "Was it Inez, maybe? One of your neighbors on the hall, isn't she?"

"Oh yes!" answered Ruby in relief at getting a name. "That's right. But the staff said that Inez was wrong and that Mickey had died of natural causes. But she didn't. I know she didn't. And they don't believe me. Or Inez."

"Well, they'd believe you both if she had any obvious wounds," said Myrtle briskly. "So I guess we're assuming that ... well, that she hadn't." She'd been going to say that they'd have to assume that Mickey had been smothered, but decided not to risk making Ruby more fractured than she already was.

"That's right," said Ruby quickly. "Because when I heard the commotion—the ambulance men and the staff a little while ago—then I poked my head out. I saw Mickey come out on a stretcher and she did look real peaceful. But I know that it wasn't her time, sweetie. I know it."

Myrtle sighed. "Okay. So I'll get Miles to take me back out there today and I'll see what I can do about getting Mickey's death investigated by someone." She stopped, realizing that Ruby hadn't actually asked her to do anything. She had only called to share her news because she probably had a piece of paper near her phone with Myrtle's name and number on it. Was Ruby going to be surprised at her interest?

Instead, Ruby sounded delighted. "Will you? That would be so good. I told the staff, but they kept ignoring me. And Inez, too. If you came—you and your friend—maybe they would listen to you."

Hanging up, Myrtle thought wryly how amazing it was that both Wanda and Ruby seemed to think Myrtle had the ability to make people listen, when usually it was the complete opposite. It just went to show that poor Wanda and Ruby were even more easily ignored than Myrtle was.

She looked at the clock again and realized there was really no reason for her to bother Miles right now. They could always investigate a little later in the morning. Pasha looked as if she wanted to go back out again to do some hunting, so Myrtle let her out the front door. As she did, she saw lights on at Red's house across the street. Not just one light, either—the house was ablaze with light. Jack was a toddler and kept odd hours and an injured Red probably did, too. Half of her wanted to talk with Red about the case and half of her was just glad to keep him out of her business. It would be helpful, though, if she could get some sort of direction to take with Red's deputy, Darrell Smith. Maybe she could ask him about Darrell without telling him about Mickey.

Myrtle walked across the street and rapped at the front door. Elaine opened up the door right away. "Myrtle," she said. "Just the person I wanted to see. I'm ready for a cup of coffee—would you like some? If I have a little adult company right now, then I think I can handle having cartoons playing in the background."

It was a testament to Myrtle's unpredictable sleeping patterns that her daughter-in-law showed not the least bit of surprise at Myrtle showing up at her door at seven a.m. Myrtle followed her in, smiling at Jack who was playing with trucks and occasionally looking up and staring at what seemed like a very frenetic cartoon where the characters would burst into intermittent singing.

When Jack spotted her, he jumped up a bit awkwardly to his feet and ran over to grab her leg for a hug. Since Myrtle was used to Jack's hugs, she was prepared by leaning heavily on her other leg and cane. Then she could give him a hug in return and not pay for it by falling on top of the poor child at the same time.

Elaine returned with steaming coffees and sat down next to Myrtle. Myrtle said, "I don't know how you do it, Elaine. You look more refreshed than I do and I know you couldn't have gotten much sleep with an ailing husband and a toddler on your hands."

"Oh, last night wasn't so bad. Jack was worn out because we were at the park all afternoon. I think Red was ready for some alone time. You know."

Myrtle knew. Red's nerves were probably starting to fray after being homebound after the surgery. And being homebound with an active toddler didn't exactly fit the definition of 'quiet recovery.'

"Well, hopefully *Red* will give *you* some alone time once he's back on his feet and policing the good town of Bradley again," said Myrtle. "I'm sure you need it. And remember that you can bring Jack by to play with his Nana at *any* time if you need a break. I love playing with trucks," said Myrtle in a convincing tone. Convincing enough that Jack ran over to hand Myrtle a dump truck for her playing enjoyment.

Elaine smiled at Myrtle. "And you know I appreciate that. But it's been going pretty well. I do feel sort of bad for Red, though." She said in a low voice, "You know how men are. When they're sick, they revert to being little boys. I think Red needs more coddling than I'm able to dole out."

Myrtle had never been able to completely understand why her absolutely wonderful daughter-in-law was so smitten with her frequently irascible son. She was smart, upbeat, pretty, and a good deal younger. She'd learned that love operates in very mysterious ways indeed and perhaps the wags who said that opposites attract really had something. At any rate, she'd decided long ago to simply accept it.

But she couldn't resist making a face at the coddling. "Elaine, that's very sweet of you. But there's a limit, right? Only so many hours in the day and only so much coddling that can possibly take place in those hours. Jack, being a toddler, requires most of them." Myrtle hesitated, and then gave a sigh. "How about if I come by this afternoon and sit with Red for a while? And then you can choose what you want to do. You can go run errands, go put your feet up, take Jack out to the playground, or put Jack down for a nap."

Elaine beamed at her. "Really?"

"Really. If Red needs coddling, he's still got his mama around, after all. I may as well be the one to do it." Myrtle squared her shoulders, feeling as if she were enlisting in the armed forces. "Maybe he can watch *Tomorrow's Promise* with me. That always seems to entertain him."

Now Elaine frowned. "Your soap opera? It *entertains* him?"

"Absolutely. It tickles him pink to point out all the unrealistic things going on, the silly names of the characters, the stilted dialogue, and the way everyone is so made-up and dressed to the nines even when they're doing yard work," said Myrtle. "I can make us some popcorn and we'll have a fine time. You just figure out how you want to spend your free time."

"My mind is racing! Wow. I'll have to give it some thought." Elaine took a huge sip of her coffee as if to power her brain to accept the challenge.

Myrtle watched Jack drive his truck up the side of the cartoon character's face on the television. "Elaine, I was wondering how Red was doing with the fact that he's not working right now. I mean, he's been police chief for so many years and is so used to always being on the job. How is that going?"

Elaine waved her hand in a so-so gesture. "It's been okay. I think he's been a little frustrated because he wants to go out and do all the things that he usually does—make his rounds, call on the older ladies to make sure they're doing all right, keep the peace in Bradley. But he can't. And, although everybody in town knows that Red is laid up, sometimes they *still* call here, even though they know they're supposed to be calling Darrell. I mean—what's Red going to do about the stray dog that's harassing Janie Mitchell? You know? He's not going to be able to chase down a dog after knee surgery. But they still call him."

"Just a habit, I guess. How's that deputy of his doing? Darrell?"

Elaine considered this. "He's okay. I don't think he's really the brightest bulb in the box, but if he were then he wouldn't be satisfied with this job. But as a fill-in sent from the county, he's doing pretty well. He's been handling a bunch of minor incidents."

"Minor incidents?" asked Myrtle. "What's more minor than the Case of the Missing Yard Statue or the Case of the Stray Dog?"

"Oh, you know. Like when Miriam Morehead imagines that there's someone in her house ... every day. So *somebody* has to go calm her down and do a thorough enough search so that she settles down and can continue functioning. That sort of thing. Hand-holding," said Elaine.

Myrtle knew that Red did a lot of handholding too, on a regular basis. "So Darrell doesn't mind that kind of thing, then?"

"Not at all. It doesn't even seem to frustrate him. In fact, Red says that he enters Miriam Morehead's house every single time as if ready to jump an intruder. He has the ability to take it seriously even multiple times a week." Elaine swiftly moved the remote control away from Jack, whose gaze had just latched onto it.

"Well, he sounds like a gift, then. Because I don't think Red has it in him to be that patient under those circumstances," said Myrtle.

Elaine said, "The only problem is that Red is worried that Darrell is coddling these old ladies. Red would ordinarily not really have to go *into* Miriam's house. He'd be able to convince her on the phone that everything was all right and that he'd be there in a flash if she *did* discover there was someone in her house. If Darrell is encouraging them too much, then Red's job is going to be a lot harder when he returns."

They heard thumping and some muttered curses and Red stood in the doorway leading from the hall. "Mama. Thought I heard you," said Red.

Myrtle tried very, very hard to keep her face pleasant but impassive. The sight of her son on a walker when he'd tried so many times to put the infernal contraption in her own house gave her a very un-Christian-like sense of satisfaction ... especially, she hurried to reassure herself, since it was only a temporary measure, after all. It wasn't as if Red were permanently disabled. And suddenly, Myrtle felt very spry on her cane. She resisted the urge to show off by prancing around the den.

"Red, you are in for a treat today."

Red's expression brightened. "You're packing your gnomes away? Or, better yet, taking a sledgehammer to them?"

"Don't be silly. No, I'm hereby naming today Mother and Son day. And very possibly Mother and Son and Grandson day," said Myrtle.

Red shot Elaine an alarmed look before giving his mother a grimacing grin. "Ah. Well, that's real nice of you, Mama. Real nice."

"Can I get you something, Red?" asked Elaine, shifting on the sofa as if she were about to get up.

"No, I'm thinking that I should do a little bit of walking. At least to the coffeemaker," grunted Red as he maneuvered the walker forward.

"It's a good idea," said Myrtle, "although I'm not sure what you're going to do with that coffee cup after you've poured it, what with pushing the walker and all." She wasn't *trying* to be a smarty-pants. Hers was simply the voice of experience. A cane offered a lot more latitude too.

Red narrowed his eyes at her a little. "Well, I suppose that's true. So I guess I'll pour it and sit for a spell in the kitchen."

Elaine asked, "Myrtle, want to move into the kitchen with us? I can give you a refill on that coffee and I've got some blueberry muffins that I made yesterday."

"Sounds lovely, but I should be heading back home. Red, I'll have a real visit with you this afternoon ... with Jack, too, if Elaine wants to head out solo. So that means I have a few things to get done before then. Y'all have a nice morning." Myrtle gave Red a cheery wave, kissed the top of Jack's head as she stood up, and gave Elaine a quick hug.

Somehow, that visit had managed to last until after eight. Surely, Miles would be up now. It felt almost like lunchtime. She walked over to his house and rang his doorbell. Instead of seeing signs of Miles moving around, though, she saw signs of Erma Sherman stirring next door as Erma shoved a couple of windows open on the front of her house. It was never a good time of day to have an Erma sighting. In desperation and rising panic, she rang the doorbell a couple more times.

Now a bleary-eyed Miles, sporting stubble, yanked open his door and stared at her, blinking in the sunlight. Myrtle pushed past him. "Erma's out there," she muttered.

"Erma *lives* there," said Miles. "Of course she's there. She's there every day."

"Yes, but it doesn't mean I have to interact with her. She makes me lose my appetite and I had such a lovely appetite for breakfast when I was walking up to your door." She paused. "Actually, I still do. Mind if I make us some scrambled eggs?"

Miles made a sweeping, be-my-guest gesture toward his kitchen. "To what do I owe the pleasure of this visit? I thought we already had a plan for today. And that the plan started out later than this."

"Oh. I forgot to tell you. Mickey is dead," said Myrtle. She opened up Miles's fridge and pulled out eggs, milk, and some shredded cheese she found. There was already a frying pan on the stove. She eyed it suspiciously. "Is this clean? And, if it's clean, why isn't it away in the cabinet?"

"It's clean and was drying on the stove last night after I used it. For heaven's sake, Myrtle, stay focused. Mickey's *dead*? The Mickey we met yesterday and thought might make a promising murder victim? That Mickey?" Miles pulled out a kitchen chair and sat down rather abruptly.

"That Mickey. And Ruby called me hours ago to let me know. The staff is acting as if it were a natural death, apparently."

"And Ruby clearly disagrees?" asked Miles.

"Yes. And Inez too, apparently. Who can blame them though, with Mickey going on and on about feeling endangered at Greener Pastures? And, of course, we have our psychic advisor indicating that there was going to be foul play," said Myrtle. She whisked the eggs and milk together, looked in the bowl and added two more eggs. They needed fortification today.

"Myrtle, I have to caution you about using the term *psychic advisor* too loosely. We're already in a position where no one is going to believe us and if we mention Wanda, then it's only going to get worse." Miles rubbed his eyes as if he were still struggling to wake up. "So...what are we going to do? I guess head on over there this morning and try to talk to someone?"

"That's right. I was going to give the staff a chance to respond. We'll tell them that Mickey said she thought she was in danger at the home and that there were definitely some people who might have wanted to get her out of the way." Myrtle put two slices of bread in Miles's toaster.

"And if the Greener Pastures staff doesn't respond appropriately?" asked Miles. "Which is what I'm guessing will happen?"

"Then we'll call the police," said Myrtle simply. "So that means Darrell since Red is out of pocket. Elaine filled me in on Darrell earlier today and it sounds as if he might be one of those incredibly earnest types ... he might actually believe us and open an investigation."

"Wait a minute ... *earlier today*? You've already been visiting somewhere else before now?" Miles stared at her.

"Just be glad that I realized you might still be asleep," said Myrtle, waving a spatula at Miles. "Yes, all the lights were on at Red's house, so I popped over there before coming here. It was fine. I'm actually going to babysit Red this afternoon, so that's why I was thinking we could go ahead and get to Greener Pastures as soon as you're ready."

There was too much talking and not enough paying attention to the skillet, unfortunately. Myrtle scraped up some eggs that were sticking to the pan. She surreptitiously looked behind her. Fortunately, Miles appeared to be deep in thought. Myrtle took the opportunity to put the dried-up scrambled egg onto some rather overcooked toast and then put a large slice of American cheese on the top to cover up any potential egg inadequacies. The slice slid off the egg pile immediately, so she quickly popped it into the microwave to melt it a little.

"Babysit *Red*?" muttered Miles. "Don't you mean *Jack*?"

"No, I most definitely mean Red. After lunch. So let's get a move on." The American cheese started popping in the microwave and Myrtle opened the door and yanked it out. How on earth could one thin slice of cheese have contributed to that much spattering in the microwave? She took a fork and tried to reconstruct the cheese on the egg top before finally pushing it in front of Miles.

An hour later, a Greener Pastures manager by the name of Darla was looking at them with a very long, serious face. Darla had artificially blonde hair and blue eye shadow. Darla's long face did not seem to have anything to do with the fact that Miles and Myrtle had just asked her to ask the police to investigate a resident's death. It seemed to be more in keeping with her general disposition and outlook on the world.

"Mrs. Clover, I appreciate your concern over our resident. But I can assure you that we hold safety in the very highest regard here. Mrs. Pelias experienced a natural death while she was sleeping, which is honestly not a bad way to go. We'll miss her, of course. But there was nothing at all untoward in her demise." Darla's clipped speech was so pat that Myrtle wondered if she'd given it before. Did Greener Pastures residents frequently ascribe foul play to seemingly natural deaths?

Myrtle felt her face flush. She was used to not being taken seriously, but it was still extremely galling. She was just opening her mouth with a hot retort when Miles quickly jumped in.

"You see, Ms. ... um ... Darla, the reason we want to report the possibility of foul play is because the resident, Mrs. Pelias, brought it up herself only yesterday. She told us that she felt her life was in danger. It seems very coincidental that she met her Maker the very same night," said Miles in a reasonable voice that Myrtle envied. She still felt as if her blood pressure were up.

Darla gave him something of a patronizing smile. "I realize that y'all think it's your duty to bring this to my attention. But there is no cause for concern. Mrs. Pelias was a bit paranoid, you see. She thought people were out to get her. Maybe it made her feel important to think that way, who knows? At any rate, she was constantly telling staff members that she felt her life was in danger—for at least a year. And every other night she was just fine. Unfortunately, we only have a certain amount of time on this earth and her time was simply up, that's all. But again, I do appreciate your concern and I'm sure that, if Mrs. Pelias was still around, she would appreciate it too."

Darla stood up to indicate that their meeting in her tiny office was over. Myrtle stood up, too, and gave her a haughty look. "It wasn't only Mrs. Pelias who felt that way. Ruby Sims called me this morning to let me know. And Inez Wilson believed it was foul play, too. "

Now Darla smirked. "Well, that's Mrs. Sims for you. She's a loyal friend, but frequently a bit confused. And Ms. Wilson is a fan of drama. Rest assured that you have nothing to worry about here, Mrs. Clover. The residents of Greener Pastures are completely safe from harm here. That's the entire reason they're here after all—to be safe. And we take that responsibility very seriously."

Darla was clearly back on script again. Myrtle grabbed her cane and her pocketbook and she and Miles walked out of the office.

"Have a safe ride back," called Darla. Her smile reminded Myrtle of a crocodile's smile.

"We will," said Myrtle. "When we eventually leave." She gave Darla a smirk before she and Miles walked off in the direction of the elevator.

"So, that didn't go well," murmured Miles. "What's our next step?"

"It went exactly as expected," said Myrtle grimly. "And our next step is to talk to the police. Well, I guess our *very* next step is to talk to Ruby and let her know we were here so she won't call me later. *Then* we can talk to the police."

Ruby seemed fairly lucid. Maybe the shock of Mickey's sudden death was responsible. Her eyes were tired when she opened the door to them. "Hi, sweeties," she said. She looked behind them into the hall as if expecting to see an army of

Greener Pastures staff or police investigators there. "Did you tell the home what happened?"

Myrtle said, "We certainly did, Ruby. We told them what we'd heard Mickey say yesterday and we told them what you heard last night." She tightened her lips for a second, irritation with Darla sweeping over her. "But, unfortunately, they didn't take me seriously."

Ruby's face fell and she nodded sadly. "I sort of thought that might be the way. Well, you did what you could, sweetie. Mickey would have appreciated it."

"But we're not through," said Myrtle briskly. "Not yet. No, we're going to talk directly to the police." She was thoughtful for a moment. "And perhaps we should speak with Inez Wilson before we do."

Ruby said, "Oh, but Inez isn't here, sweetie. She got on the bus this morning to go to the mall. And that's a long way away, you know." Her eyebrows pulled together in a worried frown. "And—the police? Greener Pastures won't like that."

"Greener Pastures is of no concern of mine," said Myrtle. "Especially in terms of what they like and don't like. We just wanted to let you know that we're on it. Miles and me. We'll come back here tomorrow and start poking around a bit more to see what we can find out."

Ruby startled Myrtle by reaching out and giving her a hug. "Thanks, sweetie," she said. Then she pulled back to give Myrtle a hopeful look. "Can you bring your cat then, too?"

Chapter Seven

As they drove off the Greener Pastures grounds, Miles said uneasily, "Myrtle, I know you have a plan and everything, but I've got a concern."

Myrtle looked over at him in surprise. "A concern? Well, share it. You're the sidekick, after all."

"You're planning on having us barge into that tiny police station downtown, put Darrell on the spot, and have him call up the medical examiner, right? And all that sounds great—as long as he complies with our request. But what if he doesn't?"

"He will," said Myrtle calmly.

"But what if he doesn't? What if we barge in and he feels overwhelmed and defensive and weird about the fact that the chief's mother is making the complaint? What if it doesn't go well? Because this is our last resort. If Darrell doesn't want to check it out, then we don't have a case." Miles was gesticulating excitedly with one hand, which made Myrtle frown. Miles didn't ordinarily get excited about *anything*. And now he was driving with one hand on the wheel.

Myrtle was eager to agree with him to ensure her personal safety. "Yes, all right, Miles. You could be right. So what's our plan, then?"

To her relief, Miles put his other hand back on the wheel, gripping it firmly in his usual ten o'clock and two o'clock positions. "I was thinking we'd run it by Red."

"Red? Are you out of your mind?"

Then she bit her lip as his hand flew off the wheel again, waving around to emphasize his point.

"I don't think you're giving him a chance. I've never known Red to shirk his duty—whether it's investigating a murder or investigating a trespassing complaint. I say we fill Red in and let *him* talk to Darrell about it. Because, sure, Darrell sounds like he might be an overzealous deputy who goes above and beyond. But we don't know how he's going to react when he comes up against a murder." Miles turned a bit in the driver's seat to look at Myrtle and nearly hit someone's mailbox.

"Fine! Fine, Miles. We'll head straight to Red's. I can show up there early for my babysitting gig and make lunch for Red while I'm at it. But, for heaven's sake, put your hands back on the wheel and focus on the road! I'm not ready to meet my Maker today. I need to get at least another couple of church services under my belt before I do," grumbled Myrtle. "And maybe a Communion."

Elaine was surprised but ecstatic to see Myrtle before the assigned time. Not wanting to test her luck, she quickly grabbed her keys and hopped into her car.

Red's eyebrows rose when he saw Miles with his mother. He'd always seemed to like Miles and enjoy talking with him, but when he saw Miles's grimly determined face, he must have realized this was some sort of a business visit. "What can I do for you?" he asked as Miles and Myrtle sat down on the sofa together.

Myrtle nodded at Miles. This was going to be his show. He had the best shot at convincing Red that there was something that needed to be investigated.

Miles took a deep breath and seemed as if he were trying to find a starting place that didn't involve Wanda the Psychic. His expression grew pleased as he found one. "We want to report a suspicious death that went unnoticed," he said smoothly. "Your mother and I were visiting at Greener Pastures yesterday when we spoke with a resident who was convinced her life was in danger. Last night she died and a couple of witnesses report hearing unusual sounds coming from that room. We tried to approach it through the correct channels and relayed our concerns to Greener Pastures—Darla was the staff member. She categorically denied that anything was amiss and basically just dismissed us. So we thought we'd report it to you, Red, since we don't know Darrell as well."

Red leaned his head back on his navy blue recliner and looked thoughtfully at Miles. "Which resident is this?"

"Mickey Pelias," said Miles.

Red nodded. "She's called me before to tell me she felt threatened there. But, of course, there's nothing I can do without an overt threat from an individual or without some kind of a break-in."

"So you believed her?" asked Miles, eyebrows raising in surprise.

"I didn't *not* believe her, let's put it that way. She wasn't flaky, but sharp as a tack. And she had the type of tough personality that might rub people the wrong way. But, again, there were no specific threats to address. It was more that she just had a sense of danger and she didn't seem like the paranoid type to me." He paused, staring at the ceiling for a moment to collect his thoughts. "So, there was a witness who heard something? More than one? And Greener Pastures didn't call the police?" This part seemed to concern him.

Myrtle and Miles exchanged glances. Myrtle said, "Well, one witness was Ruby Sims, who the staff treats as an unreliable witness. She's, as you would put it, flaky. But she called me before dawn this morning to tell me that Mickey was dead and that she had heard thumping noises from her room. Ruby was convinced that Mickey was murdered."

Red sighed. "Yes, I think I know that Ruby Sims. It's unfortunate that Ruby probably can't supply the most helpful information, but if she got the impression of a scuffle of some type, that's important to know. Who was the other witness?"

"An Inez Wilson. She's credible, but apparently has a reputation for being a bit of a drama queen," said Miles. "According to the Home, anyway."

Red nodded, thinking. Then he said abruptly, "I'll make a phone call."

Myrtle blinked in surprise. "To Darrell Smith?"

"No—to the state police. The SBI needs to handle this part. The medical examiner will need to be alerted, and a forensic team should go to Greener Pastures. I'll fill Darrell in right afterward." He was already fishing his phone out of his pocket and moved into the back of the house briefly to talk.

Jack, who'd been playing with toys back in his bedroom, came running out on his sturdy little legs and gave Myrtle a big hug. He handed her some sort of superhero toy for her to admire, and she and Miles oohed and ahhed over it to Jack's delight.

A few minutes later, Red came out from the back of the house. He had that restless, frustrated look about him as if he wished he could jump in his police cruiser and meet up with the state police at Greener Pastures.

Myrtle decided to distract him a little. "You know, Red, I'm a little surprised you took Mickey's death so seriously."

Red raised his eyebrows at her. "I take death seriously, Mama. If you can't take *death* seriously, I don't know what you *could* take seriously."

"You know what I mean. I'm surprised that you listened to Miles and me and were willing to call the SBI to check it out," said Myrtle.

"Well, I think if a twenty-year-old woman had told police that her life were in danger and then ended up dead soon afterward, with witnesses claiming to have heard sounds of a scuffle, the police would investigate. It would be shameful if the same thing happened with an elderly victim and there were no investigation." Red looked at his watch, that restless expression on his face again. "I should go ahead and call Darrell to meet the

SBI at the home." He left the room, pushing his walker impatiently.

Jack plopped down on the floor and flew his superhero around the coffee table. Miles said in a low voice, "I think you sell Red short sometimes. He does take his job seriously and he does care about *all* of his citizens, clearly."

Myrtle pursed her lips. "I never said he didn't. I just said his personal oversight of *me* is a real pain in the neck."

"Well, it looks as if the tables have turned now, right? You have an opportunity to give Red a taste of his own medicine all afternoon."

Myrtle slept hard that night for the first time in ages. Because not only had she definitely practiced some oversight of Red, who had started an odd pacing on his walker that afternoon, but she'd had Jack to keep an eye on ... and Jack had been in a very busy mood until he'd fallen asleep in pure exhaustion, curled up against Myrtle on the sofa. All the responsibility had worn Myrtle out, and she slept soundly until daylight beamed through her bedroom window.

She was just getting some food out for Pasha when there was a tap at her front door. She glanced at the clock and saw it was still slightly before seven. It had to be Miles.

It was Miles and he was holding a tray in his hands. "Blueberry muffins and Applewood-smoked bacon," he said, sweeping past her into the kitchen.

"Is it my birthday?" asked Myrtle, blinking in surprise at the food coming in.

Miles put the tray down and then moved over to start making coffee. "I thought we'd just get some real fortification before we start in on questioning suspects. Which is what I'm guessing we're doing today."

"Absolutely," said Myrtle. She peered at the tray of food. "Are these *homemade* blueberry muffins?"

"Of course," said Miles smugly. "I've been a bachelor for long enough now that my cooking isn't bad at all. Although I'd much rather have someone to cook for me. Which is why Greener Pastures was extremely appealing yesterday."

Myrtle made a face. "I'd rather make my own meals than sacrifice my personal safety by staying at the Bates Motel."

Miles said in a chiding voice, "It's not the Bates Motel, Myrtle. It's a perfectly nice and reputable retirement community."

"Where you just might end up murdered at the end of the day," muttered Myrtle.

"Honestly, the idea of being catered to is very attractive to me," said Miles, turning on the coffeemaker and tidily cleaning up the few spilled grounds of coffee. "They cook for you. They clean your room and bathroom. They take care of the yard work and general maintenance. My air conditioner broke last night and I can tell you just how tempting Greener Pastures looks right now."

"Oh, so now the truth is out why you're here so early," drawled Myrtle. "Your a/c is on the blink. You're only visiting to get some cool air."

"That's not true," said Miles stiffly.

"Whatever. Just be aware that your air conditioning issues and apparently hunger is making Greener Pastures seem like an absolutely amazing place. When, in fact, it's not. I had my purse pickpocketed when we were over there day before yesterday. That's two crimes I'm aware of in a twenty-four-hour period," said Myrtle.

Miles shrugged. "Maybe you just thought you had money in your purse. Maybe you actually either spent it or left it back at home somewhere. I really doubt that the Artful Dodger is living at Greener Pastures, Myrtle."

She glared repressively at him. "I keep tabs on my money, believe me. I don't have enough of it to be careless with."

There was a loud rap at the front door and Myrtle frowned. "Since you're here, I have no idea who else could be at my door at this time of day." She grabbed her cane and thumped to the front door.

She was starting to pull it open when Miles said quickly, "You'd better look through the window first, Myrtle." She made a shooing gesture with her hand and continued opening the door...and was punished for her stubbornness by the sight of Erma Sherman standing there. Myrtle drew back away from Erma and her legendary bad morning breath.

Erma walked in. "Most times I'd worry about visiting people this early, but I *knew* you'd be up, Myrtle." Her eyes lit on Miles. "Well now, isn't this so cozy! A breakfast for two." She gave a braying laugh and her prominent front teeth contributed to her donkey-like appearance.

Myrtle said coldly, "Miles and I are having a quick breakfast together before we visit a friend at Greener Pastures."

Miles asked politely, "Erma, would you like to have breakfast with us?"

Myrtle turned and shot him an icy look. Erma did not need to be encouraged.

"No thanks, Miles. I've already eaten." Erma wagged a finger at Myrtle. "Greener Pastures. That's actually very interesting, because it's one of the things I wanted to talk to you about. When I was driving into Greener Pastures at lunchtime yesterday, I saw you and Miles leaving. Then, when I walked in, I ran into Winston Rouse and he said that y'all had been at Greener Pastures the *previous* day, too. I found that really, really remarkable."

"I don't know why you would," said Myrtle impatiently. "There's nothing remotely interesting about visiting residents at Greener Pastures."

"As a matter of fact there *is*," said Erma. "You don't like it there. Everybody knows that. And I don't believe you really know any of the current residents there particularly well—remember, I've been your neighbor for quite a while, Myrtle."

Myrtle turned and rolled her eyes at Miles. Yes, Erma had been her neighbor for far too long.

"Miles and I have been visiting Ruby Sims," said Myrtle. "That's all. I have a real...fondness for Ruby. And I'm making sure that Greener Pastures is taking care of her because, you're right, I don't like it there and I'm not sure they have her best interests at heart."

Erma shook her head. "Nope. You're not friends with Ruby Sims."

Myrtle gaped at her. "You seriously think you know who my friends are?"

"I know pretty well. Well enough to know that Ruby isn't one of them. You see, I have a theory about what you're doing over at Greener Pastures. I think you're there to solve a mystery. After all, you're Bradley's very own senior sleuth," said Erma, grinning at her.

Miles said, "What mystery do you think she's there to solve? If you're convinced that's what she's doing."

Erma face screwed up in a hideous expression—apparently, the face she made when she was thinking. "I believe," she said slowly at long last, "that you're there to find out what happened to Evelyn Pelias, better known as Mickey." She looked back and forth eagerly at Myrtle and Miles, mouth agape at her own cleverness. "Am I right?

Myrtle was extremely irritated that Erma could be right about anything at all. But Miles seemed interested.

"Why do you think Mickey's death might be suspicious?" asked Miles.

"Because people didn't like her, of course. Especially that Fred. Have you seen him? He's grouchy and mutters to himself. He'd argue with Mickey all the time. If Mickey said the sky was blue, Fred would say it was polka-dotted. He hated her. *Hated* her," emphasized Erma.

Myrtle and Miles glanced at each other. Myrtle was aware that she should be asking Erma questions about Fred's beef with Mickey, but it was annoying to do so because it meant that she was drawing out the length of Erma's visit. She sighed and gritted out, "Why did Fred hate Mickey?"

"Mickey kept teasing Fred that she knew his secrets," said Erma, blinking quickly as if everyone should have known that. "Didn't you know?"

"What is this huge secret? Is it something silly like Fred has a crush on someone at the home? Or is it a *real* secret?" asked Myrtle impatiently.

"It's a real secret to *Fred*. Real enough to make him furious with Mickey for teasing him about it," said Erma. Her long face fell, making it even longer. "But I don't know what the secret was. Mickey said that she was going to print it in the newspaper, making it an exposé for everyone to read."

"But she died first," said Myrtle in a thoughtful voice.

"My point exactly," said Erma with satisfaction.

Myrtle didn't care for that smug tone from Erma. She said briskly, "Well, we'll check it out, Erma. Thanks for letting us know."

"So you *are* investigating Mickey's death," said Erma gleefully.

Miles gave her his most serious and repressive expression. "You've got to keep this under your hat, Erma. Otherwise, our entire investigation will be hampered. We want everyone to think that Myrtle and I are just nosy. If they know we're trying to solve a murder, we're never going to get anywhere."

Erma nodded solemnly. "Oh, I promise I'll keep my lips zipped. You've got my word." She practically wiggled with excitement. "I feel almost like a sidekick. So thrilling!"

Myrtle gave a weak smile. "Yes. Well."

Erma said, "There's something else that I wanted to come over to ask you about, Myrtle. Can you give me the number for your yardman? My mower is broken and I need someone to cut the grass this week."

Myrtle said reluctantly, "In December?"

"We had all that rain and a couple of warmer days, remember? Besides, my grass always seems to grow unevenly. It just needs cleaning up," said Erma.

Because of all the crabgrass in her yard, thought Myrtle. "Are you sure you want Dusty? You know the kind of trouble I have dealing with him. He never, never wants to come over. It's always too hot to mow, too cold to mow, too wet to mow, or too dry to mow. Then, once you threaten him enough to get him onto your property, he takes shortcuts when he mows. And his edger frequently doesn't work."

"He does a better job than Puddin, anyway," said Miles.

"Absolutely. But a child would do a better job than Puddin. At least Dusty doesn't cost much," said Myrtle grudgingly.

"Sounds perfect," said Erma. "I have a lot of odds and ends I want done in the yard, too."

Myrtle shuffled off to write down Dusty's number. She should have known Erma would like the idea of hiring Dusty. Erma's yard was a riot of crabgrass, clover, and dandelions. She and Dusty were the perfect match.

Erma took the piece of paper from her and then looked with interest at the muffin on Miles's plate. "Are those homemade? And blueberry? Because blueberry is my favorite. I guess I could find room for one muffin—"

Pasha, Myrtle's feral cat, decided at that moment to come out of the shadows of the kitchen and stare intently at Erma. Myrtle had frequently suspected that Pasha believed Erma to be a jumbo-sized rodent. The look on Pasha's face was that of a hunter studying prey.

Perhaps it was the intense predatory stare. Perhaps it was the fact that Erma was highly allergic to cats. But as soon as Erma spotted Pasha, she backed away toward the front door, tripping over Myrtle's coffee table in the process. "Talk to you later," said Erma in a high-pitched squealing voice that likely only fueled Pasha's belief in her rodent hood.

Chapter Eight

As Myrtle and Miles walked through the large front doors of Greener Pastures, Miles said in a low voice, "Where do we start this morning? I'm guessing we don't just knock on residents' doors and start questioning them about where they were when Mickey was murdered. Especially since the Greener Pastures staff is onto us."

Myrtle gave Miles an annoyed look. "You're entirely too concerned about what the Greener Pastures staff thinks about you."

"Only because I don't want them throwing away my application for residency," said Miles. "This place is looking more and more attractive by the second. I can only imagine how large the bill for the air conditioning repair is going to be when the worker comes out this evening."

Myrtle decided to ignore Miles's irritating affinity for the retirement home. "To answer your question, I think we should start with Ruby Sims. For one thing, we need to regularly show up at Ruby's door so she doesn't forget who we are. For another, I'm wondering if she knows more than she's letting on."

They entered the elevator and Myrtle pushed the button to head down to the basement level. Miles said, "You mean, you think that Ruby might be hiding something from us?"

"No. I'm pretty sure that Ruby doesn't have the faculty for hiding things. I think she might know more details about what happened the night Mickey died—but that the details might be foggy. Maybe we can go in with a defogger and pull some of those clues out of her," said Myrtle. "And maybe we can catch up with Inez, too."

Ruby seemed happy to see them when she opened her door. "Did you bring your cat?" she asked Myrtle eagerly, looking down to see if Myrtle were carrying a carrier. Her round face fell comically when she didn't spot one.

"I promise I'll get Pasha up here, Ruby," said Myrtle. "Although it might be a short visit."

Ruby invited them into her room and Miles said in a low voice to Myrtle, "Let me know when you're planning the field trip for Pasha and I'll make sure to stay at home that day."

Yes, Miles was getting entirely too concerned about what Greener Pastures might think of him. Something drastic would have to be done. Myrtle would think on it.

Ruby's room was a cluttered place. She also had an interesting fondness for baby dolls. Some of the dolls appeared to be collector's items and were in their original boxes on stands. Others appeared to be played with—recently. Miles raised his eyebrows at her as they saw several dolls on Ruby's loveseat that seemed to be getting their hair done in different styles.

"Here, I'll move the babies," she said and tenderly picked up each doll and laid it down in a separate location.

"So," she said looking at Myrtle and Miles eagerly, "did you find out who did it? Did you find out who hurt Mickey?"

Miles said gently, "Ruby, I wish I could say we have. But it's going to take some time. Myrtle and I are going to need to speak to people who may have been upset with Mickey. We're going to have to find some clues that point to the murderer."

Ruby listened intently to Miles, nodding in agreement. Then she turned to Myrtle and without any segue asked, "How many rings does it take?"

"Rings?" Myrtle stared down at her hands. She wore only the worn gold band of a wedding ring. The one that was there to frighten off any potential suitors. "For what, Ruby?"

"You know—telephone rings," said Ruby earnestly. "How many rings does it take you to get the phone?"

Myrtle shifted on the sofa a bit. These conversational roundabouts were very confusing. "Well, I suppose it depends on what I'm doing. If I'm in my chair in the living room, it likely takes me three rings. If I'm in the back of the house, it might take me four. But I don't have a very big house, so it doesn't take me too many rings. Plus, I don't get many phone calls. I don't really enjoy talking on the phone."

Ruby nodded thoughtfully again. Since she appeared not to be interested in a follow-up question, Myrtle asked, "Does it take you a while? Do you get many calls?"

"Oh, about the same, I guess. Sometimes I take naps and there are more rings before I answer. I don't get many calls." Ruby paused, frowning. "But I did get one this morning."

"Who was it?" asked Myrtle.

"I don't know," said Ruby. "It was a strange voice. Like someone trying to pretend it was their voice. It said that I needed to stop talking about Mickey's death or there would be trouble." She put her hand over her mouth. "Oops. I guess I'm talking about it now." Then her brows drew together and she said in a more confident voice, "But who cares? Mickey was my friend. I *do* know that someone murdered her."

Myrtle said, "Ruby, this is very important. The fact that someone called you trying to scare you off shows that Mickey's death *was* murder. And that the murderer thinks you know something. You need to tell the police this story."

"Or Greener Pastures?" asked Ruby.

"I wouldn't bother with Greener Pastures. They lost their chance, didn't they, when they wouldn't believe you? But you need to tell the police," said Myrtle intently.

Ruby was looking right at Myrtle, but Myrtle could tell that her mind was somewhere else. "What time is it?" she asked.

Miles glanced at his watch. "It's ten-thirty."

"In the morning?"

Miles's expression was weary. "Yes, Ruby."

"Oh. Well, we should go to the ice cream social. I think that's what we're supposed to do at ten-thirty." She stood up abruptly and started rifling through papers stacked on the floor next to the sofa. "Let's see if I can find that paper."

It would be a miracle if she could put her hands on it. The entire room was full of papers, knick-knacks and other things. It was complete chaos in there. And it seemed to reflect the chaos in Ruby's mind.

"Isn't morning sort of a funny time for ice cream?" asked Miles.

"Anytime is a good time for ice cream," said Ruby simply.

Miles looked as if he needed some air. Ruby was a bit frustrating to deal with—she was just so scattered. Myrtle said, "I'll tell you what, Ruby. Why don't we just head over to the commons area? I could use a walk, even if there's no ice cream over there."

Ruby brightened. "Okay." She walked out of her room, leaving the key on the desk.

"Don't you want your key?" asked Myrtle.

"Oh no. No, it's very safe here," said Ruby.

"Except for murderers, right?" muttered Myrtle to Miles. "And mysterious and threatening phone calls."

Miles shrugged. "It's a struggle to keep Ruby focused."

Fortunately, there *was* ice cream in the commons area. Myrtle was sure at this point that she needed some sort of fortification—and if a glass of sherry weren't available, then chocolate ice cream would fit the bill just fine. There were a good number of residents there despite the early hour.

Myrtle wasn't sure she wanted any ice cream at ten-thirty in the morning, but she did see some people she wanted to talk to at the ice cream social. One of them was Inez, who appeared to be eating a bowl of chocolate ice cream with chocolate syrup and whipped cream with gusto. The other was Fred, who Erma had been talking about earlier. Fred still looked grumpy. You'd think his mood would have improved at least marginally after Mickey's demise.

Ruby was standing in line for the ice cream. Miles made a face at Myrtle. "It makes me feel slightly nauseated to be even contemplating eating ice cream at this hour of the day."

"I think we can skip it. Let's talk to Inez," said Myrtle under her breath. "Ruby is so spacey today that we might get more done while she's busy in line."

Inez's bright green eyes narrowed thoughtfully on Myrtle and Miles as they walked up to her. She raised her carefully penciled-on eyebrows. Today she was wearing a red blouse with black linen pants, and jewelry that seemed to be ancient Egyptian-inspired. "So ... here to visit your friend again?" There was the slightest sneering emphasis on the word *friend.*

Miles said glibly, "We had such a good time seeing Ruby the other day that we thought we'd come back and spend more time with her."

"Right," said Inez. Her eyes were ironic.

Myrtle cleared her throat. "We actually came because Ruby was so distraught. Because of Mickey's demise. She called me that morning and seemed absolutely devastated. Miles and I felt terrible for her."

They turned to look at Ruby. Unfortunately, they'd picked a time when Ruby was displaying no signs of devastation at all. She was beaming at the Greener Pastures staff member as they loaded up her ice cream with whipped cream.

Inez said dryly, "I can see that she desperately needed cheering up. Look, it doesn't matter to me. You're here for a reason of some kind and I guess that's good enough for me. It's just the journalist in me who is always looking for story. You understand."

"Then you must be intrigued by poor Mickey's death," inserted Myrtle smoothly. "Purely from a professional standpoint of course."

Inez gave her a considering look. "Greener Pastures is convinced that I heard nothing. To them, any headlines about Mickey's death should read 'Old Woman Dies in Her Sleep.' Which isn't much of a headline."

"Except that she *didn't* die in her sleep. And Miles and I are privy to some more information—the police will be investigating her death as suspicious," said Myrtle triumphantly.

"Well, that's positively amazing, considering the dubious response that Greener Pastures gave my report," said Inez briskly. "I live right on Mickey's hall and I can tell you now that I heard bumping around that night. It was not a peaceful passage into the next life."

"And yet you didn't get up to investigate? To check on Mickey? You were planning on having breakfast with her, weren't you? But you couldn't spare some time to make sure she was all right?" Myrtle tilted her head to one side and used her most piercing gaze on Inez.

"I figured she knocked down some stuff off her bedside table on the way to the bathroom, that's all. And no—I certainly wouldn't call Mickey a friend. But she *was* an early bird. I dislike eating alone and it's easy to join up with Mickey in the mornings to go to the dining room." Inez shrugged.

Miles, who'd been displaying an astounding lack of attention to Myrtle's interviewing of Inez, said, "Excuse me," and hurried over to a table where Fred appeared to be searching the room for a checkers partner.

Myrtle sighed. It wasn't helpful when one's sidekick was so easily distracted. She turned back to Inez. "Still, it could make for an interesting story for your paper, if Greener Pastures allows it with the police attention and all."

"I tell you what's good for my paper. What's good for my paper is not having Mickey's silly rag around anymore. It was a distraction at best and a nuisance at worst. What people *really* want isn't scandalmongering. They want upbeat content," said Inez, a confident shine in her eyes.

"Upbeat content?" asked Myrtle although she had a sneaking suspicion that she knew the kind of content that Inez was talking about. The *Bradley Bugle* was rife with it. Even the horoscopes were happy and positive for every sign. There were cooking columns, the Good Neighbors column. Even Myrtle's own helpful hints column. The only real news the *Bugle* put out was provided by Myrtle whenever a major crime happened.

"You know what I mean," said Inez in a bored voice. "People love seeing their name in print. They *love* it. So I mention as many people by name as possible. Then I say nice things about their perky red cardigan or their jewelry, or the twinkle in their eyes, or whatever. That's what people want and it's what I deliver."

"So you don't report any hard news?" asked Myrtle.

"What kind of hard news are you talking about? The hamburgers being a bit undercooked? The fact that Greener Pastures wastes money on landscaping by not following up with watering the flowers? What?" asked Inez impatiently. She scraped her ice cream bowl to get the very last bit.

"Well—murder, obviously. And theft," said Myrtle, staring carefully at Inez for a reaction.

The reaction was more like boredom. "Theft? Why? Did you have your pocket picked? Look at it as a sign that you're one of the in-crowd. I didn't think visitors usually had things lifted from their pocketbooks."

"So there *is* theft!" said Myrtle triumphantly.

"If you want to call it that. It's pretty small-scale stuff. And whoever is doing it is very good at it," said Inez with a shrug. "Although I don't *approve*. It's wicked to steal."

"But people still leave the doors to their rooms unlocked?" Myrtle frowned. "It seems like an open invitation to trouble."

"It's never *that* much that's stolen. And it's never the same people all the time. It's more on a rotation. Half the time the victims probably never even notice their change is missing," said Inez with a shrug.

"Well, *I* do. I count my pennies. I pick up dropped change in parking lots. And I shop sales," said Myrtle. She stopped, realizing that she appeared to be going off on a tangent. Myrtle tried to regroup. "If someone *did* want to get rid of Mickey Pelias, who do you think would be the most likely candidate?"

Inez gave her a surprised look. "Her daughter, of course. She had Natalie on a leash for at least the last five years, if not her entire life. If *she* didn't want to get rid of Mickey, I can't imagine who would."

Miles would have given Myrtle a meaningful look—if he hadn't been enjoying playing checkers so much.

Inez was looking across at the ice cream stand again and Myrtle was afraid she was about to lose her attention. She asked quickly, "Tell me one thing real quick. The man over there—the one who's playing checkers with Miles—why was he so angry with Mickey?"

Inez raised her eyebrows. "Fred Lee? Who knows? Fred is the kind of person who gets mad all the time—usually over petty things. And you have to remember that Mickey wrote really cruel things in her newsletter. Maybe she said something about Fred."

"Do you remember if she did? Fairly recently?" asked Myrtle.

Inez gave her a cold look. "I wouldn't read a rag like that," she said with a sniff. And she was off for ice cream seconds.

Chapter Nine

Miles, Myrtle reflected, seemed entirely too much at home. He was laughing with Fred Lee as his checker piece got crowned.

Myrtle cleared her throat and looked hard at Miles. He flushed and put his piece down on the board.

Fred Lee, who had looked more relaxed than Myrtle had seen him, now appeared cantankerous again. "Wait your turn if you want to play a game," he said imperiously. "We're busy."

"Actually, Mr. Lee, I had a question for you," said Myrtle smoothly. "I couldn't help but notice when Miles and I were visiting the other day that you seemed upset with Mickey Pelias."

The old man jutted his chin out. His gaze was combative. "What of it?"

"What of it is that she's dead now," said Myrtle.

"Lots of people are dead. It's got nothing to do with me," said Fred, eyes narrowed.

"Well, lots of people aren't dead by misadventure," snapped Myrtle. "The police are now treating Mickey's death as suspicious. So I thought I'd ask you why you were upset with her."

Fred shifted in his seat and looked cagey. "There's no law against being upset with a person. Mickey was the kind of person that got people upset with her, that's all. Nothing against Mickey."

Myrtle noticed that every time he said Mickey's name, his mouth pursed as if he tasted something sour. "Not only that, but it's clear you didn't like her much."

He frowned at Myrtle and his eyes were wary. "No law against that, either."

"I seem to be running into a *lot* of people who didn't like Mickey much," said Myrtle.

Fred asked quickly, "Like who?"

"Oh, I don't know. Her daughter? You? And Inez didn't seem especially fond of her when I was talking to her," said Myrtle.

Fred gave a dismissive wave of his hand as if he couldn't be bothered with such stuff. "Old news. Mickey's daughter was probably irritated with her mother her entire life. Inez is too protective of her precious newspaper. As for me—as I said, there's no law against disliking someone."

"Do you have anyone else you want to add to the list?" asked Myrtle. "I'm interested in getting as many potential names on it as possible."

"All I know is that Mickey made a point of knowing everyone's secrets. She probably found out some poor ninny's big secret and threatened to publish it in that scurrilous newspaper of hers. The ninny grew a backbone and got rid of Mickey. Case closed."

"Could you tell me where you were on the night Mickey was murdered?" asked Myrtle in her most official-sounding voice.

"Are you kidding me, lady? It was the middle of the night, wasn't it? I was either asleep or else I was in the restroom." Fred was starting to sound exasperated.

"And you didn't hear any noises?" asked Myrtle.

"What, like gunfire or something?" Fred's heavy eyebrows drew together.

"No, I mean like sounds of a struggle. Someone calling for help. That kind of thing," said Myrtle.

"No. I didn't hear a thing." He turned away from Myrtle. "Now, if you'll leave me alone, I've got a checkers game to win."

Miles grinned at Fred. "Oh, feeling confident, are you? We'll see how that goes."

Myrtle sighed. Maybe she did need that ice cream. These suspects were not doing a good job at giving her information.

What's more, Miles was entirely too cozy with Greener Pastures. The last thing on earth she'd expected was that her sidekick would want to check himself into a retirement home.

She was just heading toward the ice cream stand and fumbling in her pocketbook for money (she assumed they would know that she wasn't a resident) when she felt an arm go around her back and she jumped. Myrtle turned to glare at the grinning visage of Winston Rouse—entirely too close to her. "Excuse me?" she asked coldly.

But Winston didn't appear to be able to take a hint. In fact, he seemed positively delighted to see her. "Myrtle! Did you come back to visit me?"

"Certainly not," she said briskly. "I'm here to investigate a murder. For the *Bradley Bugle*. I'm a correspondent." She nearly bit her tongue as a Greener Pastures staff person passed by and turned sharply, staring at her with narrowed eyes before continuing on to speak to the staffers at the ice cream stand.

Winston appeared not to be listening very hard. He looked deep into Myrtle's suspicious eyes. "I'm so glad you're here. You'll share a bowl of ice cream with me?"

Myrtle recoiled. Surely, he wasn't suggesting that they share a *single bowl* of ice cream? She was certain that Greener Pastures was likely a hotbed of germs with all these people living in close quarters with each other. She said in a cold voice, "Well, *I'm* going to have a bowl of ice cream. And apparently, *you're* going to have a bowl of ice cream, too. So, in that sense, I suppose we'll both be having a bowl at the same time."

Winston howled with laughter. "Myrtle, you were always so clever. So darned clever. Much more than I was, that's for sure. Yes, let's have some ice cream and then we'll talk."

"About the murder?" asked Myrtle, wanting to be very sure that something would come out of their encounter besides an abhorrent amount of flirting from Winston and her determined attempts to squash it.

"Yes! About the murder. Whatever that is. Was someone murdered? Never mind, we'll talk about it in a minute," said Winston in a booming voice that made several women in the room turn around to stare at them. Myrtle flushed. She followed as Winston strode over to the ice cream stand. She saw Inez flash a look of pure venom at her. Did it have something to do with the attention Winston was giving her? Even though the attention was purely unwanted?

Myrtle was in a severe mood and decided on a severe ice cream, asking for a plain-Jane vanilla. Winston looked at the bowl with big eyes. He scoffed, "You've got to be kidding me." To her enormous irritation, he took the bottle of chocolate syrup she was holding and squirted it on Myrtle's vanilla ice cream.

Myrtle was about to give him a piece of her mind when she stopped, biting her lip. He *was* going to talk to her about the murder, or at the very least entertain the topic. She gave him a tight smile instead.

To her irritation, Winston led them over to a cozy loveseat in the corner of the common area. "So we can converse in privacy," he said, giving her a broad wink. Miles gave her a mirthful look from the checkers table, where he was apparently still winning.

"Now, then," said Winston. He gave her what seemed to be a very practiced carefree grin and Myrtle took the opportunity to study him dispassionately. He certainly seemed well groomed and had become quite the dapper dresser with a jaunty red bow tie, sports jacket, and light blue button-down shirt. Wasn't he overdressed for an ice cream social at a retirement home? His beard was neatly trimmed and his eyes twinkled merrily at her. How could she have responded to his flirtatious nature so many years ago? Now it was only rather alarming.

"So," she said, straightening up and giving him her best schoolteacher repressive stare, "what I want to talk about is Mickey Pelias."

"Okay," he said. "Although I'm not sure why. She's annoying as the blazes. Oh, we had a short fling, I'm not going to say we didn't. But it ended pretty quickly. Did she do something to you, maybe?"

Could he possibly not have heard the news of her demise? Myrtle said, "No. Because she's dead. And she's not only dead, she was murdered."

Winston's eyebrows rose in astonishment. "Is that so? Mickey? Dead? Why, I just saw her."

"When?" asked Myrtle impatiently. "It couldn't have been that recent."

"Well, I guess it was that day when you and I were having lunch," said Winston. He seemed distracted by his ice cream, which was rapidly disappearing.

Myrtle was busily working on scraping off the chocolate syrup. "That wasn't recent. Recent is yesterday or this morning or something. At any rate, that day that I came here for lunch was the day Mickey died."

"And you're saying it was murder," said Winston.

"Ruby Sims is saying it was murder," said Myrtle. She waited for the usual disclaimer about Ruby's mental condition, but Winston only looked thoughtful.

"Is that right?" he mused. "Ruby said so?"

"Yes. And now the police are investigating Mickey's death as a homicide," said Myrtle. At least, they should be. Myrtle wondered when the state police would be arriving. She paused, and then said, "You don't seem very surprised that Ruby was the one reporting the murder."

"Well, I'm not. Not at all." He waved his hand. "Never mind all that. Go on and tell me what you're thinking about Mickey. Annoying or not, she certainly shouldn't have been murdered."

"She turned in that night and someone sneaked into her room and probably smothered her with a pillow. The staff at Greener Pastures wanted to treat it as a natural death, but Ruby overheard thumping around in Mickey's room—sounds of a struggle. As you say, Mickey was an abrasive person and she made people mad. What I'm trying to do is to find out more about who might have had something against Mickey and wanted to get rid of her," said Myrtle. She finished scraping off the chocolate syrup and took a cautious bite of the remaining vanilla.

Winston looked sideways at her. "What are you ... some kind of private eye, Myrtle? When I knew you before, you were a teacher."

"Teachers develop many talents," said Myrtle succinctly.

"I won't argue with that," said Winston, although he looked as if he sorely wanted to.

Myrtle prompted him. "So do you know who was upset with Mickey?"

Winston frowned. "Now, *I* wasn't upset with Mickey. Don't let anyone tell you otherwise. I just avoided her, that's all."

It definitely sounded to Myrtle as if he were protesting too much. "All right, point taken. But who *might* have been?"

"Natalie. Her daughter. Did you hear how Mickey talked to that girl? If she *weren't* upset with her mother, she certainly should have been," said Winston. "Plus, her mother was pretty well-off. I'm guessing that Natalie would have inherited her money. I don't know what kind of money Natalie has, but she sure didn't dress like she had much. You'd think she'd take better care of herself."

"How did Mickey talk to her daughter?"

"Very dismissively," said Winston sharply. "A couple of times I said something to Mickey about it. She told me to mind my own business."

Mickey probably hadn't appreciated the intrusion. Myrtle wondered if Mickey might somehow have made Winston a target in some way, as payback. "Anybody else?"

"Fred, of course. Fred has told just about everyone that he's upset with Mickey," said Winston. He looked sadly at his empty ice cream bowl and then gave the line in front of the ice cream stand an analytical look.

"So I've heard," said Myrtle with a sigh. "Although no one has been able to tell me why."

Winston lowered his voice, taking the opportunity to move even closer to Myrtle in order to whisper in her ear. "Mickey knew something about Fred and was going to print it in her newspaper. You know—the underground newspaper she had."

"She was definitely printing it?" asked Myrtle. "What was the secret?"

"Well, if I knew the secret, I'd be dead, too. According to you anyway, Myrtle." Winston's eyes were twinkling now. The twinkling annoyed Myrtle.

"All right. So she knew something. So that's Fred Lee and Natalie Pelias. Then we have Inez."

"We do," agreed Winston. "Inez couldn't stand Mickey. I mean, she'd go to breakfast and stuff with her because Mickey was an early bird like herself. But every morning they'd end up squabbling with each other."

"Why *was* that?" asked Myrtle, leaning in a little before correcting herself and backing away a bit.

Winston made the sign of the cross and Myrtle frowned. "You've lost me, Winston. What?"

Winston spoke in a low voice again. "A mega-religious thing. With Inez. Mickey swore like a sailor and was hard living. Inez has got a bit of religious mania, if you haven't noticed."

"I suppose that didn't crop up in our conversation," said Myrtle. "And how do *you* know? Did you engage in some sort of religious debate with Inez?"

"Not by choice," said Winston ruefully. "I was tippling maybe just a wee bit too much at the Christmas party. Inez lit into me, but good. She thinks that I'm going to ... well, that I'm not going to heaven, let's put it that way." He shook his head. "But what a woman. She has strength of her convictions, that's for sure." There was a glint of admiration in his eyes.

"Hmm. I didn't really get that impression from her. I recall her wearing a cross. I guess I thought maybe she was looking at it as an insurance policy. You know—an end-of-life insurance policy," said Myrtle.

"Not a bit. She's very vested in her beliefs, believe me. And if you hang out here enough, she may try to convert you to them, too," said Winston in a warning tone.

"I'm a believer," said Myrtle, feeling miffed. "There's no conversion needed."

"Oh, I'm a believer, too! But that didn't stop Miss Inez. And her newspaper—the one that's been officially sanctioned by Greener Pastures—is full of good news and good will. And she sticks in scripture that she feels relates to the story at hand," said Winston. He chuckled.

"Does it?" asked Myrtle.

"I guess in the same general *realm* of the story. But she alluded to Jonah when she was reporting that Suzy McDonald's grandchildren were going to visit their Nana before going on a beach trip. I just don't think that particular news bulletin needed a Biblical allusion." Winston shrugged.

Myrtle squinted. "I just don't think that was even a *news bulletin*. Who cares? Just Suzy McDonald. And if she's got particularly bratty grandchildren, maybe not even Suzy. All right, so that's a few people who had a problem with Mickey. Anyone else who didn't like her? Seems like there should be more people, since I keep hearing that Mickey was so unlikeable. In fact, I hear of only one friend of Mickey's—Ruby. Didn't she have any others?" asked Myrtle.

Winston chuckled. "Well, with friends like Ruby, who needs enemies?"

Myrtle gave him a quelling frown. "That's rather cryptic, isn't it? Do you mean because Ruby is so absentminded that it's difficult to be friends with her? She certainly seemed loyal to Mickey."

"Oh, she certainly did seem loyal to Mickey," said Winston hastily. "I'm just saying that Ruby is challenging, that's all. I mean, Ruby stuck to Mickey like glue. Would you want a friend like that?"

It reminded Myrtle of her neighbor, Erma Sherman. If Erma had her way and if Myrtle weren't so fleet of foot, then Erma would be spending about that much time with Myrtle. The thought made her feel faintly nauseated. Or maybe it was simply the fact that she was eating something very sugary before eleven o'clock in the morning.

"No, I suppose I wouldn't. But it would be very flattering. Ruby always looked at Mickey as if she were imparting some sort of wisdom from the mount," said Myrtle with a sigh.

"She did, at that." Winston's eyes were inscrutable before he smoothly flashed a toothy grin at her and said, "Myrtle, I want to ask you something. Beg something of you, if you will."

Myrtle gave him a wary look. "What's that?"

"I'm sure you've noticed that it's the end of December. In a few days, it will be the New Year. We have a party here at Greener Pastures to celebrate. Would you be my date for that event?" His expression was earnest and he reached out to hold her hand as if he were proposing marriage.

Myrtle drew back, giving him a horrified look. She was definitely going to say no, but wasn't sure how to go about it without totally alienating him—and he seemed like a good source for insider Greener Pasture info. She spluttered instead, "Greener Pastures has a New Year's Eve party?"

"In a manner of speaking. Since so many residents turn in early, we do a countdown to noon, instead," he said.

The thought irritated Myrtle. Greener Pastures was infantilizing its residents again. Countdown to noon, indeed.

Winston misread her hesitation. "It's more fun than it sounds. And we all dress up in our finery and drink white grape juice."

Myrtle said quickly, "You know, I do want to come. But Miles would be desperately jealous if I were your official date."

They both looked over at Miles who was just hooting in excitement over winning the match with Fred Lee. Fred Lee's face, in contrast, was the very definition of 'unhappy.'

Winston said slowly, "So you ... and Miles. You're not just friends?"

Myrtle crossed her fingers under her ice cream bowl. "Certainly not. We're much, much more."

Winston gave a low whistle. "Aren't you the cougar, Myrtle?" He gave her an admiring look that made Myrtle flush.

"Enough of that," she said briskly.

"But you will save some dances for me," wheedled Winston.

"If it can be arranged," said Myrtle stiffly. "And now I must go speak to Ruby really quickly." She pushed herself up from the loveseat with her cane. She paused and turned around, eyes narrowed. "But I can promise you one thing, Winston. It won't be a countdown-to-noon party we attend."

Chapter Ten

Ruby looked as happy as a child with her bowl of ice cream. "This was fun. I wish Greener Pastures had an ice cream party every week."

The heavy-set staff person behind the ice cream stand raised one eyebrow. "Ms. Sims, we *do* have an ice cream party every week."

Ruby was flustered. "Oh. Oh, that's right." She turned to Myrtle. "Did you have a nice time visiting with everyone?" They walked over to an area where there weren't any residents.

Myrtle said, "I did. Although I wasn't really visiting. I was more *questioning* people." Ruby looked foggy so Myrtle continued, "I'm trying to ask people questions so that I can find out what's happened to Mickey."

"Mickey's dead," said Ruby solemnly.

"Yes, I know," said Myrtle with a sigh.

"You know who you should ask?" said Ruby. After her forgetfulness a moment ago, she now seemed surprisingly lucid. "You should ask Mickey's daughter. That woman." She fumbled for a name, and then gave up with a shrug. "You know."

"Natalie," said Myrtle. "Yes, I do need to talk with her. But do you think that she might have some information on Mickey's death?"

"She was here then," said Ruby with wide eyes.

"When Mickey died? Where?" asked Myrtle.

"In her room," said Ruby.

"When? Around suppertime? Before eight p.m.?"

Ruby frowned in concentration. "Late. Very late. I heard her voice."

"Could you really hear Natalie's voice, Ruby? Because the walls seem fairly thick here—at least they're not super-flimsy—and Natalie has such a soft voice that I had a hard time hearing her sometimes. The woman swallows her words," said Myrtle. It was always vexing to be around young people who swallowed their words, especially when they knew they were around older people.

Ruby's mouth set stubbornly. "I know it was Mickey's daughter."

Myrtle said searchingly, "It wasn't Mickey on the phone? Or talking to anyone else?"

Ruby shook her head vehemently.

"Okay," said Myrtle. She'd somehow succeeded in getting Ruby's back up and she needed her to lower her guard again if Myrtle were to get anything else out of her. "Um—tell me about your children, Ruby. Boys, I think you said that you had."

Ruby's eyes glowed, her irritation quickly forgotten. "That's right—six sons. And nary a one in jail!" she said in a triumphant drawl.

"Certainly an accomplishment," said Myrtle once again. Really, she didn't know how to handle such a statement. She hesitated. "So do you see much of them?"

Ruby's face fell. "Not as much as I'd like. I don't have any money, just social security. If I had money, I'd give it to my boys so they could travel to see me."

"Ah. They moved from Bradley, did they?" asked Myrtle.

"That's right. They needed to make a living and Bradley didn't have any jobs for them. One of them is even sick right now and I can't get over to see him. They're smart boys—they can do all kinds of construction things. But they're far away building things, not close building things." Ruby looked as if she didn't have too much of a handle on where they actually were. Then she brightened. "Did you bring your cat? To visit? I love cats."

Myrtle rubbed the side of her forehead to try to combat the headache she felt developing there. "I didn't, no. I might have mentioned to you, Ruby, that Pasha—my cat—is not really a *pet*. She's a feral animal that chooses to spend time with me sometimes. I'd have to capture her and put her in a carrier to bring her here."

Ruby nodded, but didn't seem to have any comprehension in her eyes. "Do you have a picture of the cat?" she asked eagerly.

Myrtle tried to tamp down her impatience. "Not on me, no. I do have some at home. I'll bring them with me the next time I come over. Ruby, I heard that you told Mickey Fred Lee's secret."

Ruby blinked at her, looking confused. "Fred Lee?" she asked.

Myrtle pointed over to the checkers table where Miles and Fred were engulfed in another game. "Fred is right over there—with my friend Miles. He was angry at Mickey and said that you'd shared his secret with Mickey."

Ruby's eyebrows drew together. "Miles was mad at Mickey?"

"No, no! *Fred* was mad at Mickey."

"Oh, that's right." Ruby frowned again in concentration. "I think Fred's secret was ... well, it was ..." She stopped. "I can't remember now. But I know that Mickey was interested in it. She asked me a lot of questions, but I didn't know anything else about it. So she asked Fred."

"Was Mickey planning on printing Fred's secret in her newspaper?" asked Myrtle.

Ruby nodded her head vigorously. "Yes. But I don't remember what it was that she was going to print." Her face was discouraged but resigned, as if she'd gotten used to her memory deficiencies. And who knows, if Fred killed Mickey because she knew his secret, it was probably in Ruby's best interest not to be able to remember it.

Myrtle said, "I was speaking with ...well, someone who knows Mickey, and he was saying that Inez didn't really like Mickey very much—is that what you remember?"

Ruby's face clouded again and Myrtle tried to unobtrusively point Inez out. Ruby nodded. "No, she didn't like Mickey's swearing very much. Or Mickey's newspaper. Or, I guess, Mickey." Ruby looked intently at Myrtle. "Did you know about our New Year's party on New Year's Eve? I'm making decorations for it."

Myrtle figured that this was probably as much as she was going to get from Ruby Sims at this point. "Yes, someone mentioned it to me. A countdown to noon."

"That's right. I'm cutting out construction paper figures to hang up. It's usually fun. Are you going?" asked Ruby, looking hopeful.

"Definitely. I wouldn't miss it. But I'm going to make Greener Pastures change it to a midnight party. Counting down to noon is for children," she scoffed.

Myrtle was about to expound on this thought when suddenly Darla, the Greener Pastures manager, swooped in. *Swooped in* was a bit of an exaggeration, considering that Darla was rather heavy-set, but it felt like a swoop to Myrtle.

Darla said smoothly to Ruby, "Excuse us please, Ms. Sims, while I borrow Mrs. Clover for a few minutes." And before she knew it, Myrtle was meekly following along behind Darla on her way to her small office. Miles gave her a sympathetic look as she passed.

Darla had barely given her a chance to sit down before she said briskly, "Someone has called the state police regarding Mickey Pelias's death. What do you know about that?"

Myrtle gave her a carefully bewildered look. "Darla, I don't have the slightest idea how to phone the SBI. Do you? It's not as if I carry their number around with me."

"But your son would know their number," said Darla insistently. "Your son is chief of police."

"My son is on leave," said Myrtle coldly. "He's had knee surgery and is completely incapacitated and using a walker. I sat with him all yesterday afternoon, so I should know. He's certainly not taking on any murder cases. And that's exactly what you're faced with here at Greener Pastures—a murder investigation. The sooner you focus on that and stop focusing your energies on me, the better it will be."

"So you don't know anything about this." Darla's long face was skeptical.

"I certainly don't," said Myrtle, crossing her fingers underneath her large pocketbook. "Now, if you'll excuse me, I want to catch up with my friend so that we can get home in time for our soap opera to start."

Myrtle stood up, stretching regally to her nearly six-feet of height and staring down at Darla, still sitting at her desk. "By the way, while I'm in here, I want to relay a message to you from various residents I've spoken with. They'd all like to have a countdown to *midnight* party instead of a countdown to noon. They say that countdowns to noon are for children."

Darla's face became an alarming shade of mottled red.

"That is all," said Myrtle coolly, strolling out of Darla's cramped office.

She strode up to Miles who was just setting up the checkers for another game. "It's time for us to get out of here now." Miles, who'd apparently forgotten that he was a mere guest and not a resident, gave her a confused look. "We've worn out our welcome, okay? It's time to give Greener Pastures a little time to miss us."

Miles hurried to catch up with Myrtle as she headed toward the front door. "How did we wear out our welcome?" asked Miles a bit suspiciously. "I thought we'd only been playing checkers and eating ice cream. Did it have something to do with your being called to the principal's office?"

"If you mean Dragon Darla, then yes, it did have something to do with that. We were accused of having contacted the state police. Which, of course, I categorically denied," said Myrtle. She lifted her head righteously.

"Of course," said Miles. "Although we were directly connected to their interest in Mickey's death."

"I've found it's never good to randomly volunteer information. I especially want to avoid randomly volunteering information to Greener Pastures."

"You know, they're not so bad there," he said mildly as they sped back home. "At Greener Pastures, I mean. They seem to genuinely care about their residents. The ice cream socials were a nice touch, I thought."

"At ten o'clock in the morning?" asked Myrtle.

"It's a strange time, but older people are on odd schedules."

"I think it's *Greener Pastures* that's on an odd schedule," said Myrtle heatedly.

"You have to admit that they put on a nice social. And the ice cream was free," said Miles.

"Free, my foot! Those residents pay through the nose to live there. That ice cream is being paid for, let me assure you," said Myrtle. "And then, as I was pointing out, the Home wanted to offer the ice cream on their own terms—when it was convenient for *them*. Sort of like that silly New Year's party."

"What's silly about it?" asked Miles. "We're attending, aren't we? Actually, I think I even have a date for it."

This was the final straw for Myrtle. Her sidekick seemed to have lost all his sleuthing abilities and was getting sucked into the Greener Pastures Bermuda Triangle. "What's silly about it is that it's a countdown to noon, not midnight. And there are no alcoholic beverages, just white grape juice. It seems very much like a children's party—a *young* children's party, at that. And you do *not* have a date, Miles. I told Winston Rouse that I was going with you so that he'd leave me alone. How on earth did you acquire a date, anyway? Are you going with Fred? Because he's the only one I saw you consorting with while we were there."

Miles pulled into Myrtle's driveway and gave her a wry look. "No, I'm not going with Fred to the party. Fred has someone that he was going to set me up with, that's all. I need to phone him when I get home to cancel." He looked thoughtfully at Myrtle. "I guess that's why Winston was giving me death threats."

"Death threats? Winston?"

"That's right. He kept leaning over me when I was playing Fred and telling me that checkers wasn't his thing but that he and I should play a game of Scrabble—that he'd slaughter me. Lots of slaughtering references going on. I thought at the time that he must be a very serious and intense Scrabble fan, but now I realize that there was a whole level of subtext there that I wasn't picking up on."

"For heaven's sake," said Myrtle, frowning. "The last thing that I want is a suitor. I wish he'd leave me alone. Miles, you'll have to be especially attentive during the New Year's Eve party."

"I'll try," he said dryly. He paused. "Say, Myrtle, what did you learn with all that chatting during the social?"

Finally, some sidekick interest in all of her interviews. "I've got to sort it all out in my head—there was a lot of information. But I think the highlights were that Fred told Ruby a secret and Mickey was going to post it in her newspaper...and that's why Fred was so upset. And Inez apparently has very strong religious convictions and didn't approve of Mickey one bit. And Natalie...well, Ruby swears that Natalie was at Greener Pastures late at night when Mickey was murdered."

Miles raised his eyebrows. "And we're finding Ruby's information valid?"

"She seemed very certain." Myrtle looked in the side view mirror. "Here's the mailman."

"I'll get it for you," said Miles. He slid out of his car, greeted the mail carrier, and then brought the mail over to Myrtle.

Myrtle made a face. "Looks like a ton of invitations."

"Invitations?" Miles looked at the mail doubtfully.

"Sure. *You're invited to pay your water bill.* Lots of invitations to send money." She paused. "And one interesting bit of mail." Myrtle held up postcard with some carefully formed letters snaking across it. "From Wanda."

Myrtle stared at the back of the postcard. "It says *"muney"* is *the root of all evil.* Which is annoying."

"Annoying? I'd say it sounds very much like something that Wanda would send. I think she's trying to give us a clue," said Miles, climbing back behind the wheel.

"Annoying because the actual Biblical quotation is: *the love of money is the root of all evil.* Money is okay, loving it isn't. This is a bit cryptic, too, even for Wanda." Myrtle frowned. "And exhibiting Wanda's tragic propensity for misspelling."

"To me, it's very clear," said Miles. "It points to Natalie. Natalie was tired of her caretaker role, didn't have any money of her own, and was eager to move on to the next stage of her life. Ruby saw Natalie there that night and we know that Mickey and Natalie had a difficult relationship. Doesn't it seem obvious?"

"It's the obvious part that is so disturbing," said Myrtle. "None of these cases are obvious. No, it's likely pointing to something or someone else. Or maybe it means nothing at all. Who knows?" Myrtle was starting to feel a bit frustrated. She opened her pocketbook to stick the postcard inside and stopped short.

"What is it?" asked Miles.

"The money that was stolen from me? It's been replaced in my purse."

The roar of a lawnmower woke Myrtle up the next morning. This was shocking for a couple of different reasons. The first was that Myrtle never woke when it was light outside—it was always dark, no matter the season of the year. The second was that her ghastly yardman, Dusty, had apparently volunteered to cut her grass without being pestered.

Myrtle pushed the covers back, eager to feast her eyes on an eager Dusty. She pulled on her bathrobe, grabbed her cane, and hurried to the front of the house to peer out the side window where the mowing sounds were coming from. She was greeted by the sight of Dusty, looking a good deal more dapper and official than usual, mowing *Erma*'s lawn at an unheard of seven a.m.

"Is that a *uniform* he's wearing?" muttered Myrtle to herself. It was unheard of for Dusty to wear a uniform. Usually he wore a disreputable pair of baggy khakis that were more green than khaki and a frayed button-down shirt with some sort of checkered pattern—more of a mottled gray color. And today he seemed to be taking special care with Erma's lawn—tenderly pushing around the burgeoning weeds that he appeared to believe had been planted on purpose.

At this point Myrtle realized it was time to move away from the window. She would work herself into a froth seeing a prompt, starched, *clean* Dusty at Erma's house. It was time to take on her day. She'd start with a large coffee with an extra spoonful of sugar to help the medicine go down as soon as she'd changed clothes.

Myrtle was just contemplating whether she wanted eggs or grits for breakfast when there was a tap at the door. When she opened it, she stared in shock at the pale, dumpy woman there. "Puddin! What are you doing here?"

Chapter Eleven

"Thought your house might need cleanin'," said Puddin. She had a cigarette in her hand and quickly stubbed it out when she saw Myrtle's expression. She shoved the cigarette butt into her pocket. "Can I come in?"

Myrtle stepped aside, still looking at Puddin in shock as the woman slouched in. "Puddin, it's extremely unusual, as you know, for you to show up here to clean without my calling you first. In fact, it's extremely unusual for you to show up here to clean even after I *have* called you."

Puddin shrugged, pushing her lank blonde hair out of her eyes as she glanced around the room to gauge how much work she'd let herself in for. "I dunno. Thought you might have a dirty house, that's all."

"You didn't bring any cleaning supplies with you," said Myrtle. She pressed her lips together and shook her head. "You know how annoying it is for me when you use up my cleaners." She looked out the front window. "And you came in your own car. Not with Dusty. That's really odd. Are you ever usually awake at this hour of the day?"

Puddin didn't appear to be listening to Myrtle at all, which certainly wasn't unusual. Her eyes narrowed thoughtfully for a moment before she said quickly, "I haven't done your windows in a while. They might be dirty."

"Puddin, you've *never* done my windows."

"No time like the present," said Puddin. She loped off into Myrtle's kitchen, scrabbling under the sink until she surfaced with window cleaner and Myrtle's last remaining roll of paper towels.

Myrtle put her hands on her hips and just watched as Puddin cocked her head to one side, listening. "I think I'll start with them windows there." She shuffled over to the window on the side of the house, yanked up the blinds, and started spraying dabs of cleaner here and there on the glass as she peered outside. Occasionally, she swiped at the drips, making streaks as she went.

"Puddin, for heaven's sake! That window looks worse than it did before you started. Now, what's this foolishness about? You're no window washer. You don't get up this early. You don't volunteer to clean my house. What happened to the real Puddin?"

Puddin's chin trembled just the barest bit before she took complete control of her emotions again. She studied Myrtle's floor as if it fascinated her. "Trying to see what Dusty's up to," she muttered.

This was fairly astonishing in itself. Myrtle agreed that Dusty's actions—the early hour, the uniform, the careful workmanship—were remarkable. But Puddin had certainly never shown much interest in her husband before.

Puddin apparently took Myrtle's silence as a signal to explain herself. She rolled her eyes and said, "Dusty was excited about getting the new yard to mow. He pulled out his old uniform that I ain't never seen him wear. I think he's got a crush on her."

"On whom?" Myrtle frowned.

"Her!" Puddin jerked a stubby finger in the direction of Erma's house.

"Erma!" Myrtle's eyes felt as if they were about to bug out of their sockets. The idea of Erma involved with anyone was a nauseating concept.

"Yes, *Erma*," muttered Puddin. "That flirty man-eater. Trying to steal other women's husbands when she can't find one of her own." The words shot out like snide bullets. Puddin gave up on her pretense of cleaning and now simply stared out the window where they could clearly see a rather dapper Dusty now attacking some of Erma's weed-infested bushes.

"See what I mean?" demanded a Despairing Puddin. "Dusty don't cut no bushes. Never."

"No, he don't...doesn't," said Myrtle thoughtfully. Then, more briskly, since the very last thing she wanted on her hands was a weeping housekeeper, she said, "Have you simply *asked* Dusty? Maybe there's a perfectly good explanation for his behavior."

Puddin's eyes held a familiar combination of sullenness and stubbornness that Myrtle recognized well. "Haven't! Won't! Besides, he just done it this morning, didn't he? Left all spiffy in his uniform. Didn't have a chance to ask him about it, but wanted to find out where he was going."

"Yes, it was rather dim of Dusty not to realize you might have questions about why he was suddenly looking so professional," said Myrtle. "But that might also strengthen the case that the underlying explanation is completely innocent."

Puddin squinted her eyes. "You're not speakin' English again, Miz Myrtle."

Myrtle sighed. "I'm just saying that you've had a long and ... er ... happy marriage to Dusty. You should give him the benefit of the doubt."

"I ain't givin' that lowlife nuthin!"

Myrtle felt a sudden rising panic. The panic was one that she'd felt off and on through the years. Finding domestic help of any kind or quality was a challenge in a town the size of Bradley, North Carolina. What if Dusty and Puddin were to divorce? Puddin was a sorry housekeeper, but she was cheap and Myrtle knew how to keep her motivated enough to at least get one or two deep cleaning jobs out of her every couple of months.

Dusty was also cheap and was also difficult to motivate to work. But he was the only yardman in town who'd weed-eat with his edger around her garden gnomes. Those garden gnomes that she pulled out to irritate the stew out of Red whenever he stepped out of line were vital to keeping the peace on Magnolia Lane.

Anything upsetting this delicate balance would be a bad thing. What if Puddin were to divorce Dusty, meet some other yardman in some other town, and move away? Myrtle doubted very much that she could ever clean her own baseboards again. And the thought of chasing dust bunnies from under her bed was equally unappealing. Something would have to be done.

Myrtle was just opening her mouth to assure Puddin that Erma would not be appealing as an amour to *anyone*, even a man such as Dusty, when Puddin suddenly pinned her down with a sharp look from her small eyes. "You're a private eye, Miz Myrtle. Can you help me?"

"A private eye? Like Sam Spade? Certainly not!" That would involve wearing a fedora, drinking lots of scotch, and having a dame as a client. Puddin was no dame and Myrtle had a preference for sherry. She'd reserve judgment on the fedora. Who knows? Maybe she'd look good in one.

"Whatever. You poke around in stuff. You're nosy. You can spy on Dusty for me," said Puddin, waving her pudgy hands around in her agitation.

That sounded tedious. Myrtle was fairly sure that Dusty's day was very routine-oriented and revolved around a hearty breakfast, checking the oil in his yard equipment, complaining about working, doing a bit of work for whichever client he was most behind on, then returning home for a celebratory six-pack. "You're wanting me to *follow* Dusty?"

Puddin gave Myrtle an impatient look. "Naw! You don't drive, do you? Just watch him out the window if he shows up at your neighbor's house. That's all. Look out your windows if he's next door. You can do that, can't you? 'Cause now he's done with her yard and he shouldn't be back here later today, right?"

"What is it that makes you think that Dusty could possibly have any interest at all in Erma Sherman? Because I can assure you, she's not exactly a femme fatale."

Puddin squinted at her suspiciously. "Is that English?"

"I mean, Erma doesn't have a lot of dates," said Myrtle in exasperation.

Puddin didn't seem prepared to take Myrtle's word on this. "All I know is that he got all gussied up to come here today. And early, too. He's up to something."

"All right, Puddin. I'll keep an eye out for him, don't worry. I'll get to the bottom of it," said Myrtle with a sigh.

Puddin knitted her brows. "I don't have to pay you or nuthin', do I?"

"You can pay me back by showing some eagerness for cleaning. You can return my phone calls instead of saying that your answering machine is broken."

Puddin said quickly, "But it *is* broke."

"And you can stop telling me that 'your back is thrown' whenever I ask you to polish silver, dust, or do any other housekeeping that you don't enjoy," added Myrtle.

Puddin watched her sullenly for a few moments. Then she nodded, reluctantly. "I guess so."

"It's a deal then," said Myrtle briskly. "And I'll let you get started on your end by cleaning up around here. You haven't come for the last couple of weeks and the dust bunnies are starting to procreate."

Puddin gave a loud sigh. Then she quickly glanced around her. "That witch cat isn't here, is it?"

"Pasha? No. Pasha is busy subduing nature, I'm sure." Myrtle paused. "Actually, you know, I think I'm going to take Pasha with me over to Greener Pastures today. Ruby has been dying to see her."

"Whose car is she going to rip up?" asked Puddin with pursed lips. "That cat's a devil."

"She's a love," corrected Myrtle. "And she won't be ripping anyone's car up. I'll put her in a cat carrier like any normal, humane person would. The poor thing would be scared silly if I put her in a moving vehicle to run around and look out windows and such. The very idea."

"Just make sure you don't put her in a carrier when *I'm* around, Miz Myrtle. Don't want to get sliced to smithereens with them claws. And remember—you're keeping an eye on Dusty."

The phone rang. Myrtle called behind her as she hurried toward the kitchen phone. "Never you mind about Dusty. I know what to do. Just worry about those dust bunnies."

Myrtle grabbed the phone. "Hello?"

"Sweetie?" asked a fluttery, confused-sounding voice on the other end.

"Ruby," said Myrtle. "How are you today?"

"Sort of good," said Ruby. "They had omelets this morning in the dining hall. It's special when they have them because they make them fresh for each person. You get to tell them exactly how you want them and then they make the omelets right in front of you. So you can choose ham or spinach or bacon or turkey or broccoli or Swiss cheese."

Ruby continued listing all the possible ingredients of an omelet until Myrtle cut her off. "Ruby. You called to tell me something. Remember? What did you call to tell me?"

Ruby hesitated. "Do *you* know? Why I would have called you?"

Myrtle suppressed a sigh. "Would it have had something to do with Mickey's death? Did you find out some information? Has anyone called you again or threatened you in any way? Have you talked with one of the people we think could be involved in Mickey's murder? Have you heard from the police?" She stopped, all out of guesses.

Ruby paused on her end long enough for Myrtle to wonder if she were taking a short nap. Then she finally said, "Noooo. No, none of those are right." She stopped again, and then said, "I've got it! Mickey's daughter. That girl. She's here today and starting to clean out Mickey's room."

"You mean Natalie?" Natalie was hardly a girl, even to someone of Myrtle's advanced years.

"That's right," said Ruby excitedly. "Can you come over? So you can speak to her."

Myrtle looked at her wall clock. "I'll call Miles and we'll get over there as soon as possible."

When Myrtle phoned Miles, he sounded fairly enthusiastic about heading back over to the retirement home. Myrtle suspected that it might have something to do with Scrabble or checkers. Or perhaps the chocolate cake that he'd eaten with such gusto after their lunch in the dining hall the other day.

"Sure, sounds like a good time to talk to Natalie," said Miles in a cheery voice. "It's going to be hard to find as many opportunities to interview her as it is everyone else so let's hop on any chance we get."

"Great," said Myrtle. She paused, and then added quickly, "We'll have an additional passenger with us today."

"Wanda? You know, I was just thinking that we should probably take Wanda over to Greener Pastures. She's key to the whole investigation, don't you think? And she clearly knows something—as evidenced by her cryptic postcard yesterday."

Myrtle frowned. "Nooo...no, I don't think Wanda is key to anything. I think Wanda is taking a role of....well, maybe a whistleblowing role. And she does know a lot, but the problem with what Wanda knows is that it's all these bits of flotsam, sort of bobbing around in her head. She doesn't know how to put any of it into context. So she's *helpful*, but she's not *that* helpful."

"Not Wanda?" asked Miles. "Then who were you thinking of?"

"Pasha?" said Myrtle quickly.

"What!" Miles's voice became high-pitched in his anxiety and Myrtle moved the phone's receiver away from her ear.

"Obviously, you must have heard me, so I won't repeat it. I'm bringing Pasha with us. Ruby is dying to see her and the cat will be perfectly behaved in her cat carrier," said Myrtle.

Puddin gave a loud disbelieving snort behind her and Myrtle shot her a venomous look.

"Won't the sensation of movement drive her crazy?" asked Miles dubiously. "And are you sure that cats are allowed at Greener Pastures?"

"Pasha is too sophisticated to be concerned by the sensation of movement. Greener Pastures allows therapy animals to visit the home," said Myrtle. At least, she believed they did. They were so far behind the times that maybe they hadn't formed a policy on therapy animals.

"All right," said Miles, sounding uncertain.

While Miles was still knocked a bit off-balance, Myrtle said, "And I need you to do a favor for me, Miles. When you come over, I need you to talk to Dusty. Man-to-man."

Puddin gave a thumbs-up and an approving nod of her head.

"Talk to Dusty? Man-to-man? Myrtle, what's this all about?"

Myrtle said, "I'll give you the low-down on the way to Greener Pastures. For now, all you need to do is to catch Dusty outside, which certainly shouldn't be hard, since he's working on Erma's yard, and just have a little small talk with him. Ask him how his life is. And admire Erma—assiduously. Then see what his reaction is, or what he says."

Puddin nodded fiercely.

Miles said in a pained but dignified voice, "Myrtle, I hope there is a very, very good explanation for this."

"There is, but I don't have time to explain the problem right now, or perhaps the inclination," she said, eyeing Puddin, who was avidly and openly listening in on her conversation. "Just please do what I say. Watch for his reaction. And then let me know. We need to get over to Greener Pastures to catch Natalie Pelias before she's finished packing up Mickey's things for the day." She gently set down the receiver.

Puddin was absently pushing a filthy dust rag across Myrtle's dining room table, going over the same spot repeatedly. "What're you going to do now?" she asked.

"Capture Pasha," said Myrtle simply.

Chapter Twelve

Fifteen minutes later, she, Miles, and Pasha were on their way to Greener Pastures. Miles looked warily in his rearview mirror toward his backseat. "I'm not sure how you got Pasha in there."

The cat was silently sitting in the carrier. "She was remarkably docile," said Myrtle. "Really just a little love."

"So you put lots of treats in the carrier, did you?" asked Miles.

"Just enough to provide incentive," said Myrtle, nose in the air.

Pasha gave a hiccupping burp from the back.

"So tell me all about what Dusty said," said Myrtle. "I cannot express to you the serious nature of this business. Puddin is in a shambles, believing Dusty is unfaithful. I *must* preserve their union or suffer the consequences."

Miles gave her a sideways glance. "Hyperbole doesn't become you, Myrtle. And I don't really understand what you're talking about. I told Dusty that Erma was such an attractive woman and he gave me an appraising look and then spat chewing tobacco on the ground."

Myrtle made a face. "Sounds like Dusty, all right. So he's being cagey about it. I'll have to see what I can find out on my own, I suppose."

"Cagey? No, just taciturn as usual. Good luck getting anything out of him." Miles drove on for a few minutes and then said as he carefully maneuvered into a parking spot at Greener Pastures, "What exactly are we asking Natalie, by the way? I'm assuming we're taking a more gentle approach with her. Considering that she just lost her mom and everything."

"Gentle? You were just saying that she's our most likely candidate as suspect. In that case, we should go in with the mindset that she *orchestrated* the loss of her mom. It seems to me that being gentle with a killer is not really going to get us anywhere," said Myrtle.

"I was simply throwing out ideas. I feel bad for Natalie." said Miles.

"But you've got to be open to the possibility that there are other strong candidates for murderer," said Myrtle. "For heaven's sake—even the Greener Pastures staff could be involved."

Miles looked sideways at her as he turned off the engine. "You're not seriously suggesting that the retirement home could have something to do with her death."

"Why not? It makes perfect sense to me. Mickey Pelias was becoming a problem for them. She continued to write inflammatory stories that showed Greener Pastures in a bad light."

"We don't know that," interjected Miles.

"Sure we do. Mickey herself said that the staff took her newspapers away whenever they found them."

"I think we need to read some of these newspapers to confirm that," said Miles stubbornly. "Mickey might have been playing to her audience."

"Agreed. But how are we planning to get our hands on these newspapers? From what I heard, they were destroyed as soon as they were printed. It's a wonder Greener Pastures didn't go even farther and disable Mickey's printer," said Myrtle.

Miles thought about this. "Maybe there are some in Mickey's room? Could we ask Natalie for them? And if there aren't any in her room, Ruby could potentially have some. She thought that everything Mickey did was amazing, so it stands to reason that she might have preserved some of the newspapers."

"All right. So we'll pop in on Ruby first and let her play with Pasha," said Myrtle.

"You might want to issue a general warning regarding the sharpness of Pasha's claws and teeth," said Miles pointedly.

"We'll see if Ruby has those newspapers. And then we'll visit with Natalie," said Myrtle.

"Who is cleaning out her mother's things," said Miles gloomily. "And force her to visit with us."

Myrtle glared at him. "Are you determined to raise moral objections to everything I'm trying to accomplish today?"

Miles seemed guiltily repentant and she continued. "Anyway. We'll see if Natalie has come across any newspapers in her clearing out. Then we'll pick up Pasha, talk to the Greener Pastures staff—just enough to let them know we're onto them—and we'll head out."

Miles shifted uncomfortably. Myrtle snapped, "For heaven's sake, Miles, what is it now?"

"Only that ... that we don't need to have Pasha with us while we're grilling Greener Pastures about—whatever it is that we're grilling them about. Pasha is basically contraband. She's not a therapy animal or whatever they listed as being Greener-Pastures-approved. She's not even tame. We'll likely be kicked out and told never to return again," said Miles. His voice was vaguely plaintive.

"And that would be tragic, wouldn't it? Especially since you've gotten addicted to the chicken casserole and the checkers games over here." Unfortunately, he also had a point. This was the irritating thing about having a sidekick sometimes. "How about if I talk with the Greener Pastures staff while you monitor the rest of Ruby's visit with Pasha?"

Miles's eyes held tremendous relief. He must have been very concerned about the Greener Pastures staff's part of the day.

When Ruby opened her door, her eyes were huge as she saw Pasha in the carrier. "Look!" she gasped. "She's so beautiful!"

Myrtle felt quite smug having someone so openly admire Pasha. Ordinarily, Myrtle didn't get praised for Pasha. No one *really* understood the cat other than Myrtle. They were more scared of her or wary of her. And half the time no one even associated Myrtle with Pasha, since the cat was outdoors roaming most of the time. Pasha wasn't *owned* by Myrtle, after all. Myrtle, more likely, was owned by Pasha.

But Ruby got it. She flung her door open and ushered them inside. "Come in," she said with delight. "Can we...can we let her out of her cage?"

"It's a carrier," corrected Myrtle. "And yes, she'd probably love to be let out. I brought some of her favorite treats that you can feed her."

Miles surreptitiously took several large steps backward until his back brushed Ruby's wall. Myrtle smirked. Miles was greatly intimidated by Pasha, although recently the two had seemed to reach some sort of understanding.

Myrtle unlatched and opened the carrier door and handed the bag of treats to Ruby. Pasha cautiously slunk out from the carrier, head swinging from side to side as she assessed her new surroundings.

Ruby appeared to be holding her breath. Wide-eyed, she yanked open the treat bag and tossed out a couple of treats. Pasha gave the treats a dismissive look and Ruby's face fell, comically. "Doesn't she want them?"

"She's just checking out her surroundings, that's all. Give her a minute and she'll be eating out of your hand, Ruby," said Myrtle.

Miles coughed.

"So to speak," said Myrtle.

Miles said, "Myrtle, are you sure Pasha will be all right in here while we visit with Natalie?" He shifted uncomfortably as he watched Pasha scale a bookcase in the corner and try to peer out the tiny window near Ruby's ceiling. "Do you think she's worried about being underground?"

"Pasha is a brilliant, *brilliant* cat. But no, Miles, I really don't think she's agonizing over being in the basement of Greener

Pastures. She's simply trying to do a reconnaissance mission here in Ruby's room—she's figuring it all out. Ruby, you'll be fine in here with Pasha for a few minutes, won't you?" asked Myrtle.

Ruby was watching Pasha with delight, laughing as Pasha's eyes grew huge as she watched some ground-level creature outside.

"Ruby?" asked Myrtle again.

Ruby startled and then nodded. "I'll be fine." She was gazing at Pasha in fascination.

Myrtle hesitated, and then walked to the door. Miles followed slowly and said to Myrtle when they were out in the hall, "Are you sure that was a good idea?"

"Well, I certainly wasn't going to make poor Pasha stay cooped up in a carrier for the whole time. That really *would* have agitated her. Ruby seems content with worshipping Pasha from afar, so it should be fine. Let's go talk to Natalie before she decides she's done packing for the day," said Myrtle.

Natalie had the door to Mickey's room propped open with a doorstop. Myrtle lightly tapped on it. "Can we come in?" she asked. She hoped her voice had an appropriately solemn and mournful tone to it.

Natalie had apparently been deep in thought (and deep in packing) and jumped violently. Her hair was even more messed up than usual and she was wearing a stained cotton tee shirt and shapeless cotton slacks. She peered at Myrtle and Miles through her thick glasses. "Oh. It's you. From the other day."

Myrtle and Miles weren't getting any excited invitations to enter the room, so Myrtle decided to enter anyway. "Is it all right if we speak with you for a few minutes?" asked Myrtle in a meek voice. "You see, Miles and I simply haven't been able to sleep— no, not a wink since your mother so tragically passed away. We decided that the only way we might be able to free ourselves from this insomnia is if we told you how very sorry we are about your mother's passing. And to see if there were anything we could do."

Natalie gave them both a puzzled look. Since Myrtle continued advancing on her, she finally realized that she should offer her older guests a place to sit down. Natalie sighed and shifted the piles on the sofa to the floor with Miles quickly jumping forward to help. With space cleared, they both sat down and Natalie sank back to the floor where she'd been sorting through clothes.

"That's nice of you...uh, I don't remember your names, sorry," mumbled Natalie.

They reintroduced themselves.

"Right." Myrtle got the impression that their names had once again flown directly out of Natalie's head. "As I was saying, that's nice of you to care so much. Except I'm a little surprised. Didn't you just meet my mother the other day? Why would her death bother you so much?"

"Because it was foul play," said Myrtle simply.

Now there was an expression on Natalie's face that bordered between tired and cynical. "I see. So to whom have you been speaking? Ruby? She's the one who's convinced that Mother was murdered. And Inez for some reason, too. If that's the case, then you can consider your insomnia cured. I can assure you that Mother's death was completely natural. She was just a casualty of old age, that's all. Ruby cared a lot about Mother and was horrified by her death. Not only that, but she believed every word that Mother uttered. Even the total nonsense."

Myrtle said carefully, "So you think that your mother's concerns about her personal safety weren't valid?"

"Not valid one whit. Mother was completely paranoid and also had an inflated sense of her own importance. She was convinced that everyone was out to get her. It had gotten out of control...believe me, *no one* was taking her seriously except Ruby," said Natalie. "Besides, if Mother were truly concerned for her own safety, it seems like she'd lock the door to her room every once in a while."

Miles cleared his throat. "When you say that Mickey thought everyone was out to get her...was there anyone in particular that she'd talk about?"

"Darla was a frequent target," said Natalie dryly. "I'm not sure what exactly Mother had against Darla."

"Darla is...one of the managers here?" Myrtle frowned.

"That's right. She's the General Manager of Greener Pastures. Mother acted as if she thought she were some kind of criminal. She kept saying that Greener Pastures was wasting money on things like paint and carpeting when they should have been focusing on a higher staff to resident ratio and better care," said Natalie.

"Which sounds completely reasonable to me," said Myrtle.

"Maybe that part sounds reasonable. But Mother made all kinds of wild allegations about Greener Pastures that were a lot more colorful. No wonder they kept confiscating her newspaper." Natalie rolled her eyes, remembering.

"By the way," said Myrtle in as casual a voice as she could muster, "do you have any of those newspapers? I was just curious about them. I work for the *Bradley Bugle*, and have a real interest in...journalism."

"I'm not sure you can call Mother's paper journalism by any stretch of the imagination, but sure." Natalie rummaged in a pile on the floor and pulled out a few papers. As Inez mentioned, it was really more of a news*letter* than a newspaper. Myrtle put the papers in her large pocketbook and snapped the top together.

"Who else was upset with your mother? That you can remember?" asked Myrtle.

"Plenty of people," said Natalie with a sigh. "I guess the ones who first come to mind are that Fred guy. He was annoying about his animosity and would stop in his tracks and give Mother an evil stare whenever we were walking down the hall and saw him. I even saw her having an argument with Winston recently. I figured if she could pick an argument with Winston, she could pick an argument with *anybody*. He's always struck me as a very easy-going, nice man."

"But you don't know *why* there was tension between your Mother and Fred or Winston?" pressed Miles.

Natalie gave him a surprised look. "No, that would require me to have listened to all the nonsense that Mother was spewing. I did my best to block it out, believe me. I don't know how Ruby stood it. She must be a saint. I'm giving Ruby a lot of the junk that's in here—Mother had so much stuff that I'm not interested in all of it. Ruby seemed to be. And since Ruby was so good to listen to Mother, she really deserves it."

Or perhaps Ruby simply didn't remember Mickey's "spewing" minutes after it had happened. Myrtle said, "This is a big job for you, Natalie. Did Greener Pastures give you a deadline for moving everything out?"

"No, they've actually been very easy to work with. I think they're not in any hurry because they're not immediately moving another resident in. They said they wanted to freshen up the carpet and curtains and so forth in here. Of course, if I had some *help*, it might move a lot faster," Natalie made a face.

Miles quickly stood up. "I should have offered to help you."

"That's nice of you. But no, I'm really talking about the help that I should be receiving from my brother Tradd. He's worthless. He never lifted a finger to help me over here and rarely even visited Mother. I'm sure he'll be around to find out what Mother left him in her will, though." She spat out the words. "Not that he deserves anything. I'm the one who did all the work so I should be the only one who receives anything."

The bitterness in her voice was hard to stomach. Myrtle felt as if she needed an antacid. She nodded at Natalie to validate what she was saying, and then said, "At least *you* know that you were with your mother right at the very end of her life. You must feel good about that. Why, I've even heard that you were here late the night your mother died."

Natalie froze, staring at Myrtle. "You heard wrong," she said in a tense voice. "I was here earlier in the day. But yes, it does feel good to know I was with Mother the day she passed away."

There was a tap at the door and Ruby's round face with its china doll features peered into the room. "Excuse me, sweetie," she said to Natalie.

Miles said sharply, "Ruby, where's Pasha?"

Ruby's chin trembled. "That's just it. I don't know where she is. The door was open only a smidgeon, but she somehow got out. I've been up and down the hall and can't find her. You don't think she could have gotten upstairs somehow?"

"No. Ridiculous," said Myrtle. But her heart thumped in her chest. Pasha, when she wanted to, was very good at hiding out.

Chapter Thirteen

"Let's go find her," said Miles grimly.

One thing Myrtle liked about Miles. He was never one to say 'I told you so'.

They stepped out into the hall and looked both ways. No Pasha.

"Everyone's door is closed," said Myrtle impatiently. "She's got to be either in Ruby's room or in the commons area or the hall kitchen. She's not in Mickey's room or else we'd have seen her and hers is the only other door besides Ruby's that's open."

Natalie said, "And I'm closing the door now. It's a cat that's loose? I don't need that kind of trouble right now. Plus, I'm allergic, to boot." And Natalie shut the door tightly behind them.

They hurried down to the commons area. Myrtle swished through the window curtains with her cane, Miles squatted down to look under the tables. Ruby peered into the tiny hall kitchen that was near the commons room. "Oh dear, oh dear," Ruby kept murmuring, wringing her hands.

There was no sign of Pasha. Miles even looked under the low sofa in the commons room, just to make sure.

"We're going to have to assume she somehow got upstairs," said Miles grimly. "She honestly could be anywhere if she's up there. This is a big place."

"But a wide-open place," said Myrtle. "It's not cluttered with a lot of furniture in the hallways. We should be able to spot her."

Miles's face was doubtful. "With all those commons areas? With all those curtains and sofas? What about the dining hall? Every table is covered with a tablecloth and each one could easily conceal a cat underneath. There must be...oh, fifty tables? Something like that?"

"Well, don't sound so down about it! We'll just be methodical," said Myrtle.

"I think we should admit our folly to the Greener Pastures staff and enlist their help in finding the cat." Miles's voice was resigned. "And then they'll put my name on some sort of blacklist and I will never be allowed admittance here."

A minor blessing during a difficult day, decided Myrtle. She said, "I disagree. We don't have to tell Greener Pastures anything. I don't want to have them decide to throw us out, right when we're making progress with our investigation."

"*Are* we making progress with our investigation?" Miles made a face.

"We certainly are. And we don't need to jeopardize that. If the staff asks you what you're doing, just tell them you're doing an especially thorough job of touring the facility," said Myrtle. "They'll think you're just a very savvy senior."

"They'll think I'm a very senile senior," said Miles glumly, "if they spot me halfway underneath a table in the dining hall."

Myrtle ignored him. It was always irritating when Miles was in a dispirited mood. It was best to just overlook his deflated statements. "Let's split up, then. Miles, you're better at looking underneath things than I am. Why don't you take the dining hall? I'll look through the commons areas upstairs—more than once, just in case Pasha is playing hide and seek with us. And Ruby?"

Ruby, who had been sitting on the commons area sofa while they formed a plan, had fallen into a deep sleep.

"Let's just leave Ruby out of it," said Myrtle to Miles. "She's likely to forget what she's looking for halfway through the process, anyway."

Five minutes later, Myrtle was calling, "Kitty, kitty, kitty?" softly in an empty commons area upstairs when almost on cue,

Darla entered the area. Darla's features were grim. "Mrs. Clover? Could you have a word with me in my office, please?"

Myrtle gave a resigned sigh as she followed Darla into her tiny office. Called in to see the principal, was she? She'd been a teacher long enough to know how to get out of any kind of trouble with administrators—deny all. There never was any proof of wrongdoing, anyway.

Darla settled her stocky frame into a squeakily protesting desk chair and stared impassively at Myrtle. Myrtle silently returned her stare, nose in the air.

Since quite some time went by with no comment from Darla, Myrtle finally impatiently broke the silence. "Look, I don't have time for this. Out with it. What are my alleged misdeeds?"

"You know, Mrs. Clover. You've created nothing but problems for Greener Pastures since spending so much of your time here." Darla's eyes were really quite soulless, decided Myrtle.

"I have no idea what you're referring to. I've simply been responsible about visiting a dear friend of mine who's imprisoned at your facility. But I'm very glad you've arranged a meeting with me here today," said Myrtle, blithely overlooking the origins of her being dragged into the cluttered broom closet of an office. "I was planning on scheduling time to speak with you if you hadn't. Some of Greener Pastures' actions have been rather suspect lately."

Darla's thin eyebrows shot up. "You're trying to turn the tables and complain about *us?*" Her plain face was incredulous.

"Absolutely," said Myrtle smoothly. "After all, I want what's best for my friend. I have a sneaking suspicion that the newspaper that Mickey Pelias published was full of inflammatory information about Greener Pastures. Maybe someone is cooking the books here—perhaps cutting corners and then pocketing the difference."

Darla's face became quite red and splotchy and she began stuttering incoherently. Myrtle wondered idly if she were working up to some sort of cardiac event.

"I've noticed, you see, all the fresh paint and new carpeting. And you see, those are cheap ways to make a retirement home seem as if quality is important to the staff. But the proof is in the *care*. What's the staff to resident ratio? What's the quality of the care being offered? I believe that Mickey raised some of those concerns and perhaps others. Greener Pastures determined to find and destroy those newspapers. And now Mickey Pelias is conveniently very dead," said Myrtle, folding her hands in her lap.

Darla's eyes, if possible, got even colder. "Greener Pastures has recently been recognized for its devotion to high-quality care for its residents."

Myrtle smiled sweetly at her. "Recognized by whom? By Greener Pastures?"

Darla's hand trembled slightly as she raised it to gesture wildly in the air. "Greener Pastures and its care are not in question here today! What's in question is your behavior."

"I was under the impression that my behavior wasn't Greener Pastures' concern at all," said Myrtle coolly.

"It is when it interferes with the residents' health and wellness," said Darla, voice shaking in anger. "And when you've brought a cat in the facility—when residents might be allergic to the animal and when we're not even sure it's up on its shots?"

Myrtle had opened her mouth to argue hotly that she was very responsible when it came to Pasha's shots...before realizing that would constitute an admission on her behalf. Instead she said firmly, "You're trying to change the subject. Not only that, but you're throwing out wild allegations that have no basis in fact. I don't have a cat and I certainly didn't bring a cat to Greener Pastures today."

"Is that so?" sneered Darla.

"That is so."

"Then why did I hear you trilling 'kitty, kitty, kitty?'" asked Darla.

Myrtle gave a short laugh. "I won't hold your immaturity against you, Darla. If you don't recognize the most famous song from the 1930s, then I will try to overlook that fact."

Now Darla was looking a bit taken aback. You could see the wheels turning in her head thinking— *is this woman simply tunelessly singing an old song*?

But Darla was again on the attack. "And now we're having to change our popular countdown-to-noon party tomorrow for a countdown-to-midnight. I believe you were behind that."

"I don't know what you're talking about. Complete foolishness," said Myrtle sternly.

Darla was now looking confused. You could see in her eyes that she was trying to sum Myrtle up. Was Myrtle telling the truth? Or was she simply a consummate liar? While Darla was off-balance, Myrtle decided it was the perfect time to get a little more information. "While I'm here, is there an update on the police investigation of Mickey Pelias's death?"

Darla's eyes took on a steely look. "Did you have anything to do with that? With the police coming here and asking questions and interfering with a natural death?"

"Of course I didn't," said Myrtle, crossing her fingers where Darla couldn't see them. She'd already told enough fibs during the course of the last few minutes that she was beginning to fear that a lightning bolt would come out of the sky and strike her down. "Although you know that I don't believe it to be a natural death. And the police seem to agree with me, if they're launching an investigation. I believe the police simply feel a strong obligation to investigate any unusual death, *regardless* of age."

"There's nothing unusual about dying in your sleep," said Darla stubbornly. She continued staring at Myrtle, which was making Myrtle feel a bit uncomfortable. Myrtle resisted the urge to squirm in her seat, instead returning Darla's stare with some stubbornness of her own. Darla's head turned momentarily as they heard what sounded like someone running down one of the nearby halls. Darla frowned.

Myrtle said quickly, as a distraction, "So the police haven't updated you?"

Darla didn't appear to have heard the question. "You're *sure* you didn't bring an animal into our facility?"

"Certainly not," said Myrtle coldly.

But of course, at that moment, the sound of running feet grew louder, accompanied by out of breath panting, and Pasha bounded through the door, jumped onto Myrtle's lap, hissed furiously at a terrified-looking Darla, and then bolted back out again.

Miles burst into the tiny office as Pasha shot out. He stood, frozen, staring at Darla. "Hello," he said finally. Then, "Better go." And he was off again, after giving Myrtle a desperate look.

Darla's face was now brimming over with hostility. "Well, what do you know?" said Myrtle lamely, "It appears a cat somehow *is* on the loose. What an amazing coincidence. And how very helpful of Miles to try to contain it."

Darla's eyes narrowed. "And you have nothing to do with that—creature?"

"Of course not. How on earth could you suspect me of something like that?" asked Myrtle weakly. "But I do care a lot about animals, so I'll just pop out there and give Miles a hand. He could probably use the help."

Myrtle was standing up and trying to get out of the tiny office as quickly as humanly possible when there was suddenly a gasping, teary Ruby in there with them. "Miss Ruby!" said Darla, standing up as well. "Whatever is the matter?"

Ruby's eyes were huge and swimming with tears as she looked back and forth from the stolid Darla to the still-anxious-to-escape Myrtle. "He got me. He got me!"

"Who got you, Ruby?" asked Myrtle intently.

"*He* did! The killer. The one that got Mickey," gasped Ruby. She pulled aside the collar to her shirtdress and revealed her neck, which was quickly developing a reddish bruise.

Darla exclaimed, hurrying over and examining Ruby's neck gingerly before grimly reaching for her desk phone. "I'll call for the nurse."

"Did you see him?" asked Myrtle urgently.

Ruby shook her head, still gasping for breath and keeping a hand hovering over her neck as if she might need to protect it at a moment's notice.

Darla was talking on the phone and Myrtle quickly said in a low voice, "So you were looking for Pasha, right? Downstairs in the commons area."

"I was asleep," said Ruby in her guilty-child-manner. "But then I woke up and remembered to look for the cat. I was in the little kitchen and calling for the cat when someone came up behind me and put this cloth around my neck and pulled. And pulled!" Her voice was gruffly hurt.

"Could you tell if it was a man or woman?" asked Myrtle. "Or someone old or young?"

More headshaking. "But the person said something to me," said Ruby, eyes opening wide as if she were just remembering. "Although I couldn't tell from their voice if it were a man or a woman. You know how it is when someone is whispering? And it's sort of hard to tell?"

Myrtle nodded impatiently. Darla sounded as if she was wrapping up her phone conversation and Myrtle was worried that Ruby was going to be whisked away. "Yes, yes, I know. But what did they *say?*"

Ruby sputtered for a second, thinking.

"Surely you remember?" coaxed Myrtle. "Ruby, it was only a minute ago! What did they say?"

Ruby's eyes widened again in triumph as her memory finally delivered. "*Let Mickey rest in peace.* That's what they said. *Let Mickey rest in peace.*"

Darla dropped the phone back on the receiver with a clang. "She's on her way," said Darla grimly. "Sit down here, Miss Ruby. And tell me—what's this you're saying about an attack?" Her eyes were dubious.

Myrtle couldn't seem to stop herself from commenting, "You're doubting her? Even presented with the evidence in front of you?" She gave Darla a scornful look, and then turned to Ruby. "I'm going to go check on Miles."

"And the cat?" asked Ruby hopefully.

"Er...yes. That's right. You should be in good hands here with the nurse coming." And with another disdainful look at Darla, Myrtle swept from the office. As well as someone with a cane can sweep, anyway.

From the amount of panting and general breathlessness coming from the direction of the dining room, Myrtle assumed that Miles must be somewhere nearby.

"Kitty, kitty, kitty!" panted the voice desperately.

Myrtle rounded the corner and spotted a very disheveled looking Miles. His hair was askew, his glasses were askew, and Myrtle was certain the rest of him was likely askew as well. "Any luck?" hissed Myrtle. "Because they're onto us."

Miles gave Myrtle a baleful look. "There's really no *us* here. I was an unwilling accomplice. I'm going to assert that to my dying days."

"See, this place isn't good for you, Miles. You have dying on the brain. And let me assure you that you should have absolutely no interest in residing in this combat zone."

"Combat zone?" Miles rolled his eyes. "You really have no idea, Myrtle."

"No, *you* really have no idea. Because while we've been searching for Pasha and getting the third degree from the gulag, Ruby Sims was attacked downstairs."

"What?" Miles's eyes were huge behind his rimless glasses.

"That's right. She was warned off and nearly strangled by some thug," said Myrtle.

Miles frowned. "But she got away."

"No thanks to us. To think there was a killer running around downstairs and we had the chance to have caught him in the act!"

"Right, yes. But I saying—she got away. Doesn't that seem odd to you?" asked Miles. "Why would the killer have let Ruby go?"

Myrtle sighed. "Well, with all the hubbub, I didn't have a chance to ask her many questions. We'll ask again later. Maybe she fought back. Maybe the killer heard a noise. Maybe Pasha leaped out at him and scared him to death. I'm simply thankful she was able to get away from the fellow. Besides, this falls into the same category as the ominous phone call that Ruby received. A warning. Apparently the killer is fonder of Ruby than he was of Mickey."

"Who wouldn't be?" muttered Miles. Then he seemed to steel himself. "All right. Onto the next challenge...Pasha. Although I'm not holding out much hope. That cat is determined to bolt as soon as I catch sight of her."

A blur of black caught Myrtle's attention. "Pasha?" she asked eagerly. And soon the black cat bounded up to her, rubbing lovingly against Myrtle's legs. She crooned to the cat and Miles awarded her a look of extreme exasperation.

"Now what?" he asked. "Pasha's carrier is downstairs, isn't it?"

Myrtle glanced around them. "I'll just borrow one of these tablecloths. I'll wrap her up securely and carry her downstairs to reunite her with her carrier."

Miles said, "How many arms do you think you have, Myrtle? There's no way you can hold a cane and hold a feral cat at the same time."

It always irritated Myrtle to be reminded of her infirmity, no matter how minor she considered it to be. "Well then, *you* carry my cane and hold out your arm and I'll lean on it while I carry her. *You* certainly can't carry Pasha...she won't stand for it."

She sat down in one of the dining hall chairs, removed the tablecloth after putting the salt and pepper shakers and vase of flowers on another chair, and reached over to carefully wrap a compliant Pasha in the cloth. Myrtle cautiously stood, clutching Pasha like a baby in the voluminous fabric.

Chapter Fourteen

"There," she said with satisfaction. "Now let's get downstairs before she starts getting too heavy."

They started off in the direction of the elevators, but heard a lot of staff talking near Darla's office. Myrtle grimaced. "We shouldn't go that way. All those staffers will be congregating around Ruby and we don't need them to see how friendly we are with Pasha or they might think she's our pet."

Pasha emitted an unhappy growl at the noise down the hall. Miles gave Pasha an uneasy look. "I don't think anyone would make the mistake of assuming that Pasha was *anyone's* pet. She doesn't seem particularly tame right now."

They walked down a parallel hall toward the elevator, Myrtle stopping to shift Pasha into a more comfortable position a couple of times. But before they could reach the elevator and as they walked near the front entrance of the Home, a tall, thin young man barreled toward them. He wore a police uniform and gave Myrtle and Miles a puzzled look as he hurried in their direction.

"He thinks we're carrying a baby," muttered Miles. "We must look like parents who *really* put off having offspring."

Myrtle cleared her throat. "Darrell?" she asked. "Darrell Smith?"

The young man stopped short and for a second Myrtle thought he was going to salute her. She said briskly, "I'm Myrtle Clover, Red's mother. You're his fill-in deputy, Darrell, aren't you?"

Darrell's face broke out into a large smile and he said in a deferential voice, "Yes ma'am, I sure am. It's good to meet you, Mrs. Clover. I've heard a lot about you from Red."

"I'm sure you have," murmured Miles.

Myrtle shot him a look. "And this is my friend, Miles."

Darrell looked uncertainly at the bundle in Myrtle's arms. "And that is...?"

Pasha, who was not a fan of unfamiliar voices or smells, emitted an ominous growl. Darrell, startled, opened his eyes wide.

"Myrtle's granddaughter," said Miles quickly, still clearly worried about his chances for future admission to the Greener Pastures retirement community.

Myrtle pulled Pasha closer to her so that Darrell couldn't see the cat. "She's shy," added Myrtle. She shot Miles a look. Now he'd put them in a pickle. She changed the subject, shifting Pasha's weight a bit. "I'm glad to see you, Darrell," Myrtle lied. "I was hoping you could tell me what the state police found to be the cause of death for Mickey Pelias."

Darrell looked toward the office area. "Well, I can give you a real quick update, Mrs. Clover. Then I've got to interview an assault victim."

Myrtle nodded. "Ruby Sims. Yes. And pay close attention when you speak to her. She may seem addled, but she seems to know a lot. Now, about Mickey Pelias?"

"Forensics found that Mrs. Pelias was suffocated," said Darrell in his slow, musical drawl. "So I'll be helping them investigate." He stopped and shook his head sorrowfully. "Can you imagine? What's the point of violence in a place like this?"

"Oh, I don't know, there's a lot about Greener Pastures that brings out the violence in me," said Myrtle dryly. Her bundle gave another low growl and Myrtle rubbed her back. "I should get my granddaughter out of here now—it's time for her nap."

"Right," said Darrell, still giving the bundle a puzzled look. "Maybe she's hungry, too. Is that her...stomach growling?"

"The child has a voracious appetite."

Darrell still seemed uncertain, but apparently decided to let it drop. "Okay. Tell Red I hope he's better soon. And that I have a whole new level of respect for what he does on a daily basis."

Myrtle watched him hurry off, and then called after him, "You know, Darrell, I think I might join you as you interview Ruby. To give her moral support, you know."

Miles looked alarmed. "What about ...?"

"Here. You can watch Baby for a while, Miles. Make sure she has a good nap." And she firmly deposited the growling bundle in Miles's arms and quickly followed Darrell back to Darla's office.

Darla was none too pleased to see her. "I thought you were on your way out of our facility, Mrs. Clover," she said smoothly.

"Oh, sweetie!" said Ruby, beaming at her. "Thank you for coming!"

"I simply thought I'd be a good friend to Ruby and hold her hand through this upsetting process," said Myrtle. And, of course, to get information on this attack before Ruby forgot it, herself. Because Greener Pastures certainly wasn't going to be helpful in that respect.

Darla pursed her lips in displeasure. She appeared to be about to firmly evict Myrtle when Darrell said in his placid drawl, "That's very nice of you, Mrs. Clover. Anything that helps Mrs. Sims relax and give a thoughtful statement would be helpful."

Darla nodded but her eyes were steely.

Darrell said kindly to Ruby, "So, Miss Ruby, take your time and tell me what happened to you."

Ruby drew in a deep, shaky breath and trained her eyes on the ceiling of Darla's office as if her story were written up there among the peeling paint. "I was downstairs in the commons area. I'd just woken up from a very short nap. When I woke up I started looking for ..." She hesitated and looked down at Myrtle "... for my reading glasses." Ruby gave Myrtle a wink. "But I couldn't find them in the commons area. So I walked into the kitchenette to look for them in there."

"Your reading glasses," said Darla in a disbelieving voice. "The ones that are hanging on a lanyard around your neck?"

Ruby's hands jumped up to her chest and fingered the purple reading glasses, which were indeed hanging around her neck. She beamed at Darla. "How clever of you!"

Darla rolled her eyes and Darrell gave Darla a reproachful look. "I'm *very* interested in hearing what Mrs. Sims has to say." He paused. "If you don't mind, Ms. Benton, I'd really appreciate a glass of ice water. It's been a busy day so far and I'm parched."

Darla raised an eyebrow. "Does one get parched in December?"

Myrtle gave her an annoyed look. "One can get parched at any point one is low on fluids."

Darla flounced out and Darrell seized the opportunity to gently question Ruby, taking notes the entire time. His expression and constant nodding gave the impression that he was completely fascinated by her story and that Ruby Sims was the only person in the entire universe right at that moment of time. Myrtle eyed him closely. He wasn't nearly as slow as she thought he was supposed to be. He was actually very sharp, although his cleverness was hidden behind the good old boy exterior and the heavy drawl.

Ruby sounded even more addled than usual, but Darrell seemed to take her entire account as gospel, questioning her deferentially as she told her tale.

"And then," said Ruby, eyes opened wide as she reached the climax of the story, "a cloth slipped around my neck and a gruff voice told me to *back off*! Or I'd never see tomorrow. And the cloth squeezed and *squeezed* on my neck until I thought my eyes would pop out of my head! I really did."

Darrell continued his sympathetic nodding. "And you're positive it was a piece of cloth around your neck."

Ruby looked hopelessly lost and confused and Myrtle shifted impatiently in her seat. Ruby looked at Myrtle for clarification.

Myrtle carefully kept her annoyance out of her voice and explained, "You felt a terrible pressure around your neck—but do you know for a fact it was a bit of cloth? Not someone's hands?"

Ruby blinked with confusion. "That's right. Cloth. At least—I think so."

"And what do you think the person meant by *back off*?" Darrell asked gently. "Have you had an argument with anyone recently? Any problems with any of the other residents?"

Ruby said, "Oh, no. No, I really like the people here. A lot. They're very nice. Most of them anyway."

"So why would someone want to hurt you?" asked Darrell in a soft voice.

Ruby looked to Myrtle for help again.

"Perhaps," said Myrtle with a small cough, "it's because of what you said about Mickey?"

"Oh! Yes." Pleased to have remembered, she turned back to Darrell, her words falling all over themselves as she said, "When Mickey died, I was the one who said it wasn't an accident. Because it wasn't. And I told ... her ... about it." Here Ruby gestured to Myrtle, having clearly forgotten her name again.

"You were the one who got the police investigating her death?" asked Darrell, still nodding as he jotted down his notes.

"Well, I didn't tell the police. But I told Greener Pastures! They didn't believe me, though." Ruby deflated in her seat a bit at this memory. "But then I told...sweetie here...and she told the police. And here we are."

Darrell said, "You didn't get any ideas about who your attacker was? How tall they were? If they were male or female? And how did you finally get away?"

Ruby shook her head sadly. "I was so surprised. They didn't want to be seen, either. It could have been anybody. The only reason I got away is because he pushed me down to the floor and ran off."

Myrtle said to Darrell, "So it was only meant to warn her off. I guess her attacker didn't realize the police were already looking into Mickey Pelias's death. He must have believed that she hadn't yet persuaded them that there was foul play."

Darla came back in at this point with a glass of ice water for Darrell. He thanked her and took the glass of water, taking a large sip before setting it down on the desk in front of him. He softly closed his notebook and smiled at Ruby. "You were very helpful. Thank you. I should be heading out now. I've got more calls to make." He snapped his fingers. "Although first I need to talk to Natalie Pelias. My understanding is that she's here today."

Darla confirmed this with a quick nod and a curious expression.

"The autopsy did show that her mother was smothered," explained Darrell.

A look of anger flashed on Darla's face and the look she shot Myrtle was accusatory.

Myrtle gave Darla a haughty look in return and then said to Darrell, "You've had more calls today?" asked Myrtle, arching her eyebrows. "That's a little unusual, isn't it?"

"Yes ma'am, more calls would definitely be unusual. These are other chores I need to take care of. Mrs. Ellenbee told me that she needed help untangling her garden hose, for one."

Myrtle frowned. "What in the name of all that's good does Mrs. Ellenbee need her hose for? The last I saw, the forecast was for cold, wet weather. Does she think she needs to water her grass?"

"I didn't trouble her to ask," admitted Darrell. "She sounded real concerned about it, so I thought I'd relieve her mind real quick and just pop by there and take care of it. And while I'm on her street, I always bring Mrs. Patterson's newspaper and mail to her front porch. It's a challenge for her to get to the end of her driveway sometimes, the poor lady."

Myrtle's opinion was that Mrs. Patterson was as fit as a fiddle. She didn't even have a cane, for heaven's sake. Myrtle herself was in poorer condition than Alma Patterson. And Alma was probably twelve years younger than she. Red was going to have a conniption fit when he heard the news that Darrell was making these old ladies dependent on him. And Myrtle strongly suspected that they were making up problems so they could receive visits from the young policeman.

It was a fairly quiet ride back to Myrtle's house, other than the low growling coming from Pasha's carrier. Miles appeared rather put out for some reason. Myrtle finally broke the silence to say, "I can't imagine what's bothering you, Miles. It's not like Pasha did anything really dreadful. She was just out of her usual environment and freaked out a little. Greener Pastures makes *me* want to freak out, too."

Miles looked at her coldly before turning back to concentrate on the road. "I didn't want you to bring her in the first place."

"But Ruby was so excited," said Myrtle weakly.

"And then Ruby nearly gets herself killed while she's looking for the missing Pasha," said Miles sternly.

Myrtle was quiet for a few moments, accepting the truth of this. "At least we found out some information."

"Did we?" asked Miles. "My recollection of my time at Greener Pastures was that I spent the bulk of it searching for a missing feral cat while pretending that I wasn't searching for a cat at all but taking myself on an extraordinarily detailed tour of the facility as I peered under tables."

"Of course we learned information. We found Mickey's underground newsletters and were able to question the Home about them. Darla was very defensive about Greener Pastures' treatment of its residents...suspiciously so. Natalie reinforced the fact that we're on track with the suspect list we've put together—and she mentioned that her mother had a bad habit of not locking her door. Ruby's attack demonstrated that she did in fact have credible information about the night that Mickey died. And Darrell Smith confirmed that Mickey was indeed murdered." Myrtle shrugged. "I think that's a fairly successful outing."

"Dare I ask what our plans are for tomorrow?" asked Miles. "Are we planning another insurgence at Greener Pastures? Perhaps this time involving more advanced weaponry?"

Myrtle narrowed her eyes at him. "Your tone really doesn't suit you, Miles. And no—we have other plans at Greener Pastures, remember?"

Miles frowned.

"It's New Year's Eve. So we're attending the party over there. You have to be my date since I told Winston you were," said Myrtle.

"Oh, that's right." Miles's voice was relieved that only a party factored into their plans. "So we'll head over there before noon then."

"Actually," said Myrtle with a small cough, "I was able to have the schedule for the event changed. Now it's a countdown to midnight instead of a countdown to noon. Since countdowns to noon are for children." It still miffed her to think of it.

But the news didn't appear to make Miles happy. "So we'll have to be heading home from Greener Pastures after midnight? With a bunch of intoxicated drivers on the road? In the dark?"

"I've seen you drive in the dark a million times," said Myrtle in a bored voice. "It gets dark here at five o'clock in the winter— you're certainly driving after five in the dark."

"Not in an ice storm," said Miles.

"Who said anything about an ice storm?"

"Channel Nine," said Miles.

"Channel Nine must hold stock in area grocery stores," said Myrtle with a sniff. "They always say it's going to snow or sleet or ice over and then everyone hysterically dashes out to the grocery store for bread and milk. These storms never come to pass. I do believe Channel Nine is lining its pockets with ill-gotten gain."

"But what if they're right this time? What if it ices over?" asked Miles.

"Then we'll sleep on Ruby's floor. Maybe we should do that anyway, considering that she appears to be in mortal danger. But I bet we'll be fine," said Myrtle. Miles pulled onto Magnolia Lane. "See you tomorrow night at ten-thirtyish?"

Miles muttered something under his breath. Myrtle decided to take it as a delighted affirmation of their plans.

Chapter Fifteen

Even Myrtle had to admit that the New Year's Eve party was nicely staged. There were glittery stars hanging from the ceiling of a large activity room and there was a table of noisemakers and party hats. Another table held champagne cocktails for the countdown and there was a table with a variety of different foods, including black-eyed pea salsa (black-eyed peas being vitally important in the South for good luck in the New Year), mini quiches, cheese in crescent rolls, and artichoke dip.

Myrtle and Miles both paid a Greener Pastures attendant for admission and Miles appeared to be determined to get his money's worth as he loaded a plate full of food. The lights were slightly dimmed to provide atmosphere, but not enough to create hazards for the guests. A large screen television was playing a countdown program. And the staff had music playing—it sounded like a selection of hits from the forties, fifties, and sixties. Everyone seemed to be having a good time and there was a lot of loud laughter.

There was a tap at Myrtle's shoulder, and she turned to see Inez Wilson giving her an insincere smile. "Good to see you here, dear. And who are you wearing tonight? I'm doing a story for the paper."

Myrtle felt as though Inez was trying to rub it in her face that she was a reporter, too. It was very annoying to have Myrtle's position at a town newspaper compared to Inez's retirement home newsletter. Knowing she needed to have Inez cooperative, though, she forced a smile. "Whatever do you mean, Inez?" she asked. "Do you mean *what* am I wearing? In that case, I'm wearing a black button-down shirt dress with a belt and a festive red scarf." It seemed festive to her, anyway. Miles kept asking her on the car ride over if she were cold, so maybe he thought it was purely functional.

"No, I mean *who* are you wearing?" asked Inez with something of a superior look. "The designer."

Myrtle frowned at her. Did people wear designers at Greener Pastures? This was yet another sign that she didn't belong here. "I believe the designer is Mr. Wal-Mart, Inez. Maybe I shouldn't be included in your piece."

Inez smirked. "Not at all, Myrtle. I also wanted to profile visitors to Greener Pastures. Here, let me take your picture."

Myrtle bared her teeth for the cell phone camera that Inez whipped out of her stylish purse.

"There!" said Inez in a pleased voice. "That wasn't so bad, was it?"

It was. But Myrtle wouldn't give her the satisfaction of saying so. She decided that she really didn't like Inez much. Her eyes combed the room, wanting to change the subject. "Have you seen Ruby tonight, Inez?" She was starting to feel as if Ruby might require a bodyguard.

Inez's voice was bored. "No, and I don't care if I do. I'm convinced that Ruby is a thief."

Myrtle knit her brows, remembering the stolen items from her pocketbook. And the one return. "Why do you say that?"

"I went on the Greener Pastures van to the grocery store and took the trouble of getting myself a bag of veggie chips. They're my *favorite* type of chip and they're not even that bad for you. Helps me keep my figure." Inez gestured with some pride to her thin physique clothed in a glittery black evening dress that nearly reached the floor. Myrtle decided that Inez was decidedly overdressed for the occasion.

"I put the chips in the cabinet in our hall's kitchenette. The very next day I went into the kitchen to make some lunch and my chips were gone." Inez's eyes were wide and her mouth trembled for a second. Myrtle was becoming very concerned that Inez might cry over the loss of the chips.

"What makes you think it was Ruby?" asked Myrtle briskly. "There are plenty of other people who live on your hall. Or Natalie Pelias could even have taken them if she needed a snack while she was clearing out her mother's room. *Anybody* could have taken them."

Inez stared at her with dislike. "Anybody *could* have taken them. But Ruby actually saw me put the chips in the kitchen when I returned from the store. And then she had crumbs on her top when I saw her at lunch. Orange and green crumbs. The kind of crumbs that veggie chips might make."

"She might have been eating anything," said Myrtle with a shrug. "She might have had crumbs from something she ate in the dining room. Who knows? You can always replace chips. You don't have enough evidence to blame Ruby for the missing chips."

"I should make her replace them," brooded Inez.

"I don't think Ruby is exactly loaded with extra cash," said Myrtle, shooting Inez an exasperated look. "Especially not for buying expensive chips that she probably didn't even steal from you."

Inez leaned in closely and Myrtle fought the urge to step back away. "I've heard just the opposite. I've heard that Ruby is loaded."

"Loaded?" Myrtle shook her head disbelievingly.

"Well, she's *about* to be loaded. I hear that Mickey left most of her money to Ruby," said Inez.

"To Ruby?" Myrtle realized she was starting to sound like a Greek chorus.

"That's right. Oh, she didn't *totally* cut Natalie out, but she didn't give her nearly what she probably thought she'd be getting. Of course, my understanding was that Winston was supposed to get some money, too," said Inez in a knowing voice.

Myrtle somehow stopped herself from repeating '*Winston?*' but instead just gave Inez an inquiring look.

"Winston was Mickey's boyfriend for a while here. A good, long while." Myrtle was intrigued by the jealous flash in Inez's eyes. The woman did seem to hold a torch for Winston.

Myrtle made a face. She hated the word *boyfriend* when it was applied to anyone older than a teenager. Still, there didn't seem to be a good alternative to the word. Companion and partner both left something to be desired she thought.

"How long were they together?" asked Myrtle.

"For several months," said Inez.

"Several months is a long time?"

"Here it is," said Inez in irritation. "Greener Pastures is sort of like junior high. Three months is a long time to be together. Anyway, she was supposed to be leaving Winston something in her will. She'd been bragging about how she was going to "take care" of Winston. It must have made her feel powerful or something. But then they had a falling out of some kind."

Now Myrtle was paying more attention. "What kind of a falling out?"

Inez pursed her lips. "Well, I'm not one to snoop. Or to gossip. And I don't actually know what the problem was—except that Winston was desperately trying to make up with Mickey. All I know is that I heard Mickey yelling after Winston when he was leaving her room. She was screaming that she was going to have her lawyer come out and she'd change her will."

Myrtle raised her eyebrows. Surely, this would be motivation for murder. Wouldn't Winston want to get rid of Mickey before she changed her will? She'd have to see what she could find out from Darrell or maybe even Red. "When did this happen? Was it a while back?"

"Heavens, no. It all happened in the last couple of weeks."

Myrtle asked thoughtfully, "Did Mickey's daughter, Natalie, know that her mother had changed her will in favor all of these other people?"

"I doubt it. Because then Natalie wouldn't have been as motivated to wait on her mother hand and foot. And Mickey wouldn't have had anyone to boss around. No, I'm pretty sure that Mickey would have kept that information from Natalie. I don't even think that Ruby knew that Mickey was planning on leaving her money. And Winston wouldn't have told Natalie about his potential windfall because then Natalie would have tried to talk her mother out of it," said Inez. Then she made a face. "I should go take some more pictures." She hurried away.

Myrtle turned to see Winston wink at her. She froze.

Someone stopped Winston to talk for a minute, but he was definitely heading her way. She looked around desperately for Miles. Shouldn't he be dancing with her and saving her from Winston? Myrtle spotted him going back for seconds at the food table and hurried over there.

"Miles," she hissed. "You're not being nearly attentive enough. Winston looks like he's on a mission to dance with me."

Miles stared sadly at his plate. "I was going to just have a little more to eat, that's all."

"Plenty of time to eat later. Just put that plate down somewhere."

"Someone might take it!" said Miles in an affronted voice.

"Greener Pastures certainly won't be *that* much on top of cleaning up. They probably won't clean until after the party. Hurry up!"

Miles put his plate down on a table, Myrtle propped her cane against the wall, and Miles and Myrtle started dancing.

"You're not a bad dancer," said Miles in surprise.

"Of course not. Neither are you," said Myrtle graciously. Although she felt her toes might have had a near miss a moment or two ago. "The music helps. They *have* done a good job picking tunes."

Miles had a thoughtful look on his face. "I remember this one," he said.

"I should hope so."

"I was in elementary school at the time," said Miles in a reminiscent type of voice.

Myrtle gave him a withering look and then froze. "He's coming over!" she said in alarm, watching Winston's progress. "He's going to break in."

"Well, I can hardly refuse to relinquish you," said Miles dryly. "I doubt I can fake that type of fervent jealousy. And I *do* want to hear the story about the two of you. There must be quite a tale."

Winston, dressed in a dark suit with a red and green striped tie, sidled up to them and made a bow to Myrtle. "May I have the extraordinary honor of dancing with you, Myrtle?"

Myrtle couldn't seem to help the sour expression she felt forming on her face.

Winston carefully overlooked any signs of displeasure and turned to Miles to implore, "Do you mind? It's just a dance."

Miles's eyes twinkled at her. "I don't mind at all. But Winston, if you could steer her toward her cane at the end of the dance. It's propped against the wall there."

Winston pulled her in a bit too close and she shoved him until they were dancing at nearly an arms' length. "Just like the old days, isn't it, Myrtle?"

"Except for the presence of a cane," noted Myrtle. And the fact that although she'd once cared far too much for Winston, she only wanted to avoid him now.

"Say, though, it was grand of you to come to our New Year's Eve shindig tonight. And for arranging the countdown to midnight...I understand that was your doing."

"A countdown to noon was absurd," said Myrtle simply with a shrug.

"I think that you've become a woman who knows how to get things done," said Winston thoughtfully. "And knows how to get her own way."

"From what I hear, you're able to get your own way, too," said Myrtle. "I hear that you had Mickey Pelias so infatuated with you that she was planning on leaving you money in her will."

"Planning?" asked Winston quickly. "She *did* leave me money. It was a friendly gesture, that's all, Myrtle. Mickey had plenty to give away and the thought of giving money to help out a friend pleased her. Besides, she probably thought that I would predecease her, right? Men always croak before women do."

Myrtle disapproved of the word *croak*. "So to you, it was merely a gesture. Not something that you expected to receive."

"Of course," said Winston smoothly as he spun Myrtle around.

Myrtle wasn't expecting to be spun and she took an extra few steps to stabilize herself. The fact Winston kept knocking her off-balance both literally and figuratively was annoying. It made her more determined than ever to press him for information. "But you had a falling out with Mickey, I understand. A falling-out that made you very anxious because Mickey threatened to bring her lawyer in and change her will.

"Minor posturing from Mickey," said Winston. His tone was one of fond reminiscence. "She didn't mean a word of it."

"At the ice cream social, you told me that you didn't have any problems with Mickey," said Myrtle.

"Did I?" Winston pulled Myrtle a little closer.

Miles's eyes were full of merriment as Winston steered Myrtle past him.

"You certainly did. While we were eating ice cream," reminded Myrtle crisply.

"Well, that might have been because I hated to speak ill of the dead and bring up any past disagreements. I'd been very sad that entire day about poor Mickey. And being sad affects my brain chemistry. It's science, you know," he said.

Myrtle raised an eyebrow. "That's very interesting. Particularly since you told me that you hadn't heard anything about Mickey's death. You led me to believe that I was the one who informed you about it."

Winston colored a bit. Myrtle couldn't tell if he was coloring from the exertion of the dance or from embarrassment at having been caught in a fib. Because, clearly, it was a fib. Why would he lie about not having heard about Mickey's death? Or about having an argument with her?

"Well then, it must not have been grief that eroded my memory at the ice cream social. It must have been the fact that I really didn't think our disagreement was any big thing. Mickey could be a diva, you know. She was simply being melodramatic that day. I was giving her some space to have a cool-down period. Mickey was bound to be over any minor irritation in a few days," said Winston.

"Do you know what kind of a windfall you're in for?" asked Myrtle. She was feeling quite sour now. It might have been all the spinning around. She believed that Winston was trying to show off how nimble he was.

"I haven't the foggiest," said Winston. But he didn't look at her. "The lawyer hasn't contacted the beneficiaries yet. I suppose these things take time."

"Especially when there's a murder investigation going on," said Myrtle. "Wouldn't want anyone to benefit from a crime, you know."

"Now you really *are* sounding like a private eye," said Winston. "Does Greener Pastures have you working for them as an undercover agent?"

The idea of working for Greener Pastures in any capacity was bile inducing. "Certainly not," said Myrtle briskly. "And I believe you're trying to change the subject."

"What was the subject again? Can't concentrate on conversation when I'm dancing with such a beautiful gal," said Winston gaily.

Myrtle's gaze was scathing. "Murder. Murder is the subject. And I have a couple of questions for you."

The song stopped and Myrtle bit her lip in annoyance. Now Winston would probably try to escape. But instead he simply steered her back close to her cane as instructed and then gestured to a couple of chairs that were on the back wall. "Sure, Myrtle. Let's have a seat."

They sat down, Myrtle somewhat gingerly after her unexpectedly strenuous exercise.

Winston studied her for a moment. "You've changed, Myrtle. Oh, you were always absolutely brilliant. The cleverest person I knew and the most underemployed. You should have been working at a think tank or something instead of trying to make young people learn their native tongue."

"Nonsense." But Myrtle felt a warm glow.

"The difference is that now you'll speak your mind."

"I've always spoken my mind. Sometimes people just haven't listened. Foolish people. Now, the couple of things I wanted to ask you," said Myrtle. "First off, where were you yesterday morning? Were you in your room?"

Winston chuckled. "At what time? I was in my room until I woke up—which was rather late, about nine forty-five. I walked to the dining hall to see if I could still beg some food from the staff, but they weren't having it."

"So you walked back to your room around ten?" asked Myrtle. That must have been around the time that Pasha was on the loose.

"I got a muffin from my room and then walked to the kitchenette to warm up the muffin in the microwave," said Winston.

"Did you see Ruby?" asked Myrtle.

"Ruby?" he frowned. "Where? On our floor?"

"Probably. Either in the commons areas or in the kitchenette."

"I didn't see Ruby at all," said Winston. "And I probably would have noticed if I *had* seen her, because she's usually doing something odd." He suddenly gave Myrtle a grin showing that he still had all of his teeth in perfect condition. "You know, if you're looking for a better sidekick, I'd be happy to take Milo's place. I could use the excitement."

"His name is Miles," said Myrtle dryly. "And I'm not looking to replace him."

"Seems easily distracted," mused Winston. They watched as Miles made another surreptitious trip to the food table. "These young fellows frequently are, though. Say, Myrtle, do you still drive?" There was a longing look in his blue eyes.

"When I feel like it," said Myrtle with a sniff. "My license was very recently renewed." She gave him a wary look. For this age group, admitting you could still drive was like admitting you were a millionaire. It was just as attractive to singles. But her pride wouldn't allow her to fib about it. She *was* very proud that she could still handle an automobile. At a reasonable speed, of course.

"That's the thing I miss most," said Winston sorrowfully. "Driving. No car now, even if I *could* drive."

He looked intently at Myrtle's right hand. "That's a beautiful ring you're wearing. An old-fashioned setting for the stone, too."

Myrtle decided that she was going to have to distract Winston. She certainly didn't want to encourage him and Miles was going to take their fake relationship only so far. Plus there was the fact that she really didn't care for Inez very much. So she said rather curtly, "Thanks. It was my mother's ring." She cleared her throat. "Speaking of rings, did you see the beautiful jewelry that Inez is wearing tonight?"

Winston didn't appear very interested. "I'm sure she's wearing plenty of jewelry. She always does."

Myrtle leaned in closer. "If you promise not to make it obvious that I told you, I know a secret about Inez."

Winston's eyes widened. "What? What did you find out?"

Myrtle decided to play coy. "Oh, I don't know if I should tell you."

"Tell me what? Just go ahead and fill me in—you might as well." Winston was now hanging on her every word.

"Well...okay. But remember—you heard *nothing* about this from me. Or *anyone*. But Inez confided in me that she really likes you."

"She...does?" Winston's gaze circled the room until it lit on Inez, still busily snapping pictures of residents and jotting down notes on her clipboard. His eyes narrowed in a considering way.

"That's right. But she didn't know how to tell you," said Myrtle. "And if you come on too boldly, you'll probably scare her off."

"Scare *Inez*?" Winston stared across the room at Inez in wonder.

Myrtle had to admit that this last bit was something of a stretch. They watched as Inez gave some hapless resident's dress a dismissive look as she jotted down something likely scathingly critical in her notebook.

"Well, what do you know?" asked Winston in a bemused voice.

Myrtle smirked to herself. She'd figured that Winston's ego would be such that he would take her story hook, line, and sinker. "Just remember—you've got to really *woo* her. You know. Anonymous love notes. Flowers from her secret admirer."

Winston was looking concerned. "And she'll like this?"

"She'll love it." Or else she'd at least be kept very busy wondering who was behind it. And Myrtle would be left alone.

Winston mulled this over quietly for a moment. "Might have to give up some stuff. To date Inez, I mean."

"Like pickpocketing?" questioned Myrtle succinctly.

Winston startled. "You mean you know about that?"

"I sure do. I know you took money from *me*, even."

Winston said quickly, "But I gave it back to you." He shifted uncomfortably. "You won't say anything about it, will you? Really, it's almost like a game to me. And I'll give it up. Especially to be with Inez. I know she wouldn't want to be with me if she knew."

Myrtle was feeling quite smug now. She'd provided even more of a public service than she'd at first imagined.

Miles, plate again quickly depleting, finally joined them. Winston said in a courtly manner, "I'll leave you two lovebirds alone now. Thanks for the dance, Myrtle."

Chapter Sixteen

Miles and Myrtle both made a face at the word *lovebirds*. "Seems like you were able to dispatch him relatively quickly, Myrtle. Did you step on his toes a lot?"

"No, but I should have. His dancing was exhausting. But I've created what I think will be the perfect diversion for him. I intimated that Inez had a crush on him."

Miles's eyebrows flew up. "Inez?" He glanced over at Inez who had her hands on her hips and was looking at the drinks table in a disapproving way. "She seems a little straight-laced to be interested in Winston."

"She is. I made it up. Besides, I really don't care for Inez very much. She has this very condescending air about her and forever has an expression as if she's smelled something disagreeable," said Myrtle. "So I've crafted some revenge to spring on her." She squinted as a figure approached them. "Here comes grumpy old Fred. Probably wants to grab you for a game of checkers again."

Miles's face clouded. "Ordinarily I wouldn't mind, but we're getting pretty close to midnight. I'd like to be part of the countdown. And maybe have some champagne."

"You're having entirely too much fun," snapped Myrtle. "You really need to be focusing on the project at hand. Which is, if you've forgotten, finding out what happened to Mickey and who was behind it. And, if possible, who might have been behind Ruby's attack yesterday. You could help me question Fred about it. If I do *all* the questioning, people are going to start running away when they see me coming."

Miles appeared to be pressing his mouth shut tightly as if to keep ill-advised words from popping out unbidden.

Fred did indeed want to play checkers with Miles. "Feel up to a game?" he asked. "I had a winning streak yesterday and I'm feeling lucky. Maybe we can even wager on it."

Miles looked at his watch. "It's getting very close to midnight now, Fred. I have a feeling I'm not at my best right now."

Fred gave him a canny look. "Too much champagne to play?"

"No, it's not that. It's just been a long day and I want to play when I'm fresh." Miles sounded apologetic.

Myrtle interjected quickly before talk could continue on the topic of checkers, "Fred, I was wondering if you could tell me where you were yesterday morning."

"Yesterday morning?" Fred frowned at her. "Well, I do the same thing every single day, so I would have been following my routine. I got up at seven. I showered, dressed and headed to breakfast. I read the paper in the commons area in our hall. Then I changed my shoes and took a walk around the perimeter of the retirement home."

"Inside or outside?" asked Myrtle.

"Inside, naturally. I wouldn't want to walk outside and freeze my tail off. It's cold out there!" Fred's wrinkles all collaborated in a ferocious frown.

"Did you see Ruby Sims at all?"

"Certainly not. If I had, I'd have avoided her. Silly woman, always broaching some sort of nonsense or another," said Fred in a crabby voice. Then he hesitated and reluctantly said, "I might have seen her in the basement commons area when I was just unfolding my paper. I remember feeling fortunate that she hadn't seen me."

"Where was she when you saw her?" asked Myrtle.

"Just coming out from the kitchenette, I think. Why on earth does this matter?" Fred cast a longing look at the drinks table.

"Because there was an incident yesterday and I'm trying to get a better handle on what happened. Did you see anyone in the kitchenette with her?" asked Myrtle.

"In the Greener Pastures kitchenette? Of course not! Are you telling me that there are romantic liaisons occurring in the kitchen? That will put me off of snacking, for sure." Fred looked disgusted. "There are rooms for that sort of behavior. I can tell you with all certainty that I heard and saw nothing but Ruby exiting from the kitchenette and by that point I was hiding behind my paper."

"So if someone *had* come out of the kitchen after Ruby left, you wouldn't have seen them?" asked Myrtle.

"Not unless they stuck their head around the business section of the newspaper," said Fred firmly. "Now, if you'll excuse me, I see Ruby heading our way now. Which I'm quite sure is my cue to leave."

Ruby was wearing quite possibly the loudest Christmas sweater that Myrtle had ever seen. It was bright red with bright green ornaments all over it. She approached Myrtle and Miles with a smile, but a bit of a foggy look in her eyes—a look that was becoming very familiar to Myrtle.

"Hi sweetie," she said, "Happy New Year. Glad you could make it to the party. Have you seen my drink anywhere? I had it in my hand and then I stuck it down somewhere."

Myrtle said dryly, "Considering that Greener Pastures marked all the glasses with names, I'm sure you can reunite with it."

"It makes sense, if you think about it," said Miles rather defensively. "They wouldn't want anyone exchanging germs during flu season."

"I don't think it has a thing in the world to do with flu season. I think it has to do with the fact that they don't want to have to wash more than one glass per person," said Myrtle. She peered around the room. "Ruby, there's a glass right there on that table. See if that one has your name on it."

Ruby swung around and her face brightened. "That's it!" She picked up her glass and took a big sip. "Say, what do you think of all the decorations? Don't they look great? I helped out a lot with them."

"They look wonderful," said Miles. "I especially like all the stars hanging from the ceiling."

Ruby beamed at Miles. "I cut most of those out, myself. And I put glitter glue on them, to make them sparkle."

Myrtle had had enough of Greener Pastures party décor. "Have you been taking special care the past twenty-four hours, Ruby?"

Ruby's face clouded again. "Special care?"

"Just being careful. Making sure you're not by yourself in the commons area. Being watchful if you are." Myrtle saw that there still wasn't much comprehension on Ruby's face. "Because you were *attacked* yesterday, Ruby!"

"Oh! Oh, right," said Ruby rather sheepishly. "Yes, I've been very careful. I look both ways when I open my door and make sure that no one is lurking out there. It's so awful to think that some bad guy is hanging around Greener Pastures and trying to hurt people."

Myrtle and Miles exchanged a look. Could Ruby really be naïve enough to think that this was a crime by a stranger? If she was, she needed to be disabused of that idea.

Myrtle said, "Ruby, it wouldn't make sense for a stranger from the community to do this. This is an inside job. Someone you know here at Greener Pastures wishes you ill. The phone call, the attack on you—they're all intended to scare you off. Somebody must think that you know something about Mickey's death. That person wants to make sure that you're not going to say anything to the police."

Ruby frowned. "But I don't know what I know."

"Well, if you figure it out, call me. You still have my number, right? Let me know as soon as you think of it," said Myrtle.

Myrtle felt eyes on her back and turned to see Wanda's cousin, Randy, staring at her. He raised his eyebrows and rolled his eyes, and then headed over to Darla, who was standing near the food table.

"Uh-oh," murmured Myrtle to Miles. "Something must be up. Randy looks very purposeful as he's heading over to the staff."

Miles looked glumly at his watch. "Typical. It's nearly midnight. Time to break up the party, right?"

But the countdown to midnight had already started and the voices of the residents were loud enough to drown out the conversation between Randy and Darla. She impatiently gestured to him to follow her out into the hall.

"Five, four, three, two, one! Happy New Year!" shouted the residents. Ruby bounced off to more closely watch the countdown on the television. There was a cacophony of party horns and some kissing and embracing among both residents and staff.

Myrtle and Miles clinked champagne glasses and took a big sip.

Darla, who rather grimly clinked a spoon against a glass, cut the revelries short. She cleared her throat. "Happy New Year, everyone. Unfortunately, I've just received a report that the ice storm that was predicted has transpired. Randy has been listening to local radio and the police are urging that no one drive tonight. This means that any guests tonight need to spend the night on the premises." Darla turned a sour look toward Myrtle and Miles. "And staff that was intending to leave for home needs to stay put, as well."

"I guess we're the only guests here," murmured Miles.

"Guests can either find a friend to room with for the evening, or else the staff can make up a bed...somewhere." Darla looked rather displeased by the entire prospect.

Suddenly, Fred was next to them again. He said to Miles, "Unless you want to sleep in an extra bed in the memory care unit, I suggest you hang out with me tonight. I've got a sofa in my room that doubles as a day bed." He looked at Myrtle. "I guess you'll take Mrs. Pelias's room." He turned and walked away as another resident called his name.

Miles glanced over at Myrtle. "What are you thinking of doing? Staying in Mickey's room, as Fred was saying?"

"I'm staying with Ruby, naturally," said Myrtle. She scanned the room for Ruby, which was a little difficult to do since the residents were now heading back to their rooms. "Now I just need to find her. It seems like Ruby is always around when you aren't looking for her, and then she disappears when you need to see her."

Miles sighed, "Poor Ruby. It shouldn't be hard to spot her. Those red and greens made her look like a Christmas tree gone mad."

Myrtle frowned. "I know. That's why it's weird that I can't find her." She increased her already considerable height by standing on her tiptoes. "That's strange—she's asleep on the sofa over there."

"Well, it *is* really late," said Miles. But then he added a bit uncomfortably, "It is a little odd that she's asleep. She seemed like she was pretty excited about seeing the New Year come in. Maybe she drank too much?"

"There's no way. Remember? She'd lost her drink for half the time. Let's go check on her," said Myrtle.

Ruby was indeed passed out cold, her head lolling on her Christmas sweater-covered chest. The room emptied from revelers except for the staff and Myrtle, Miles, and Ruby.

"Ruby?" Myrtle shook her by the arm. "Ruby, wake up."

Ruby's arm was completely limp and her head swung to the side.

Myrtle put a hand to Ruby's neck. "She's alive, but unconscious. Get the staff. Someone besides that miserable Darla."

Unfortunately, the miserable Darla was right there next to them and giving Myrtle a baleful look. "What's going on now?"

"My future roommate is unconscious. I don't know if it's a medical-related thing or some sort of criminal mischief," snapped Myrtle. "But she needs medical attention."

Darla rolled her eyes, leaned forward and studied Ruby closely. "She's asleep. Sound asleep. Probably not used to staying up until such a late hour."

Darla's eyes told Myrtle that *she* wasn't used to staying up, either, and would rather be at home in her bed right now.

This time it was Miles who pushed back. "Darla, I think you'll find upon closer inspection that Ruby is most definitely *not* just asleep. If you're unable to wake her, and I believe you will be, then I suggest you call for an ambulance."

"In this weather?"

"Naturally, in this weather!" said Myrtle. "Emergency vehicles and personnel are *always* out. Including my son. Usually."

Darla, clearly not wanting ownership of any further problems tonight leaned forward and shook Ruby's arm insistently, calling her name as she did. Ruby was unresponsive. Darla scurried away and found a cool rag from the kitchen and swabbed at Ruby's face. Ruby didn't even move.

With a frustrated exclamation, Darla pulled a phone from her pocket and started dialing for help.

Within minutes, an ambulance had arrived and taken Ruby away on a stretcher to the regional hospital. Darla clearly didn't want to arrange accommodations for Myrtle, but another staff member named Cindy, who had pleasant features and a rather heavy physique, said that Myrtle was welcome to stay in Ruby's room "since she was her friend and all."

"Thanks," said Myrtle to Cindy. "Are there any toothbrushes at the infirmary or anywhere that I could use? That's the one thing I'll really miss."

"Oh, sure. We keep some in the infirmary for residents. If you'll follow me, I'll find you one."

Myrtle said to Miles, "I guess I'll see you tomorrow morning. Good luck with Fred."

Cindy moved a lot quicker than her large frame would suggest and Myrtle was fairly breathless when they arrived at the infirmary. Once she caught her breath she said, "Cindy, could I ask you something? It seemed to me that maybe Ruby had an overdose of sleeping pills or something. Do you think that's a possibility?"

Cindy's eyes widened in surprise. "Oh, no ma'am. Miss Ruby isn't allowed to take her own medication anymore. We come by and bring it to her."

"So there are no sleeping pills in Ruby's room? She couldn't have accidentally taken some?" asked Myrtle.

"Even if she *was* allowed to have medication in her room, there wouldn't be any sleeping pills in there. Miss Ruby sleeps real, real good," said Cindy.

"But as well as she was sleeping tonight? I mean, you're always able to wake her up, though, right?" asked Myrtle.

"Oh, yes, ma'am. Because sometimes she's napping when we come by with her medicines and she opens the door right up when we knock. But then she'll fall back asleep again as soon as we leave. Sleeps like a baby, she does," said Cindy fondly. She handed her a toothbrush. "Here you are. And you know how to find Ruby's room, don't you?"

"I do. Except I don't have a key," said Myrtle. "Could you let me in?"

Cindy clucked. "That one doesn't lock her door. We tell her and tell her, but she doesn't do it. You can call me at the infirmary extension if you're locked out—but I'd be shocked if you were."

Myrtle took her toothbrush, walked to the elevator, and traveled down to the basement. As she walked to Ruby's door, she gave a little shiver. She definitely didn't like the subterranean feel of the floor, no matter how cheerfully Ruby accepted it. It had a sinister atmosphere at night with the small lights on the walls throwing eerie shadows around the hallway. There was no sign of life on the hall—everyone must have already turned in and Miles must have settled into Fred's room.

She tried Ruby's door and sure enough, it opened right up. Myrtle made a face. Ruby wasn't the brightest bulb in the bunch sometimes.

After entering the room, Myrtle turned to automatically turn the lock, but then hesitated. No one saw Ruby's ignominious departure from the Home by ambulance. The New Year revelers had all filed out before they'd discovered how incapacitated Ruby was. What if the culprit tried to take another crack at Ruby's glass tonight? Wouldn't it make sense for Myrtle to lie in wait and then attack the surprised killer with her cane or some other weapon?

Myrtle decided to lock the door only momentarily while she got ready for bed. She wanted to be fully prepared if she were to be attacked. Once she'd finished in the restroom and borrowed some of Ruby's decidedly loud pajamas, Myrtle unlocked the door again. She slid into the bed, laying her cane on the bed beside her. And she propped up on pillows. She'd rather be sitting if someone came into the room. She gazed around the room slowly. Ruby's baby doll collection was unsettling. The dolls all seemed to be staring at her. She turned off the light.

Myrtle hadn't intended on falling asleep. The possibility of falling asleep hadn't actually occurred to her. After all, she was an insomniac who didn't sleep in even the most relaxing of circumstances—which sleeping in a retirement home resident's bed with a murderer hanging around didn't qualify as. The last thing she remembered, she'd been thinking about Ruby and how very vulnerable she seemed. She'd been staring ferociously at the door, almost daring it to open and for someone to be foolish enough to come in. She'd been gripping her cane hard.

But apparently, as unlikely as it seemed, she *had* fallen asleep. Because the very next thing she remembered, she jerked awake to the sound of the door being very gently opened.

Chapter Seventeen

The biggest problem was that, being in the basement, there was really no light at all. And Myrtle was still just the tiniest bit groggy, which later she would attribute to the aftereffects of the champagne she'd consumed. But she woke quickly and held onto her cane with a tight grip, knowing that the intruder wouldn't be able to see *her* either, and believed her to be Ruby.

As she waited for the inevitable attack, Myrtle frowned. What was this intruder doing? Why was it taking so long? And what was the rustling sound she kept hearing?

She kicked impatiently at the bed sheets that were curled around her legs. But apparently there was something on the bed—something she hadn't noticed in the puffy comforter when she'd climbed into the bed. Whatever it was fell to the floor with a resounding crash.

There was a muffled curse from the intruder, who darted for the door. Myrtle scrambled to get out of the bed with its cloying sheets. But in her hurry, the cane fell off the bed and she was left to fumble frantically for it before scrapping the cane completely, and charging out of Ruby's room while holding onto the walls and bed as best she could.

Myrtle opened the door into the hall just in time to see Fred yanking open the door to his room and closing it back behind him.

Two seconds later, she was at Fred's door—pounding on it since he'd hastily locked it behind him. And a couple of seconds later, Miles opened the door with a very groggily confused expression on his face. "Myrtle? What's going on?"

Myrtle hissed, "What's going on is that your roomie and checkers partner just broke into Ruby's room...that's what. I guess he thought that Ruby was in there and he was planning to finish her off, or ensure that whatever sleeping pills he'd given her earlier had done their job."

The look on Fred's face was such that Myrtle could easily envision him twirling a mustache and saying, "Curses! Foiled again." Instead, he said coldly, "I don't know what you're talking about. Clearly you were having a nightmare."

Miles demurred. "Actually, Myrtle doesn't have nightmares. Myrtle doesn't sleep as a matter of fact. So Fred, it does sound as if you have some explaining to do."

Fred cleared his throat and stalled for time as he seemed to search for reasonable explanations. "Ruby and I had a romantic assignation planned?"

"*Very* doubtful," said Myrtle. "I think you'll have to do better than that. Or don't even bother to do better and I'll just go ahead and call my son up, since he's chief of police. You can explain it to him." Which Myrtle had absolutely no intention of doing, but Fred wouldn't know it.

"Well, whatever I was doing, it didn't have anything to do with killing Ruby," said Fred defensively. "And where is Ruby, by the way? I thought you were sleeping in Mickey's room, Myrtle."

"Ruby had to leave Greener Pastures via ambulance tonight," said Myrtle giving Fred a level stare. "Someone laced her champagne glass with sleeping pills. I'd decided to be Ruby's roommate tonight, but since she is probably getting her stomach pumped, that wasn't possible."

Fred's face relaxed in relief. "There you have it. We've got proof that I didn't mean Ruby any harm. I knew nothing about Ruby's glass being tampered with or the fact that she wasn't in her room. For heaven's sake, if I thought *you* were going to be in there, I'd never have opened the door."

Miles made a snickering sound that he quickly turned into a cough when Myrtle glared at him. He said, "So Fred, stop beating around the bush. If we were playing checkers, you'd know you were cornered by now. Tell us the truth—what were you doing in Ruby's room?"

Fred took a deep breath, flushed slightly, and gave them both a resentful glare. "All right, all right. I'll tell you. But I don't want it getting out. That's the whole point about secrets—they don't need to get out!" He hesitated. "I was looking for an old newspaper in Ruby's room. It was actually a paper that belonged to Mickey, but apparently, Ruby asked Mickey's daughter for any of Mickey's effects that Natalie didn't want. Which was a lot of stuff, I guess."

"Was it a Greener Pastures newspaper?" asked Myrtle.

"No. Thankfully, it's not. That was the whole reason I was relieved that Mickey was dead—so she couldn't expose this information she had." He shook his head in irritation. "That's not to say that I had *anything* to do with Mickey's death. I was just relieved she wasn't around to plague me anymore. No, this was a *Bradley Bugle* newspaper that Mickey and I were both featured in from long ago. It was pure chance that Mickey had it. She'd kept it because it had a nice write-up of her graduating from Duke University. You know how the *Bugle* does these fluff pieces."

Myrtle gritted her teeth, but didn't say anything. Miles looked amused again.

"Anyway, the same edition also had a piece on my dad's hardware store. My dad was quoted in there saying that he was proud of me for foregoing college to help him out with the store," said Fred. The words seemed pulled out of him against his will.

Myrtle nodded. "And I assume that you've been telling people that you did graduate from college."

Fred shrugged. "Who'd know the difference? Who'd even care? Yes, I mentioned for years that I'd graduated from an Ivy

League school. It was the only hole in my resume and I was a clever guy—I figured I could fake it. And that little fib helped me to get my first job in banking. And my second. Until pretty soon I was manager of a bank branch in Charlotte, back in the day. There was no internet back then, you know. Keeping track of pieces of paper with records on it—and fact-checking them—was time-consuming."

Myrtle nodded. "And you thought you'd gotten away with it."

"Gotten away with it? By that point, I believed it, myself! I'd been spinning that yarn about graduating from an Ivy League school for decades," said Fred. "You know how it is with a lie. After you've lied so many times, it becomes the truth. I could even talk about my college days with a certain amount of fond remembrance."

"And you talked about it here?" asked Miles. "At Greener Pastures?"

"Certainly. Why not? It's like any other place. You introduce yourself ... you try to make friends ... you give little facts about yourself," said Fred.

Myrtle nodded. "But Mickey found out."

Fred said, "It was really a perfect storm. There was a woman here who had been a friend of mine when we were growing up. Sally. She's passed away now, and had sadly gotten to the point where she had dementia before passing. What happened minutes ago was gone to her, but what happened when she was twenty was clear as a bell. She talked to me as if we were both kids again. And she remembered hanging out at my dad's hardware store while I was working there. She'd get a soft drink and sit on a stool and we'd chat all day. It was a much more slow-paced time then, you know."

"So Mickey heard her talking about you and the hardware store," said Myrtle.

"Mickey was her friend, too, both from when we were kids and now. And Mickey was sharp, very sharp. She recalled my saying that I'd gone to an Ivy League college and she tried to reconcile that to what Sally was saying. After all, we grew up in the same town. I should have been more cautious once I moved back to Bradley from Charlotte. I should have known that someone might remember that I hadn't gone to college at all. But it had been *decades*. An entire lifetime. These were old people. How good could their memories be? But Mickey's was very, very good. And there was another problem. Mickey kept *everything*. She was a real packrat," said Fred irritably.

"Not only that, but Mickey also liked finding out people's secrets. She liked holding this knowledge over their heads. And she had a certain underground newspaper in which she was fond of writing exposes," suggested Myrtle.

"That's correct," said Fred. He rubbed the side of his face and his eyes didn't meet Myrtle's eyes.

"It would certainly have worked out better for you if Mickey were no longer around," said Myrtle.

But Fred flatly refused to take the scenario farther. "I had absolutely nothing to do with that. Yes, it made my life easier that she wasn't going to be around to print her findings in her ridiculous newspaper. But I had nothing to do with her murder."

Myrtle gave him a hard stare. "You were in Ruby's room tonight. Was that because you were trying to find that newspaper story?"

"And destroy it once and for all. Sure," said Fred. "Why wouldn't I? Ruby is forever leaving her door unlocked. I'm not sure I've ever seen her use a key to get into her room. I figured I'd just get in there, use my little pen-flashlight to find a stack of papers, pull the article out, and then get out of there. That way I wouldn't have to worry about it anymore."

"But Ruby wouldn't even recognize the importance of the article anyway," said Myrtle impatiently. "Even if she saw it, it's likely she wouldn't recognize either your picture or even your name in the story."

"Sure," said Fred. "But if you were in my shoes, you wouldn't want to take the chance. Maybe she'd have a rare flash of lucidity. Or maybe Mickey wrote instructions on the paper to point out its importance. Maybe someone visiting Ruby would idly read the paper. No, I wanted the thing destroyed. Still do." His eyes narrowed.

"That's going to be impossible," said Myrtle. "You've got to realize it gives you a real motive in this case. Mickey *was* murdered. You had a secret you'd kept a long time that you'd like to keep concealed. This is something that the local police need to hear about."

Fred's eyebrows drew together and his entire body tightened with stress.

Miles said quietly, "Fred, think about it. It doesn't really matter anymore. The police may never release this information. Myrtle and I sure aren't going to go around telling people about it. Even if it somehow were to get out, it's not as if you're currently employed and your employer might let you go. The information simply isn't as devastating as it could have been decades ago."

Fred stared at him silently before giving a curt nod. "All right. I understand—you've got to go to the police with this."

"It might be better if you talked to them *with* us," said Myrtle.

"No. I want nothing to do with it. If you want to tell the police, they can come to me with any questions they have. I'm not voluntarily tattling on myself," said Fred crisply.

"Well, I'm certainly not going to sit on evidence. But I'm not calling the police at this hour, either. Besides, Darrell Smith is probably all over the town by now, trying to rescue people stuck in the New Year ice storm. It'll wait until the morning when things have defrosted outside a bit." Here Myrtle leveled a look at him that made the ice outside look warm. "However, I'm issuing a warning to you, Fred. Don't come back to Ruby's room. I'm locking the door tight. And I'm keeping that article on my person, so there's no need to come lurking around for it anyway, unless you're in good fighting shape. Which I don't believe you are." Myrtle gave a sniff. "And now I'm off to sleep."

Her dramatic exit with her nose in the air was somewhat ruined by the fact that the door was a lot closer than Myrtle had remembered it being. She grunted under her breath as her hip connected with the door handle. Quickly pretending it didn't happen (and that Miles's unmanly giggle behind them didn't happen, as well), Myrtle sailed out through the open door.

She was still so incensed by the entire episode, and the hall was so very dim, that the realization that a very slight man was standing outside Ruby's door made Myrtle give an undignified jump.

A gruff voice said, "Tried not to scare you Miz Myrtle, but you was deep in your thoughts when I said your name."

A wave of relief washed over Myrtle as she recognized the very Wanda-like voice. She whispered, "Oh, Randy, it's you. You scared the living daylights out of me. I guess you're stuck here tonight, too, aren't you? Here, come on in Ruby's room and we'll talk."

The Greener Pastures custodian, smelling something of old nicotine grandly held the door to Ruby's room open for her to enter. He even did a quick check around the room. "Won't hurt none to check the room for bad guys," he muttered. "Since nobody locks doors around here." He gave Myrtle a reproachful look.

"I know, I know. But I was chasing someone out of here at the time, Randy."

He narrowed his eyes. "Trouble?"

"Sort of. No one was trying to murder Ruby, or me for that matter. He was just trying to find evidence against him to destroy it. You know—just everyday life at Greener Pastures." She pushed aside some clutter on Ruby's sofa and sat down. Randy hesitated and Myrtle said, "Oh, have a seat, Randy, and tell me to what I owe the honor of this visit."

Randy seemed to relax a bit and he gingerly sat down on Ruby's loudly floral sofa after moving several wide-eyed dolls. "I've been wanting to talk to you, Miz Myrtle. But whenever you're here, it don't seem like the right time. What with chasing cats and being at parties and whatnot."

"Agreed," said Myrtle. "It does tend to be a bit chaotic whenever I'm at Greener Pastures. And I blame Greener Pastures for that. I certainly don't believe that chaos follows me wherever I go." Although her son would perhaps disagree.

"And I heard tell from Wanda that you don't sleep ever. I couldn't sleep on that cot they set up for me tonight, so I thought I'd head over here and see if you was up. And you was." Randy bobbed his head at her. "So here I am. I wanted to tell you about Miz Inez and Miz Mickey."

"Excellent. Because no one in this place talks about anything. It's the most secretive bunch I've ever seen and I've seen a lot of folks with secrets before. So tell me. They didn't get along, those women, right? But why? Was it Mickey's fault or Inez's fault?" asked Myrtle, leaning back on the sofa.

"Well, I don't know as I can dole out the fault. Isn't my place, is it? But I can tell you that Miz Inez disapproved of Miz Mickey because she thought she was wicked. That's what she called her— wicked." Randy gave an emphatic nod that made his ponytail bob.

Myrtle frowned at this. "That seems rather silly. I'd have called Mickey loud. I'd have called her coarse. I'd have called her self-centered. But I wouldn't have called her wicked. Sounds like hyperbole from Inez."

The word hyperbole apparently knocked Randy for a loop. He muttered it under his breath a couple of times before giving a small shrug and casting it off. "Don't see as how I know about that. But I do know that Miz Inez didn't like Miz Mickey's cussing. Nor her wine But not only all that—she was also upset that Miz Mickey told her that she'd given away a baby for adoption once when she was young."

"Adoption? What on earth is wicked about that? It seems like a perfectly lovely thing to do—to bless someone else with a child. What an odd woman Inez is," said Myrtle, shaking her head.

"I was cleaning windows nearby, so I heard it all," said Randy blandly. "What I heard was Miz Inez saying that it was wasteful. That Miz Mickey hadn't understood what a gift a child was. But Miz Mickey just laughed like she was surprised. She told Miz Inez that she *did* know what a gift a child was. Which is why she *re-gifted* the baby to someone else."

"Ha! Clever of Mickey," said Myrtle. "She certainly wasn't a stupid woman. What did Inez say to *that*?"

"She stomped off in a huff, she did. But before she did, she told Miz Mickey that she herself hadn't been able to have no children. So she could call it a waste if she wanted to. And told Miz Mickey that she was the wickedest person she'd ever known. In this real mean voice, she said it, and sort of like she was about to start crying. That's when she left," said Randy.

"What was Mickey's reaction to all that?" asked Myrtle.

"She just looked real thoughtful. I'd turned around at that point, to make sure Miz Mickey was all right. And she gave me a smile and then made a face, nodding her head toward where Miz Inez had left and said, 'I done made myself an enemy, Randy.'"

Or words to that effect, thought Myrtle.

"You liked Mickey, didn't you Randy?" she asked.

He sighed and looked down at his scruffy tennis shoes. "Yes ma'am, I sure did. She always said hi to me—and by name. I don't even have my name on my shirt, but she asked me the first day she come here what my name was and she never had to ask again—her memory was that good. She gave me candy sometimes, too, from the store. I liked her a lot."

"And you were worried about her, clearly. Enough to tell your cousin about it," said Myrtle.

"Yes. Wanda said that you can't change the future, but you can get revenge," said Randy.

"It won't be revenge, it'll be justice," said Myrtle in a stern voice, echoing Wanda's words on the matter. *Justice must be meted out.*

Chapter Eighteen

Myrtle actually did end up clocking a few hours of sleep after Randy left. But she must have had one ear or eye open the whole time, listening for trouble, because she woke up feeling as if she'd been awake the entire night.

"Might as well make use of the time I've got left in here," she muttered. She needed to find Fred's newspaper and put it in her pocketbook to secure it. She also wanted to have a look and see if there was anything else in Mickey's pile of papers in Ruby's room. Maybe Ruby was the owner of a huge bundle of blackmailing material and was completely unaware of it.

After about forty-five minutes of searching, Myrtle was beginning to get stiff and irritable. Half of her wanted to just head over to the dining room and be the first in line for coffee and breakfast, but the other half was certain that she needed to make sure she'd taken the opportunity to thoroughly go through these papers while she had the chance.

Finally, she found the newspaper that had both a story on Mickey's graduation (she was dressed in a carefully ironed dress and was wearing a smirk on her face) and Fred's interment at his father's hardware store (a resigned look on *his* face). Myrtle found neither story to be particularly interesting or well written. "Silly of Fred to care about this so much," she muttered.

Myrtle folded the newspaper and stuck it into the depths of her large pocketbook. As she did so, she realized there were a couple of pieces of notebook paper underneath that paper.

One of them was a to-do list of Ruby's from last week that had gotten mixed into the fray. In her careful hand, she'd written down the date, a list of tasks involving laundry, things to buy at the Home's on-campus store, and meals that she particularly wanted to eat at the dining hall. But the other was a note of *Mickey's* that was covered in a sideways scrawl and lots of exclamation marks.

On closer examination, Myrtle saw that it was a printed-out picture of Winston Rouse. He was sitting next to an old woman in the dining room and his hand was inside the purse hanging on the back of her chair. On further inspection, Myrtle saw that the old woman was *her*. Mickey must have been following Winston around trying to get proof of his activities. How she'd managed to give Natalie the slip long enough to shadow Winston was the question. Probably sent Natalie on another fool's errand and then hurried out to see what she could see. Obviously, Winston would have had the best opportunity to pick someone's purse or pocket at mealtimes or other community events.

Under the printed out picture, Mickey had scrawled *Winston Rouse strikes again*. So...had Mickey been tracking this? Had she perhaps suspected that Winston had taken things from her—or her room, if he'd been visiting there? Had that been the reason they'd fallen out enough to warrant a big argument and Mickey's statement that she was going to revise her will?

Myrtle jumped at the tap on her door. She relaxed a bit when she heard a voice calmly state, "Myrtle? It's Miles."

She pulled open the door and Miles raised his eyebrows at the fact that Myrtle was still in Ruby's pajamas. "Thought we'd head over to breakfast. You're not ready."

"Oh, I've been awake for ages, but I've been going through all Mickey's stuff. Now it's all Ruby's stuff, I guess." She yanked Miles into the room and closed the door for privacy. "I've made some interesting discoveries."

After she filled Miles in, he said in a surprised voice, "So, old Winston, is it? I can't say I'm too sorry. I never really warmed to him, especially since he seems to consider me his romantic rival for some reason."

"That's all old news, Miles. He's obsessed with Inez now. I fixed it," said Myrtle, waving her hand impatiently. "Do try to keep up. And I'm not sure that Winston is the perp at all. He's certainly a strong suspect, though. I'm pretty steamed that he took my money."

"But he gave it back," said Miles. "Remember that?"

"Apparently because he realized I'm not exactly infused with funds," said Myrtle stiffly. "It was an act of charity—reverse pickpocketing."

"Well, at least he didn't *donate* any money, he just gave yours back to you. He was clever with it I have to say. Wish I could see him in action—that's a lot of sleight of hand," said Miles. He looked a bit wistful. Then he frowned at the pajamas again. "Can't we go to breakfast? I'm starving."

Myrtle grabbed her clothes from Ruby's sofa and stepped into Ruby's bathroom, closing the door behind her. As she quickly got ready, she said, "There's nothing noble about him, you know. He's a generic thief. I guess Mickey figured out what he was doing and decided to catch him in action with a camera."

"I wonder what she was going to do with the information," said Miles in a musing tone. "Surely Mickey wouldn't have blackmailed Winston. It appears that he doesn't have much money."

"Maybe she was going to put something in her newspaper about it. Maybe she was just going to enjoy knowing something that no one else knew. Maybe she wanted something back that she was convinced he'd nicked from her. Maybe she wanted to stop him from pickpocketing other residents," said Myrtle as she tugged on her dress from the night before.

"Maybe you don't need any coffee at all this morning, since your brain is already running on all pistons," added Miles dryly. "Didn't you sleep at all last night?"

"With people breaking into my room and custodians dropping by for chats? Unlikely," said Myrtle. She opened up the bathroom door, smoothing her hair down as she walked back into the living room/bedroom. Her hair was determined to stand up on end this morning.

"Custodians?" Miles frowned. "Wanda's cousin dropped by?"

"Directly after I left Fred's room," said Myrtle succinctly.

"And the purpose of his visit?" Miles raised his eyebrows. "The middle of the night isn't ordinarily a good time to chat."

"Randy seemed aware of my proclivity for insomnia," said Myrtle. "And his mission was to inform me that Inez thought Mickey was wicked. Especially for giving a child away for adoption."

"Rather twisted, don't you think?" asked Miles, making a face. "Who on earth sees adoption that way?"

Myrtle shrugged. "Inez, apparently. She's clearly unhappy with the way her life turned out. No children. Planned something very different, I guess. And that unhappiness made her bitter. And remember, Mickey didn't seem to realize what a gift *either* of her children were—the one she gave up for adoption or the one who she was constantly harping on. Natalie's efforts certainly didn't appear to be appreciated."

They left Ruby's room, Myrtle carefully locking the door behind them. Miles muttered, "Makes me like Inez even less than I did already."

Myrtle smirked at him. "Oh, don't worry. I have plans for Inez. I think she'll get what she has coming to her."

"In what way?"

Myrtle said in a low voice, "Remember? I'm setting up Inez and Winston."

Miles's eyebrows shot up into his hairline. "Playing matchmaker? That doesn't sound like you, Myrtle. It's very generous of you."

"Not so much. Inez is such a pain to deal with that I figured if I could get her set up with Winston maybe she'd get a little sweeter. And if we keep Winston busy, perhaps he won't take our watches. Besides, I think they deserve each other," said Myrtle darkly.

"You're still not sharing what happened between you and Winston all those years before," said Miles.

Myrtle glared at him in response as they got into the elevator.

Miles added reproachfully, "You know I'm not going to tell anyone. I'm just curious, that's all. It's so long ago I'd think it would be water under the bridge. It sure seems to be water under the bridge for *Winston*."

Myrtle rolled her eyes and then looked at her feet with great determination. "Let's just say that Winston lied to me about his intentions. Let's say that he intimated that he intended to marry me. Let's say I was smitten—I was young, and foolish. Well, young at the start of our relationship, anyway. Winston was one of the few men in Bradley who was as well read as I was—which was an attractive quality to me. By the time I'd wised up and realized the man had no intention of marrying me, I was the only one of my peers who hadn't married."

Miles said in a confused voice (Myrtle steadfastly refused to look at him), "That's not like you. I don't get it."

Myrtle gave an exasperated sigh. "I suppose it was easy for me. I didn't have to go out and try to be pleasant or engaging ... because I had a beau. I didn't have to dress nicely or wear makeup or even comb my hair...because I had a beau. And it wasn't as if Winston were always around. He was away in the service for ages. We wrote letters, that kind of thing. For heaven's sake, Miles, he wasn't always old and silly! Once upon a time he was rather charming and nice looking, well-read, and very clever."

The elevator doors shot open and Miles courteously held them open for her to stomp her way out. It was most annoying to start one's day with a discussion such as this.

Miles murmured, "Still, it seems like you'd have caught on."

"When I was ready to catch on, believe me, I caught on!" said Myrtle hotly. "I dumped him right then and there and sent him off with a flea in his ear. Apparently his memory isn't completely intact because it was quite a dumping, let me tell you. Then finally my eyes were open and I noticed that there was a very nice principal at my school by the name of Stanley Clover. Before long, we were married and then came little Red. And that's the end of the story."

Miles seemed to want to argue that it was the end of the story. Myrtle cut him off. "And there's Inez," hissed Myrtle. "This is the perfect opportunity for me to put a little flea in her ear about Winston."

Miles was tagging along as she approached Inez so she stopped walking. "Miles, I don't think Inez will want to discuss secret admirers with you around. If you head over to breakfast, I'll be right there."

Inez seemed surprised to see her but then said, "Oh, that's right. You got stuck here with the ice storm. Lucky we didn't lose power, is what I say. Usually we do. I suppose you should be able to leave by this afternoon. The news said they're putting salt and sand on the road. Besides, the temperatures are supposed to be way above freezing today."

"A good thing," said Myrtle. It was getting most disconcerting to be at Greener Pastures for so long. She was starting to feel as if she were an inmate here.

Inez gazed curiously at her. "So where did you stay last night? To sleep, I mean. Did they put you up in the infirmary?"

"No, I stayed in Ruby's room."

"Crowded in there, wasn't it?" asked Inez, raising her eyebrows. "Still, I think Ruby mentioned that she has a sofa bed in there. Or loveseat bed. Whatever."

Myrtle frowned. Was Inez pretending to know nothing of Ruby's hospitalization? Or was she being truthful? It would have been easy for Inez to have put sleeping pills in Ruby's drink last night. Of course, it actually would have been easy for *anyone* to put sleeping pills in Ruby's drink since Ruby lost her drink for a good portion of the New Year's Eve party.

Myrtle filled Inez in, just in case. Inez tut-tutted the entire time.

"Well, I can't say that I'm completely shocked. Ruby really isn't in the *best* of health. Still, it's a pity that her bad eating habits would catch up with her at a party. I'm assuming it was a heart or circulation-related issue?" asked Inez.

"Not at all. In fact, they're working from the assumption that there was something in Ruby's drink," said Myrtle coolly. This was a bit of a stretch, but Myrtle was sure they'd discovered the issue at the hospital.

Inez made a face. "Really, Myrtle. Who would want to kill *Ruby*? I've never heard anything so silly."

"Ruby apparently knows something that the killer wants to keep under wraps," said Myrtle sternly.

"Ruby knows *nothing*. Why, she barely knows my name. In fact, I don't think she *does* know my name."

Inez was clearly not going to be swayed. And Myrtle hadn't had any coffee yet, so she tamped down her natural desire to completely flatten the annoying Inez. Instead, she decided to change gears. "Whatever! I guess we'll find out more later on. Even though the evening ended on a sad note with poor Ruby, I have to admit that I enjoyed the Greener Pastures shindig last night. I had an interesting conversation with Winston Rouse there. We spoke of you as a matter of fact," said Myrtle, faking what she hoped was a genuine smile.

"Of me?" asked Inez, eyes open wide with surprise.

"That's right. He only had eyes for you the entire evening. Didn't you notice?" asked Myrtle.

"Um, no. No, I was busy asking everyone what they were wearing and writing up a story." Inez flushed. "Are you sure about that, Myrtle? Maybe I was just standing too close to the food table and Winston was staring over at the fudge brownies."

"Absolutely not! He told me himself that he was smitten," said Myrtle chidingly. "Said that he'd wanted to speak to you about it for a long time but that he was too shy."

"Winston? *Shy?*" Now there was suspicion in Inez's eyes. "Hmm ... what about the fact that he's been hanging out with Mickey for so long? I thought he and Mickey were an item. *Mickey* thought they were an item."

"Only because he thought you wouldn't be interested in him. If you'd shown any interest in him, then he'd have been right at your side," said Myrtle.

She and Inez were now walking into the dining room. Inez stopped short, blushing furiously. "Look! A note at my usual spot at the table. And ... a rose!"

Myrtle frowned. "There are not supposed to be reserved seats here! That's in the owner's manual. Most distressing that they don't abide by their own policies here. And how on earth would Winston get hold of a rose in the middle of an ice storm?"

"Oh, they sell them in the gift shop and it's already open. But *I've* never gotten one."

Myrtle watched in interest as hard-as-nails Inez positively glowed.

Miles finished off his scrambled eggs and carefully set his fork across the top of his plate. He dabbed gingerly at the corners of his mouth with his napkin and said, "So this is what I was able to find out. The roads are quickly melting and we should be able to leave here whenever we're ready. I also heard that there will be a memorial service for Mickey here at the home tomorrow."

Myrtle frowned. "People can't get from here to the funeral? Really? I'd think they'd have a dedicated bus route between Greener Pastures and the cemetery."

Miles gave her a repressive glare. "Myrtle! Surely, that's uncalled for. Apparently, that's just the way they do things here. Sometimes folks go to the funeral, yes. But the most popular thing is to attend the memorial service here in the chapel. The family comes and the chaplain performs the service. It's supposed to be nice."

The debatable niceness of a memorial service at a retirement home ignored, Myrtle mused, "I suppose Natalie will be there. I can ask her about last night. Ruby's drink and all."

Miles stared at her. "You're not suggesting that Natalie Pelias has anything to do with Ruby's supposed poisoning? She wasn't even here!"

"She certainly was here," snapped Myrtle. "She was busily clearing out her mother's room, remember? We're only *assuming* that she left Greener Pastures at all. She could have been lurking around."

"What, in disguise?" Miles shook his head. "Somehow I don't see that."

"Why not? She could have pretended to be a staff member. Or just melded into the woodwork like she usually does. Natalie isn't the type of person you notice. She'd only have had to be in the room for a few minutes. Everyone was drinking and watching the ball drop. It would have been a piece of cake."

"Okay," sighed Miles. "We'll keep Natalie as a suspect for Ruby's poisoning, too. Although I still strongly favor Winston."

"Which is quite shortsighted of you, Miles, considering that your checkers partner sneaked into Ruby's room last night. It seems to me as if Fred Lee has a huge motive in this case." Myrtle quickly stopped talking as a herd of old ladies approached their table, looking with interest at Miles. Myrtle gave them a ferociously discouraging stare and they hurried off to another table.

"So what's our plan?" asked Miles impatiently. "Where do we go from here?"

"We go home to regroup," said Myrtle. "We'll check for messages from Wanda. We'll make sure Pasha has had enough to eat. I'll ensure Red isn't driving Elaine completely up the wall.

Most importantly, we'll catch up on our soap opera since neither of us saw yesterday's episode."

Miles nodded. "In a day's time, babies could now suddenly be teenagers. Our favorite characters might somehow now be in the ICU in the hospital. All chaos might have been let loose."

"Exactly. And then we'll come back for that memorial service. It's time to knock this case out, Miles. I certainly don't have faith in the pleasant Darrell Smith to solve it."

Chapter Nineteen

The ride home wasn't a bit treacherous, despite the residual ice on the roads. When Miles pulled onto Magnolia Lane, he said in a perplexed tone, "I can't believe my eyes. Your wayward housekeeper appears to be cleaning your home. Without your badgering her or even being there. Has Puddin had a mild stroke?"

Myrtle frowned. "That Puddin. She turns up like a bad penny. No, she wouldn't be there if it weren't for Dusty. I guarantee you that Dusty is at Erma's doing something. Remember? She's gotten it into her head that Dusty is running around on her with Erma."

Miles made a sound that was halfway between a chortle and a coughing fit as he pulled into her driveway. When it had subsided, he said, "There are so many things wrong with your last statement that I don't even know where to begin."

"Then let me help you unpack it," said Myrtle smoothly. "Dusty couldn't possibly be attractive to anyone but Puddin. Erma couldn't possibly pose a threat as the "other woman" in any relationship. Dusty doesn't ordinarily, however, put himself out to do yard work for anyone, so how on earth is Erma luring him there as much as she is? Erma doesn't care a flip about her yard— evidenced by her crabgrass infestation, so why is she intent on having Dusty there? Yes, I know, it's all baffling. The only part I understand is that Puddin is pretending that I need her over to clean so that she can spy on Dusty."

Miles shook his head. "It's even more complex than our soap opera's plotlines." He stared at Erma's yard. "Wow. She's got

Dusty picking up limbs that broke from the ice storm. That's pretty amazing."

Myrtle nodded and opened the passenger door. "Here, let me check the mail real quick before going in to calm Puddin down. I've got to keep their marriage intact, you know. If Dusty runs away with Erma and Puddin divorces him and remarries ... what on earth will I do about my yard and house? Red will stick me in Greener Pastures for sure." She reached in her mailbox and pulled out a couple of bills and some junk mail. "I don't see anything here," she said, disappointed. Then she flipped through the junk mail and a postcard fell out. "Hold on. Looks like we received another cryptic missive from Wanda."

"What's it say?"

"I guess Wanda is obsessed with money," muttered Myrtle. "This is yet another hint that it's financially-motivated. Wanda's preoccupation probably has something to do with having all of her utilities cut off. It says: *it's all about the muney*."

"Not very helpful of Wanda," said Miles morosely. "She could at least give us a name or something."

"She claims it doesn't work that way, remember? But this really takes the cake. This could point to just about any of our suspects, especially if we bring blackmail into it," said Myrtle in disgust.

"There's nothing else on there?" asked Miles. He sounded disappointed.

Myrtle squinted at the postcard. "Well, there is a smudge or something near the bottom. Like an afterthought. Wanda's penmanship is ghastly and she's misspelled everything she's written so far." Myrtle tilted the postcard in the sun. "I can't make it out without my reading glasses."

Miles opened a glasses case that had been resting on his dashboard and put his glasses on. "Here, let me have a go." Myrtle handed over the postcard and Miles studied it for a minute. "It appears to say, *not whut they seem*.'"

"For heaven's sake!" spat Myrtle. "Wanda can't even use pronouns correctly? What's the help in saying *they*? She can't use *he* or *she* and at least point us in the right direction?"

"Somehow, I don't think Wanda got much instruction in the dos and don'ts of pronoun usage," said Miles. "At least she's trying. So what are you going to do now? Check on Red?"

"I'm feeling too cranky to call on Red right now," said Myrtle huffily. "I've got to wind down. Oh, and deal with Puddin. No, I'm thinking that it's time to watch *Tomorrow's Promise*. Then Red. Then maybe I can just think things through a little before we go to that blasted memorial service and deal with Ruby's fogginess again." She paused, remembering something. "I don't suppose you want to watch the soap with me, do you?"

"I'll pass," said Miles, holding his hands up. "If you're feeling cranky, I don't think I want any of that directed at me right now. I'll check in with you later. Good luck with Puddin. At least you'll be walking into a very clean house."

"I doubt that very much," said Myrtle grimly. "The dust bunnies will probably be terrorizing the dirty dishes."

But when she walked into her house, she looked around her in wonder. The silver and brass weren't tarnished. There didn't appear to be any dust on any surface. The floor was well vacuumed. The dishes that had been left to soak (or really to just sit around dirty) had been washed and put away. Instead of feeling delighted, Myrtle felt alarmed. Had Puddin perhaps suffered a small stroke? Did she need medical care?

"Puddin!" called Myrtle.

Puddin surfaced from the back of the house. Her eyes were puffy as if she'd been crying. Or, perhaps, it was the effect of the dust storm that must have arisen when she started so vigorously cleaning Myrtle's house.

"Mmm-hmm?" answered Puddin. Her small eyes looked toward the window where sounds from Erma's yard indicated that Dusty was assiduously clearing out the broken limbs.

Myrtle noticed that some things never changed, though. Puddin was clutching an industrial-sized bottle of all-purpose cleaner ... that was Myrtle's bottle. And it was nearly gone. No wonder the house smelled like a pine forest.

"Puddin, is everything okay? You don't seem to be acting like yourself. Is it Dusty? You're worried about Dusty?"

Puddin nodded miserably and to Myrtle's horror began to wail. "He's in uniform—again! And he's picking up sticks! Dusty hates to bend over. I ain't never seen him pick up sticks before, not ever."

Myrtle said severely in her best schoolteacher voice, "Puddin, get a hold of yourself. Right now!"

On cue, Puddin stopped her keening and gave Myrtle a resentful look at interrupting her crying spell.

"Now listen to me. Dusty is *not* interested in Erma Sherman. It is a biological impossibility. There is absolutely nothing beguiling about Ms. Sherman—nothing! She is completely revolting in every way...in fact, she's developed repugnance into an art form. So here's what I'm going to do," said Myrtle.

Puddin broke in, heatedly. "I'm gonna leave him! I'm gonna take up with somebody who loves me."

"Certainly not! You don't even know the facts, Puddin. You're jumping to a bunch of hastily conceived conclusions. I *will not* allow this to happen. I'm going right over there and getting to the bottom of this. No more speculation. Just cold, hard facts." Myrtle squared her shoulders, dragged a coat around her, and headed for her front door. Now that she'd had to deal with Puddin's nonsense, she was going to deal with Dusty's. It really wasn't a great start to the day.

Dusty was stooping to pick up a variety of sticks and larger limbs from Erma's side yard when Myrtle approached. Myrtle could hear popping and snapping sounds that she at first figured were the limbs before realizing they were coming from Dusty.

Clearly, he wasn't in the best of shape to be doing so much bending over.

"Dusty!" said Myrtle sternly.

The old man jumped and wheeled around. When he spotted Myrtle, he relaxed. He said something completely unintelligible before continuing to chew on something in his mouth.

"I can't understand you around your chewing tobacco, Dusty," said Myrtle. "And you know how I feel about that stuff."

He shifted the gob of goo around in his mouth, giving her a sour look before saying, "I just said hello. That's all. What's wrong, Miz Myrtle?"

"That's exactly what I wanted to ask *you*. What's wrong?"

Dusty squinted at her. All of his wrinkles from years of sun exposure bunched up when he did. "Ain't nothing wrong, is there? I'm cleanin' up Miz Sherman's yard after the storm."

"In a uniform? And meticulously?" asked Myrtle incredulously.

Dusty looked down at his uniform as if he'd forgotten it was there. "That's just because I done growed out of my work pants, Miz Myrtle. And torn a hole in two of my favorite yard shirts. Besides—it's horrible cold out here. The uniform is warm. Meticulous—I don't even know what that is, so I sure ain't been doing it."

"But I've never even laid eyes on you in a uniform before, Dusty," said Myrtle. She leaned on her cane and looked down at the shorter Dusty. "It seems to me that a uniform bought long ago would surely not fit if you've gotten too heavy for your work pants." Dusty did appear to have gotten a bit of a belly. It made for an odd sight—the scrawny man with wiry arms and the spare tire around the middle.

Dusty gazed scornfully at her. "That's just because when I bought it, I ordered the wrong size. Was too big. Couldn't send it back because it had my name on it, didn't it?" He patted a calloused hand on the red cursive *Dusty* over one shirt pocket. "But now I growed into it. Might as well get some use out of it."

It made sense. But then, Dusty frequently made more sense than Puddin did. So she'd confront him on his apparently inexhaustible drive to spend time with Erma Sherman. "Something else, Dusty. I have to practically threaten your life to get you to come over to my house to do work. Am I right?"

"In the summer, maybe," growled Dusty. "That's because it's busy then. You doesn't need your grass cut and your weed-eatin' done in the winter."

"Granted. But it seems to ... well, Puddin and me ... that you are eagerly volunteering your time next door at Miss Sherman's house. You're there quite frequently. In your uniform, which I now understand is from necessity," explained Myrtle.

Dusty continued squinting at her. This time he tilted his head to one side as if thinking it through. Then he shrugged, giving up. "Say again, Miz Myrtle?"

"Why are you working so hard for Miss Sherman?" reworded Myrtle impatiently. "You're here all the blasted time, Dusty. I can't look out my window without seeing you slinging stuff around in her yard. It's worrying Puddin to pieces having you behave so out of character and I *won't* have my life in disarray by losing my yardman and housekeeper!"

Dusty's face cleared. "Puddin is worried?" They both glanced toward Myrtle's house in time to see the pudgy, pale Puddin peering at them before ducking quickly out of sight. "What d'ya know? Aw. Naw, ain't nothin' but needing the money. Puddin should know that! That woman never listens to a word I say. I need new work pants. My string trimmer done bit the dust. In winter, business dries up. Miz Sherman needs my help right now because she got some sort of man-cousin coming to visit her soon and she wants all the mess in her yard carted off. Seeings how I need the money and she needs the mess out, it was a good deal for both of us." He shrugged bony shoulders. "That's it."

Myrtle blew out a gusty sigh of relief. "Well, thank heaven for small mercies. Emergency averted. All right. I'll explain things to Puddin and go watch my soap. Carry on, Dusty."

But the yardman stopped her. "Naw. I'll talk to Puddin. She was real worried?" He frowned at this. "What d'ya know?"

Myrtle sighed. She supposed she was expected to dawdle in her freezing cold yard until Dusty had patched things up with Puddin. Since he was a man of limited vocabulary, she both expected and fervently hoped that the process would be a short one. She was greatly relieved a few moments later to spot a brief embrace through her very clean window and Puddin's face go from anxious to its usual rather petulant expression.

When she saw that transformation, Myrtle headed inside. She wasn't about to turn into a Popsicle in her yard. Sure enough, as she walked in the front door she saw everything had returned to normal. Dusty was on his way back out to finish up with the limbs and Puddin was lounging on Myrtle's sofa.

"My back is thrown," she offered succinctly. "And your house is clean. Can we watch your soap?"

Myrtle, who ordinarily wouldn't want to encourage a bad habit, was so relieved to get Puddin back that she wordlessly grabbed the remote and plopped down into her favorite chair. She was still fumbling to get the recorded soap up when Puddin gruffly said, "Thank you, Miz Myrtle."

Myrtle was very much afraid Puddin would shed tears of relief at getting her blasted Dusty back, so she said briskly, "Don't mention it, Puddin. Happy to do it." But she felt something soften in her toward her problematic Puddin. And she sighed.

The plotting of this installment of *Tomorrow's Promise* was as convoluted as usual. But ridiculously watchable, also as usual. It was like junk food for the mind. Puddin's eyes were open wide in her absorption, her mouth was slightly open and she looked quite dense, which Puddin decidedly wasn't. Puddin was a lot brighter than she wanted to let on. "What's goin' on with Marlene?" she muttered to Myrtle at one point.

"Marlene is blackmailing Cheyenne. Marlene lost her money to that con man who was going to marry her, remember? And Marlene knows Cheyenne has stolen money from the spa where she works," said Myrtle. She made a face. It was amazing how much of this dreck she remembered.

Puddin continued droning out questions about the plot points but Myrtle wasn't even listening to her now. Something she'd just said or thought was important. She frowned. Marlene. Blackmail. Con man. Stealing. Puddin. She couldn't figure out what it was. Was it the fact that Mickey knew Winston was stealing money from residents? That Fred lied about his education? That Natalie needed money like Marlene did? Myrtle mulled it through but couldn't find the connection she needed.

"It's nice to answer people," said Puddin reproachfully.

Myrtle said absentmindedly, "Just pay attention, Puddin. And you'll figure it out." Just as Myrtle would.

The next day, Myrtle studied herself critically in the mirror. Her funeral dress was actually in good shape today, without any of the inexplicable stains it somehow attracted. She'd even been able to comb her white hair into some semblance of order.

She glanced at her watch. Where on earth was Miles? It wasn't like him to be late.

Finally there was a light tap at the door and Myrtle hurried to get it. "There you are!" she exclaimed as she pulled open the door.

Miles was clearly crotchety. "My toaster oven caught on fire," he said. He was quite disheveled, which was most-unlike Miles. His dark red tie was askew against his snow-white button down. Well, snow-white aside from what appeared to be a coffee stain. Myrtle reached up to smooth down several strands of his hair that were standing up on his head like Myrtle's usually did.

"You know," said Miles hotly, "if I lived at a place like—"

"Stop!" bellowed Myrtle. "I shall *not* listen to you extoll the virtues of Greener Pastures another time! No more! That place is a death trap and I shall *not* allow my friend to go there because of a silly toaster oven overheating event. Now let's get over to this memorial service. I certainly hope it's a short one."

Myrtle's hopes were dashed as soon as she sat in the small activity room and met Chaplain Amy. Chaplain Amy was one of those incredibly earnest people who believed deeply in what they were doing. That's an important attribute, true, but when combined with a tendency to like the sound of one's voice too much...it's a problem. Chaplain Amy's greeting alone took ten minutes. And her voice had a grating high-pitched drone that sounded like a broken fan set on high speed.

Miles's expression was bleak. "Think we're here for the long haul," he intoned.

"Shh!" Myrtle hissed at him.

"I don't think we've really even started yet," said Miles miserably. His gaze seemed fixed on the wall clock.

Inez was there in a shockingly bright red suit that looked great on her but she certainly didn't seem very mournful. She appeared to be taking notes on a legal pad, probably for the Greener Pastures paper. And she was *smiling*. She gave Myrtle a jaunty wave when she caught her eye. Could it be that she was mooning over *Winston*? Inez seemed to be in an incredibly chipper mood despite the somber event she was covering.

Ruby was dressed in a black top and black pants. She was sound asleep in her chair and gently snoring, head on her chest.

Natalie was there and looking as rumpled and frumpy as usual in a long, black dress that was too tight on her. She sat next to a man who was very dapper in comparison. Myrtle assumed it was Natalie's brother—the one she always complained about not helping enough with Mickey. He spotted her looking in his direction and winked at her. Myrtle gave him a disapproving frown.

Chapter Twenty

Chaplain Amy droned on. She decided to start out with the Lord's Prayer and somehow managed to muff it halfway through. Apparently, during the weighty decision of choosing between *trespasses* and *debts*, she completely lost her place in the prayer and had to abandon praying altogether while the rest of the congregation continued on.

A hymn followed. Although Myrtle had always thought "Holy, Holy, Holy" a lovely hymn, there was unfortunately someone sitting behind Myrtle and Miles who was convinced he was an operatic quality singer. He croaked out the holies in a bellow that woke Ruby from her nap, making her fumble red-faced on the floor for her dropped service notes.

The door opened as they ended the hymn, and an old lady with a determined expression grabbed a vase of lilies. "Meant for these to go to the memorial service down the hall," she said defensively to Chaplain Amy before nimbly scurrying away with the flowers.

Miles was making muffled coughing sounds and Myrtle looked at him in alarm. Sure enough, his eyes were full of merriment and he appeared to be on the verge of laughing. She gave him a repressive glare. "For heaven's sake, Miles!" This resulted in more strangled noises.

Chaplain Amy cleared her throat and picked up a large pile of papers that Myrtle was very worried were her notes for the homily. If so, they might be there until kingdom come. Chaplain Amy took the reading glasses that were hanging on a chain around her thick neck and put them carefully on her nose. In a very deliberate tone, she set about reading her notes.

The door flew open and an old man wearing a tee shirt and shorts that exposed toothpick-like legs stood there glaring at all of them. He was clutching a dumbbell with .5 on it. "Is this the Breathing Easy class?" he demanded.

Chaplain Amy appeared rather taken aback. "Ahh...no. No, this is Mickey Pelias's memorial service."

The indignant would-be exerciser appeared to take umbrage to this. He waved an orange flyer in front of him. "This flyer says that the class is today at ten. It's ten."

Chaplain Amy tugged at her collar as if it were choking her. "It can't be today. It's mistaken."

The man squinted at the flyer. "Wait a minute. Is today Tuesday?"

Miles now exploded into giggles, which he hastily concealed by coughing. Myrtle pounded him on the back with rather more force than was perhaps required.

"No, today is Friday," said Chaplain Amy helpfully.

The man, no longer irate, quietly closed the door behind him. But the process was interrupted by a lady in a wheelchair coming in with a large cup of coffee. "Sorry I'm late," she grunted.

Myrtle reflected later that the interruptions were key in making Chaplain Amy decide to ditch her notes and just ad-lib her homily. This resulted in a much shorter service than they were originally slated to endure. She saw that as soon as the service was over, Natalie appeared to be quickly gathering her things and preparing to make a fast exit. Didn't she know she was supposed to hang around and chat with the attending mourners?

Myrtle caught her before she could leave. "Such a moving service," said Myrtle, hoping she sounded sincere.

Natalie gave a doubtful shrug. "Nice of you to come," she said politely.

Then she gave a resigned sigh as the rest of the congregation came up to give her a hug and hug the man next to her who she identified as her brother Tradd.

Finally, everyone but the chaplain, Myrtle, Miles, and Natalie's brother trickled out of the room. The chaplain was beaming at Tradd as he appeared to be charming her with some apparently hilarious story about his mother.

Natalie watched grimly. "Figures. Tradd always *could* charm the birds out of the trees. But Mother saw right through him. Thank goodness. *She* couldn't be tricked."

"In what way?" asked Myrtle.

"Mother didn't leave Tradd a thing in her will. Not a penny. She knew exactly the kind of person he was and she'd have none of it," Natalie said with a fierce pride. Then she made a face. "Of course, she basically left me nothing in her will, either."

Miles looked appalled. "Nothing? Really? After all you'd done for her? Day in and day out? All those long hours ...?"

Natalie gave him an irritated look. "I know, I know. I'm not going to be destitute and she did leave me some property that I wanted. Actually, that's really *all* I wanted. But Mother was an individual. A free spirit. She gave her money where she wanted it to go."

Chaplain Amy tittered a laugh again and Myrtle, worried that their conversation might be interrupted, said hastily, "To whom? To whom did she give it?"

"Different people. To Winston, for one. Well, some to Winston. A pretty hefty bequest, but not the bulk of her money. That went to Ruby Sims. She was a loyal friend. And a friend who believed everything Mother said, which was unusual. Mother even gave something to Inez."

"Well, now you *are* surprising me," said Myrtle.

Natalie gave a small smile. "It was a very garish piece of costume jewelry that Mother despised. She seemed to think that Inez would make good use of it. And I see that she is wearing it today."

They could see Inez out the glass window looking into the commons area. She was wearing a sequined parrot pin on her red suit jacket.

"But nothing for Fred?" asked Myrtle.

"Fred who?" inquired Natalie with a frown.

"Fred lived on your mother's hall," said Myrtle.

"You mean that very grumpy guy who didn't like Mother? No, she didn't give him a thing...why would she?"

Myrtle needed one more bit of information and she decided to fib to get it. "By the way, you were lucky you didn't get stuck at Greener Pastures on New Year's Eve. You *didn't* get stuck, did you? I know somebody mentioned you were here that night and I didn't see you the next morning."

"Oh, that was a long night! Yes, I was there on New Year's Eve. I hadn't gotten everything out of Mother's room and I'd dropped and broken my cell phone so I thought I'd run by and get Mother's, since hers was still activated and I was paying the bill, after all. Especially since they were predicting icy weather. A friend of mine was having a New Year's Eve party and I was going to slide by before midnight. Then the ice storm moved in faster than the forecasters said."

Myrtle said, "You were stuck at the Home?"

"No, I got out of Greener Pastures all right. But I had to have help getting my car back on the road when I slid off into a ditch. The car was towed out and I never made it to my friend's house. At least I had Mother's phone to make my distress call," said Natalie. She saw Chaplain Amy and her brother looking her way and she quickly said, "Excuse me."

"What now?" murmured Miles.

"Now we see if we can pick up any other information," said Myrtle. "Let's see who's out there. Fred? Winston? Inez? We can mill around. Maybe you can play checkers. We can see what we can find out." They headed to the door and Myrtle spotted a thin figure with a ponytail standing on the other side. "Looks like

Wanda's cousin is here to clean after the memorial service. Let's see if he knows anything."

Randy was shifting from foot to foot, peering into the room and looking anxious.

Myrtle sidled up to him. "Everything all right, Randy? No other bodies, right?"

Randy shook his head until his ponytail swung from side to side. "No ma'am. I'm just wanting to clean in there so's I can get my smoke break."

Myrtle relaxed. "Oh, okay. You were looking so fidgety that I thought maybe something could be wrong." She paused. "You haven't had any cryptic messages from Wanda, have you?"

Randy squinted at her.

"I mean, have you spoken to Wanda? Has she given you any clues?"

Miles added helpfully, "Wanda said that someone here wasn't what they seem."

Myrtle flinched a little at the pronoun construction in Miles's sentence.

"That what she said?" asked Randy. He scratched a thin finger along the side of his face. "Could be anybody, couldn't it? Could be *me*. I'm not just the custodian—I'm also sort of spying on everybody. Like a double-agent almost. Except on the side of good." He seemed pleased by this idea, a faint smile tugging at the corners of his mouth. He looked younger when he smiled.

"So, as a double-agent, what have you heard?" asked Myrtle. "Anything good?"

Randy mulled this over. "Anything good. Hmm."

After a quiet minute, Myrtle revised. "Anything *at all*?"

"Sure. Sure, Miss Myrtle. But I don't know as you're interested in that stuff."

Myrtle said, "Try me. But only about the people who are involved in this case."

They walked a bit farther away from everyone, although Randy was still keeping an eye on the room in the hopes of working that cigarette break in. "Okay. So Mr. Winston, he's been real keen on getting his bequest thing from Ms. Pelias's estate. He's been spending money left and right, you see. New clothes. A fancy pair of sunglasses. New hair products. And he smells real good, too. I think he done spent all of it already."

"Sure sounds likely," agreed Myrtle. "What else?"

"Miss Natalie was telling her brother off. Called him a leech. He said that she was just as much a leech as he was—that the property their mom done gave her was worth more than everything put together. Then Miss Natalie said that maybe her brother was a vulture then, instead of a leech." Randy shrugged at this. "Sounded like they argue all the time."

"Again, sounds very likely. Anything else?"

"Miss Ruby was talking on the phone with her son. Apparently, he's real sick and doesn't have any insurance. She was talking about hospitals and treatment and stuff," said Randy. "But she's just as upbeat, no matter what her problems are. Sunny personality."

Myrtle said, "It's amazing her son could keep her focused on the topic at hand while she was on the phone. Although I guess when it's your child, you work harder to listen. Okay, what else, Randy?"

Randy looked at Miles. "I know you like Mr. Fred, but truth is, he runs his mouth a lot— talks about himself, likes to brag. But he's been real quiet the last few days. Real quiet. Sorta unlike him."

Miles nodded thoughtfully.

"And Inez?" asked Myrtle. "How has she been lately?"

Randy eyed her closely. "She's been very nice. Even told me 'good mornin' when she ain't never done that before. Reckon she's in love. Somehow. Maybe that's why Mr. Winston is spending so much money to smell good."

Myrtle nodded. "It all makes sense. Good observations, Randy."

"And now, if you'll excuse me, I'm going to head over and clean up the room the service was in. And get that smoke break." He was gone in seconds.

"I'm feeling like putting my feet up," said Myrtle. "That memorial service was simply too much."

"Don't think you're going to have a chance of that for a while," said Miles. "Ruby Sims is heading our way."

"Great," said Myrtle grumpily. "Because all I need now is some extra foolishness in my day.

Ruby's round face was cloudy as she approached them. "I was looking for y'all, sweeties, but couldn't find you. Wasn't that a lovely service for Mickey? But it made me feel sad. I think she would have liked to have heard all the nice things Chaplain Amy said about her."

Myrtle's opinion was that Mickey Pelias probably wouldn't have given two figs, but nodded. "And I had a nice talk with Natalie afterward. Although she was telling me something sad."

Ruby's eyes widened. "Sadder than Mickey's being dead?"

"Maybe. Because when it's a young person, it does feel sad. Natalie was saying one of your sons was sick. Is that so? I remember your saying one of your sons was ill, but I thought it was a flu bug or something when you mentioned it."

Now Ruby's face wasn't just cloudy. A tear trickled down one snowy white cheek. "Cancer," she said in a trembling voice. "Pretty bad cancer. So the doctors have got to try real hard to fix him."

"I'm sorry," said Myrtle gently. "That's got to be hard to handle."

Ruby's voice grew louder as she said, "It's very hard. But there's something else hard, too. I'm too scared to sleep now. So last night I had my light turned on and tried to sleep sitting up with a baseball bat in my lap."

Miles said with surprise, "A baseball bat?"

"One of my boys gave it to me for protection," said Ruby with pride. "Six sons. And nary a one in jail!"

Myrtle suspected this was a popular refrain of Ruby's. She tried to hurry the conversation along. "But nothing else happened, right?"

Ruby slowly shook her head. "No. But that doesn't mean that nothing will be happening. What if I get another scary phone call? What if someone comes up behind me and tries to choke me again? What if someone puts sleeping pills in my drink again?"

Miles and Myrtle glanced at each other. It was just as well that Ruby didn't know anything about Fred sneaking into her room early on New Year's Day.

"So I didn't sleep," repeated Ruby sadly. "And someone told me that I snored during Mickey's memorial service. I feel bad. But I'm so tired."

Myrtle said, "Fortunately, you know an insomniac."

"Do I?" Ruby's eyes were wide again.

"Me," said Myrtle, giving a small bow. "You can sleep while I stare at the ceiling."

Miles frowned, "Myrtle, are you sure?"

"I'm sure. I won't be sleeping at home anyway. Might as well be awake with Ruby," said Myrtle.

The logistics of it all seemed to trouble Miles. "But where will you sleep? Ruby will take the bed and there's only the sofa." He stopped politely before detailing the fact that the sofa was in fact, covered with piles of papers.

"You've not been listening, though. I'm *not sleeping*. So I can sit up on the sofa or put my feet up on the sofa and just think thoughts. Or whatever. I won't need a spot to sleep since I won't be doing it," explained Myrtle.

Miles's expression was uneasy.

"It will be fine, Miles. I'm not sure there's a better way to trap the killer. And I'll be very careful."

Miles said in a soft voice, "But you'll be trapped at Greener Pastures. I won't be here."

Myrtle gave him a delighted smile. "So you're backing off your convictions that Greener Pastures represents a little piece of nirvana? Gotten over your toaster oven rage?"

Miles looked at her coldly. "Just be careful, that's all, Myrtle. We're dealing with someone who isn't just playing around. They mean business." He hesitated. "Do you need me to run by your house and pick up some toiletries and some...well...night garments for you?"

Night garments. Miles sounded as if he was a contemporary of Myrtle's instead of so much younger. "No, I don't think I'll be requiring any night garments. And I still have the toothbrush here from my stay the other night, unless Ruby got rid of it."

Ruby said excitedly, "I sure didn't, sweetie!" Her face clouded again. "At least—I don't remember getting rid of it."

Or perhaps she used it herself. Myrtle made a face. "I'll simply get another toothbrush from the infirmary. No worries. And maybe I can put an end to all this nonsense. This particular killer seems to think that he can do *anything* and get away with it. It's time to disabuse him of that notion."

Miles looked levelly at her and then reluctantly nodded. "All right. I'll check back in with you tomorrow morning. And call me if you need me. Or anything."

Chapter Twenty-One

The worst part, reflected Myrtle that afternoon, was that she was starting to feel the teensiest bit at home at Greener Pastures, which was completely abhorrent. But sure enough, there was a sort of rhythm to life there that was easy to fall in step with.

First she joined in a Scrabble game with two very sharp-looking women who were both wrapped up in fluffy sweaters and scarves as if it were winter *inside* the retirement home. Myrtle was beaming when she won the match, even though she hadn't played Scrabble for ages. The daily crossword puzzles were key, she decided.

Lunch was rather uneventful and not as good as the meal she and Miles had had their first time there. It was a shame Miles wasn't there to witness its blandness.

When it was time to watch *Tomorrow's Promise*, Myrtle hesitated. She really did want to watch the episode today and not only to find out what had happened between Marlene and Cheyenne. She'd love to pick back up on her train of thought from yesterday—the train of thought that had almost revealed the killer to her.

The only problem with watching *Tomorrow's Promise* could be Ruby. Myrtle cleared her throat as she and Ruby walked on the way back from the dining room. "Say, Ruby, do you ever watch soap operas?"

Ruby frowned in concentration. "I think I used to. Which one do you watch?"

"*Tomorrow's Promise*," said Myrtle. "You don't have to watch it with me, but if you're not planning on watching anything else, I'd like to watch it on your TV if you don't mind."

Ruby's TV was a tiny set with questionable reception, but Myrtle didn't feel like watching the soap out in the commons area with everyone milling around.

"Well, sure!" said Ruby, beaming. "I'm happy to share my TV. I'll watch it with you."

Unfortunately, the soap opera watching was a real bust. Ruby, even more than usual, had no idea what was going on and asked a lot of questions. And she asked some of the same questions more than two or three times.

"Who is the girl with the black hair again?" she asked in a concerned voice. "And why is she hiding outside the blond man's house?"

Miles never interrupted with silly questions when they watched *Tomorrow's Promise* together. Although Puddin had. But who could expect more from Puddin?

Then there was supper. She and Ruby were running slightly late and couldn't find a place to sit. Finally, they spotted two free chairs at Fred's table. Fred rolled his eyes as they approached. Myrtle supposed that he didn't much like Myrtle knowing his secret about not going to college. She put a thumb and finger to her lips and mimed zipping them. Fred glowered at her.

Myrtle decided that when Greener Pastures was having a bad day in the kitchen, it was a *bad* day. Supper was meatloaf (she supposed) with some sort of cold, salty sauce on it. The accompanying peas were just short of frozen, and the bread was stale.

The rest of the table was engaged in conversation so Myrtle leaned closer to Fred and murmured, "You can relax, you know. I'm not here to disclose your secret."

"It's annoying that you're here at all," said Fred. "You're not a resident, but you're staying over just about as much as one. You don't even have Miles with you this time. He's probably gotten fed up with all your nonsense and investigating."

"Miles had a toaster oven to replace," said Myrtle serenely. "He likely had other errands to run, too."

"That's the best part about living here," said Fred. "I don't have to worry about toaster ovens breaking. If they break, it's not my problem."

He sounded smug. Smugness was incredibly irritating.

"At least when I'm at home, I don't worry about people sneaking into my bedroom and trying to murder me in my sleep," whispered Myrtle. Most of the time.

Fred flushed and answered in a low voice, "I'm expecting you'll have a very quiet evening tonight."

"With hopefully no visitors," said Myrtle sternly.

"If you leave me alone, I'll leave you alone," muttered Fred. He hesitated. "You haven't spoken to Darrell yet, have you? About...you know?"

"No," sighed Myrtle. "I wanted to. But then life happened." And soap operas and nonsense with her domestic help.

Fred frowned. "Now what? Here comes that Darla person. Is she coming to speak with *you*?"

Myrtle stifled a groan. "Probably. She seems to have it in for me for some reason."

Ruby quickly intercepted Darla before she could approach Myrtle. "Did you hear? Sweetie here is going to spend the night with me in my room and make sure nothing happens to me. Isn't that nice? So y'all don't have to worry about it."

Darla's eyebrows drew together. "Now Miss Ruby, we talked about this, remember? That there is *nothing* for you to be concerned about in terms of your personal safety."

Ruby's mouth trembled. "Did we? But I still feel so worried."

Myrtle cut in. "How can you possibly state that, Darla, when Ruby has had threatening phone calls, was nearly strangled, and was poisoned with sleeping pills?"

This statement had the effect of completely shutting down conversation at the table. Everyone stared at Myrtle.

Darla gritted her teeth. "Mrs. Clover, if we can meet in private?"

Fortunately, Myrtle was done with the unappealing supper. As she stood up, Fred smirked at her for being dragged off by Darla. She stuck her tongue out at him.

She followed Darla to the hallway outside the dining hall. Darla took a deep breath. "Now, Mrs. Clover. The last thing we want is for Ruby to get excited again."

"Why on earth not? Do you think she should just placidly agree to be murdered like a good little lamb?" Being hungry wasn't helping Myrtle's disposition, she decided.

Darla looked at the ceiling as if for support. "No, of course not. But I still don't think Miss Ruby is in any danger. I can see that you and I should agree to disagree on that point."

"Precisely."

"So I'll move on to my next point," said Darla smoothly. "I'm expecting no trouble out of you tonight. My understanding is that Ruby has asked you to stay as her guest."

"That's right. And as her protector."

Darla's gaze rested doubtfully on Myrtle's cane and generally elderly figure. "All right. Let me just reiterate. No matter what the reason is behind your visit, I'm expecting it to be very quiet."

Myrtle raised her eyebrows. "I'm hardly planning a toga party."

Darla flushed. "Quiet. That's all. Quiet."

"Naturally."

Darla hesitated and Myrtle got the impression she was dying to say something else. But then she caught herself. "All right. Carry on," Darla muttered.

It did start out very quiet that night. Aside from the fact that Ruby loved watching reality television shows until quite late. Myrtle was about to despair that she was ever going to have any peace when Ruby finally turned off the television.

"I guess we should go to sleep," said Ruby, sounding not a bit sleepy.

"We should," agreed Myrtle fervently.

Fifteen minutes later, Myrtle settled on the sofa, feet up and back supported by one of Ruby's large, fluffy pillows. The dolls had been put in Ruby's closet to make room for Myrtle. The door was unlocked and Myrtle had her cane lying across her lap. Ruby was lying in the bed, a baseball bat next to her. Myrtle couldn't see her at all in the dark, but she could tell that Ruby wasn't in any mood to sleep.

"Does Pasha come in at night or stay outside?" asked Ruby.

Myrtle sighed. "She doesn't really enjoy spending much time inside, Ruby. She's outside most of the time, including nighttime."

"What kind of cat food does she like? Does she come when you call her? Will she sit in your lap sometimes?"

Myrtle felt a headache coming on. She answered all Ruby's questions and then felt a sense of relief when silence descended on the room.

The silence was quickly shattered when Ruby kicked the covers off the bed and headed past Myrtle for the small bathroom. "Need a glass of water," said Ruby apologetically.

Myrtle heard water running and some vigorous glugging of water as Ruby drank. Then she tripped a bit on the way back. "Sorry, sweetie, sorry," she whispered.

Twenty minutes later, Ruby was up again and headed for the bathroom. "You asleep, sweetie?" asked Ruby with whispered concern.

"No, Ruby."

"Oh, okay, Myrtle. Just heading to the restroom, that's all. Forgot to brush my teeth."

No wonder Ruby napped half the day if she were wandering around so much at night. And Myrtle noticed that she actually remembered her name for once.

After Ruby had returned to bed and tossed and turned a bit more, Myrtle took a deep, relaxing breath and decided she'd busy her mind by mulling over the case. And there was plenty to mull over.

But what she kept returning to was Wanda's note. The note with the unfortunate pronoun usage. '*Not what they seem.*' This could really apply to nearly all the suspects. Natalie was unexpectedly more gracious about receiving a pittance in her mother's will. Winston was an unlikely thief. Inez appeared very cold and removed but had gone gaga over Winston when given the very slightest nudge. And Fred—well, Fred was quite obviously not the well-educated man that he said he was.

Everyone but Ruby, actually. Myrtle snorted as she thought back to that afternoon and the

frustrating attempts to watch her soap opera with the constantly chatting Ruby. It was almost like watching the soap with Puddin. She frowned at a sudden ping of awareness she felt. She'd been watching the soap with Puddin, who'd been just as annoying as Ruby. But the point was that she'd thought to herself how dim-witted Puddin had looked when watching TV...when Puddin wasn't dim-witted at all. She was actually sly as a fox.

Like Ruby?

Myrtle caught her breath as she thought back. Ruby's lack of money. Her pride in her six sons (and, yes, nary a one in jail). Her son with cancer and his lack of health insurance. Ruby's sudden fogginess that had come on her quickly. That very organized and thoughtful—and recent—to-do list that Myrtle had come across when she'd been looking through the pile of papers the night Ruby was in the hospital. It hadn't seemed to be the list of someone who was slipping.

Ruby could have bruised her own neck.

Ruby could have doctored her own drink.

Ruby could have lied about the phone call she got.

Not what they seem.

"Are you awake?" whispered Ruby in the dark.

Myrtle didn't say a word.

Myrtle listened as Ruby slipped out of the bed once more. She slowly sat straight up and waited as Ruby padded toward her. Her hand tightened around her cane.

And as soon as she felt Ruby hovering over her, Myrtle swung the cane as hard as she could and connected somewhere on Ruby.

Chapter Twenty-Two

There was a very startled and angry and very coherent spate of cursing from Ruby as Myrtle dashed for the bathroom and turned on the light. Where was the lock on the blasted door?

"Did you know there are no locks on the bathrooms here?" Ruby's voice was a disturbing singsong. "Just in case the staff needs to help us, you know. Always so thoughtful here at Greener Pastures."

Myrtle spotted the call button on the wall and pounded on it before bracing herself against the bathroom door.

A tinny voice came from the call box. "Miss Ruby? Do you need some assistance?"

Myrtle groaned. It was Darla, of all people.

"It's not Ruby, it's Myrtle Clover. And, yes, I'm in dire need of assistance. Your resident is a homicidal maniac!"

There was a pregnant pause on the other end. "I'm sorry, Mrs. Clover, I don't think I heard that correctly."

"You heard it! She's going to kill me if you don't get down here right away," roared Myrtle.

A pause again as if that might be very tempting to Darla. "All right," she finally said. "I'm on my way."

The pressure against the bathroom door stopped and Myrtle eased up a little bit, catching her breath. Could she hold Ruby off until help came? What was Ruby doing over there?

She found out a moment later as Ruby screeched and slammed what Myrtle presumed was the baseball bat against the bathroom door. "Hi-*yah*!" bellowed Ruby.

Part of the door started splintering. Myrtle waited until Ruby yelled out a second hi-*yah* and then jerked the door open as wide as it would go and Ruby fell into the bathroom as Myrtle scurried around her into the bedroom and to the outside hall.

Myrtle swung her head from side to side searching for curious faces sticking outside of residents' doors. But apparently, everyone in the basement slept like the dead. No one was looking out. And Myrtle could hear Ruby coming toward her.

Myrtle jogged a bit stiffly down the hall, whacking her cane against various doors and yelling, "Help! Help!" Finally, seeing Ruby's furious face, she pulled the fire alarm which set in motion an ear-piercing, light flashing pulsing alarm that would have raised Lazarus, Myrtle was sure of it.

Finally a door was yanked open and Fred, wearing red and white striped pajamas, blinked angrily at her. "What in the Sam Hill—" and Myrtle plowed him over, scrambling to lock the door.

"It's Ruby!" she panted. "She's the killer. She's lost it."

Fred raised a dubious eyebrow. "It sounds to me like *you've* lost it. Ruby lost it ages ago, don't you remember?"

"She's been faking her fogginess," said Myrtle urgently. "It's all been a hoax."

Ruby gave a strangled scream on the other side of Fred's door and commenced hitting it with the bat.

Fred's eyes grew huge.

"As I was saying. Can you call Miles? And Red, maybe? Or Darrell, the deputy?" Myrtle heard fire trucks in the distance. "Never mind about the police. If the firemen are here, the police will soon follow."

Ruby continued pounding at Fred's door with the bat.

"Miss Ruby!" came an absolutely furious voice from down the hall, barely discernable over the cacophony of the alarm and the yelling and the door beating. "Stop this *at once*!"

Whereas Myrtle appeared to have no effect on Ruby, Darla's voice, to Myrtle's profound relief, did. The pounding stopped immediately.

Fred nodded his head. "Darla is obnoxious, but she does know how to handle this kind of thing."

"You can't mean you've had something like this happen *before*," said Myrtle.

In minutes, other staff voices joined Darla's and with soothing voices, it sounded as if Ruby was being led away from Fred's door. Myrtle cautiously opened it and peered out.

Darla spotted her. With the alarms still blaring around her, Darla hissed, "I said I wanted it *quiet*!"

Ruby just glared balefully at her as she was led away.

Red, on a walker, stared at his mother in the Greener Pastures retirement home. Since Red wasn't supposed to be driving yet, Miles had driven Red over there. Red's deputy, Darrell Smith, was also there since he'd been in the area on another call. It was now getting close to four a.m. Miles was sipping a coffee and looking amazingly alert. Darrell was, too. Red, however, was still looking halfway asleep.

"You know you really shouldn't be out of the house yet, right?" said Myrtle censoriously. "You need to stay off of your feet."

"Agreed, Mama. Except I really couldn't pass up an opportunity like this. When I got the phone call from Darla, she said that my mother—who is practically allergic to retirement homes—had spent the night at Greener Pastures. And that you'd accused your roommate there of trying to murder you with a bat. And that you'd pulled the fire alarm. And caused any number of other disturbances."

"That's all true," said Myrtle in a stiff voice. "However, I was provoked. And Greener Pastures is a ghastly place, Red."

"I believe I've heard this tune before," Red sighed looking at the ceiling.

Darrell Smith cleared his throat and looked apologetically at Red. "If you don't mind, I'd like to hear some more about how your mom went from thinking of Ruby Sims as a friend and started thinking of her as a killer. I swear I didn't see it coming. Mrs. Clover, you've got some powerful deducing abilities," he said admiringly.

Myrtle preened. It was nice to have her investigative skills recognized—finally.

"Yes, Mama," said Red, leaning in, "Tell us exactly how you realized that Ruby Sims wasn't flaky at all but was a cold-blooded murderer."

Myrtle shot him a look and then said directly to Darrell, "Well, you see, I have this housekeeper named Puddin."

Red rolled his eyes. "I guess I should be thankful that your epiphany didn't involve your soap opera."

Myrtle cleared her throat. "As a matter of fact, Puddin was finished working and she and I were watching my favorite soap opera, *Tomorrow's Promise*."

Darrell's eyes brightened. "Oh, I like that show, too."

"I realized something was reminding me about the case. At first, I just thought it was Marlene and Cheyenne."

Red's face was completely blank.

Darrell nodded in comprehension. "Because of blackmail? But I didn't know Mickey Pelias was blackmailing anyone."

"In a manner of speaking she was," said Myrtle. "She was really more of a collector of information. She sort of curated it. She knew secrets about both Winston Rouse and Fred Lee. But that wasn't what clued me in to Ruby. In fact, I couldn't put my finger on it until tonight. When Puddin watched the soap with me, she suddenly had this very foggy, dim-witted look on her face. It was like television turned her into a zombie or something."

Red raised an eyebrow. "Isn't Puddin always sort of dim-witted?"

"Not a bit. She may not be educated, but she's very clever. In a way, it reminded me of Ruby. Ruby *also* wasn't foggy or feebleminded. She was only pretending to be. And I had a postcard from my psychic friend Wanda that said someone wasn't who they were pretending to be."

Red rubbed his forehead, a characteristic gesture that he seemed to employ whenever he was in his mother's presence. Especially when there were psychics mentioned.

Darrell's eyes widened. "A psychic?"

"Yes. And the real thing, not some wannabe phony. Anyway, it also made me remember that I had spotted a list that Ruby had made. Nothing elaborate, just the sort of to-do list that you and I might make at the start of the week. But it was very detailed. It was divided by day, it had subcategories of various tasks. And it was recently written," said Myrtle. "It wasn't the sort of list that someone with dementia might make."

"Well, my goodness," said Darrell, smile stretching across his pleasant features. "If that don't beat all."

Miles said in a thoughtful voice, "I'm still having such a hard time wrapping my head around all this."

"You and me, too," muttered Red.

Miles continued, "Could you walk me through how sweet Ruby Sims would *want* to murder her friend Mickey? And you?"

"Absolutely. The fact of the matter is, Miles, you and I were duped. I'm quite irked by it, actually. At least we weren't the only ones. Ruby's fellow residents were duped, her friend Mickey was duped, and even the staff was duped. The catalyst to Ruby's sudden decline was when one of her sons developed cancer," said Myrtle.

Darrell snapped his fingers. "You know, I think somebody was telling me about that. He is pretty sick. And the only thing that might could help him was an experimental drug of some kind."

Myrtle said, "I didn't know anything about the severity of the cancer, the spread of it, or the need for expensive experimental treatments. But I did know that Ruby, besides being crazy about cats...if she wasn't faking that as well, was also crazy about her six sons. I also heard that the son didn't have any health insurance or enough coverage or something. At any rate, it sounded like Ruby needed money. I don't know when she discovered that her son had cancer, but I do know that everyone says Ruby experienced a very rapid decline in her mental acuity and faculties. To me, it makes the most sense that the decline would have occurred right after hearing about her son's condition."

Miles nodded slowly. "Ruby knew Mickey had money. Did she know that Mickey intended leaving her money?"

"I'm going to assume that Ruby and Mickey were friends before all this happened. I think Ruby did respect and enjoy Mickey's company and that Mickey was flattered by the attention. Mickey liked to sort of throw her power and influence around, so let's imagine that she decided to tell Ruby that she planned on leaving her a nice nest egg in her will. Mickey was paranoid too remember. She really *did* believe that she was in danger. And she *was* in danger. But she was in danger from the person she'd allowed to be closest to her," said Myrtle.

Darrell seemed moved. "That's really very sad."

"Ruby decided she was in no position to wait for this money. Her son desperately needed the help now. As soon as she had set everyone's expectations that she was no threat to anyone and was rapidly losing her memory, she decided to eliminate Mickey. Ruby knew, as Mickey's friend, that she never locked her door. Even if she *had* locked her door, she'd have opened it to Ruby. But the night Ruby killed Mickey, Mickey's door was unlocked. Ruby slipped in, took a pillow, and smothered Mickey," said Myrtle.

Red grunted. "And figured it would look as if Mickey had died in her sleep. She probably thought it would go unnoticed."

Myrtle shrugged. "And why would it? Old people sometimes pass away in their sleep. Mickey wasn't young. But someone had heard something. And Mickey was a light sleeper. Light enough to put up quite the struggle."

Darrell said, "Right. Inez Wilson was the one who reported hearing suspicious noises in the room."

"Pity she couldn't have reported them when they were happening," grunted Red. "Would have saved us all a lot of grief and probably would have saved Mrs. Pelias's life."

Myrtle shook her head. "But Inez is a fairly selfish woman. She probably just rolled over and didn't think anything else about it until the next day when the staff was stating that Mickey had died in her sleep."

Miles said, "But Ruby corroborated Inez's story."

"Yes, but only because she was trying to divert suspicion away from herself. This is also why she pretended to be senile, why she lied about receiving a threatening call, why she choked herself, and why she doctored her own glass with sleeping pills. And it worked. We believed her," said Myrtle crossly.

"For a while," said Miles loyally. "But then you saw through her lies."

"It took a long time," said Myrtle. "She must have really thought I was a complete idiot to agree to spend the night in her room."

Red said, "So exactly what happened there?"

"Oh, Ruby kept making excuses to get up and walk past my sofa. She was trying to see if I were asleep so that she could smother me, too. But I hardly *ever* sleep. Especially under those circumstances. I faked it, though, and when she came closer I managed to escape. Noisily," said Myrtle.

"Under those circumstances, I think it was understandable," said Red. He shook his head. "What a mess. But Mrs. Sims is now locked up where she won't be trying to smother people ever again."

"Amazing," said Darrell, still looking starry-eyed. "You really just pieced everything together with no forensic evidence or anything. Just by using your brain."

"And now," said Myrtle, "I'd like to give my brain a rest. And then I believe I'll write a magnificent story for the *Bradley Bugle*. An exposé, I believe. Miles, could you take me back home?"

Red said, "I'm sorry, Mama, but you're going to need to repeat all this to the state police...they're on their way. But after that, you can definitely go home and rest. It will be well-deserved."

Myrtle was pleased to see a flash of admiration in Red's eyes. Perhaps she should pack her punitive garden gnomes back in the shed until Red's next infraction.

It was a couple of hours later when Miles was finally pulling into her driveway. "Are you planning on trying to go to sleep?" he asked. "Do you think you even can? Or will you have visions of being smothered with pillows when you do?"

Myrtle said, "Considering it is six o'clock in the morning, I'm thinking I might as well stay up. Maybe I can nap some this afternoon, although I also need to start working on that story for the *Bugle*. Besides, I wanted to see my taped soap opera from yesterday. That blasted Ruby was asking so many questions that I could barely listen to the show, myself."

Miles said, "By the way, you'll be glad to hear that any thoughts I might have had in the direction of considering Greener Pastures as a potential residence have now been discarded. This whole episode has left a bad taste in my mouth."

"You're lucky you didn't have supper there last night. That really *would* have left a bad taste in your mouth," muttered Myrtle. "I'm delighted to hear that you've come back to your senses."

Miles made a surprised sound. "Oh no. It looks like poor Wanda is here and huddled on your front step. She must be freezing." He squinted through the dim light. "What on earth is she holding?"

Myrtle beamed. "It's Pasha! Pasha is sitting in Wanda's lap!"

Miles turned off his car. "If Wanda's here, I might as well visit for a little while. She must have walked here again and I'll have to drive her back." He stifled a yawn. He was looking a bit less fresh than he had when they were at the Home.

Wanda stood to greet them, still holding Pasha. Pasha kept her eyes focused on Miles. Although the two of them had reached some sort of understanding, it was clear that Pasha still wanted to keep an eye on him. They all walked inside and Pasha jumped from Wanda's arms to follow them in.

Wanda said gruffly, "Started to sleep tonight and had the most horrible vision ever. Couldn't shake it. Worried I might have sent you into the lion's den." She shoved a bony hand into her pocket. "Here. Wrote this before I left. But figured I couldn't get it to you in time anyway. Hoped you'd be alive for me to hand it to you. I knew I couldn't sleep, so I just walked over here."

Wanda offered the crumpled postcard to Myrtle and Myrtle solemnly took it. It read in Wanda's careful but nearly illegible scrawl: *Too many trips to the restruum.*

"Isn't that the truth?" said Myrtle. "Ruby kept trying to see if I were asleep."

Wanda nodded her head mournfully. "Pity the visions don't work in the most helpful way sometimes." She gave Myrtle an anxious look. "Did they get her? And lock her up?"

"They most certainly did," said Myrtle decidedly.

"Justice was meted out," intoned Wanda.

"In every way."

Wanda slumped in relief. "Well, I guess that's all that I needed to know," she said. "Reckon I'll head back home now."

"No, no, no. There will be no heading back home yet, Wanda. We're going to light a fire."

"Are we?" Wanda looked doubtfully at the fireplace.

"Yes. Well, Miles will," said Myrtle airily. "It's the least he can do after abandoning me at Greener Pastures last night."

Miles gave her a baleful look. "Has that chimney been cleaned recently?"

"You know how Red stays on top of those things. It's clean as a whistle. Anyway, we'll sit in front of the fire, have a lavish breakfast, and watch the soap opera I taped yesterday," said Myrtle. "And good times will be had."

And they were.

About the Author:

Elizabeth writes the Southern Quilting mysteries and Memphis Barbeque mysteries for Penguin Random House and the Myrtle Clover series for Midnight Ink and independently. She blogs at ElizabethSpannCraig.com/blog , named by Writer's Digest as one of the 101 Best Websites for Writers. Elizabeth makes her home in Matthews, North Carolina, with her husband and two teenage children.

Sign up for Elizabeth's free newsletter to stay updated on its release:

http://eepurl.com/kCy5j

Other Works by the Author:

Myrtle Clover Series in Order:
Pretty is as Pretty Dies
Progressive Dinner Deadly
A Dyeing Shame
A Body in the Backyard
Death at a Drop-In
A Body at Book Club
Death Pays a Visit
A Body at Bunco
Murder on Opening Night
Cruising for Murder (2016)
Southern Quilting Mysteries in Order:
Quilt or Innocence
Knot What it Seams
Quilt Trip
Shear Trouble
Tying the Knot
Patch of Trouble (2016)
Memphis Barbeque Mysteries in Order (Written as Riley Adams):
Delicious and Suspicious
Finger Lickin' Dead
Hickory Smoked Homicide
Rubbed Out
And a standalone "cozy zombie" novel: Race to Refuge, written as Liz Craig

This and That

I love hearing from my readers. You can find me on Facebook as Elizabeth Spann Craig Author, on Twitter as elizabethscraig, on my website at elizabethspanncraig.com, and by email at elizabethspanncraig@gmail.com. Sign up for my free newsletter to stay updated on new releases:

http://eepurl.com/kCy5j

Thanks so much for reading my book...I appreciate it. If you enjoyed the story, would you please leave a short review on the site where you purchased it? Just a few words would be great. Not only do I feel encouraged reading them, but they also help other readers discover my books. Thank you!

Interested in having a character named after you? In a Myrtle Clover tote bag? Or even just your name listed in the acknowledgments of a future book? Visit my Patreon page at https://www.patreon.com/elizabethspanncraig .

Thanks so much to Karri Klawiter for her beautiful cover, Judy Beatty for editng, and my family for their support.

Printed in Great Britain
by Amazon